Just Moving On

Dia Webb

Published by Dia Webb
Publishing partner: Paragon Publishing, Rothersthorpe

ISBN 978-1-78792-033-0

Cover illustration © Cheryl Thornburgh
cherylannthornburgh@gmail.com

Book design, layout and production management by Into Print
www.intoprint.net
+44 (0)1604 832149

For all those people who pulled together under difficult circumstances during wartime, and for all the American soldiers who did not make it home.

Chapter 1

The train was waiting on the platform at Waterloo Station when they arrived, out of breath from their efforts to get across London in order to be in good time. The weather was relatively mild for January and it looked as if the sun might come out. They found themselves over-dressed in their winter coats.

'We needn't have rushed after all, Emily,' her mother said, 'but you never know if you'll be held up somewhere.'

'You didn't have to see me off, Mum. I'm not a child. I could have managed.' They walked towards a third-class carriage and put down the luggage on the platform.

'Look love, there's an empty compartment. Get in and I'll pass everything in for you.'

'I can carry my suitcase, Mum. I'm not helpless.' Emily climbed in and put her handbag on a window seat facing forward and lifted her suitcase up onto the rack. She returned to her mother on the platform.

'Here's your violin, Emily. Now don't look at me like that. I know you don't feel like playing it yet but maybe, when you start to feel better – ' Her voice trailed away.

'I know you mean well, Mum but I just can't; I don't feel fit for anything. I just feel a failure and now I'm leaving you and – '

Her mother cut in quickly. 'Nonsense, love! You need some time away, somewhere different, and going to stay at Little Bridge Farm with your Auntie Barbara and Uncle Fred will be a sort of convalescence; just what the doctor ordered, in fact.'

'I don't want to be a burden to them, Mum. They have enough to do as it is, and so do you.'

'They will love having you there. Your cousin Helen is away farming with her husband on Exmoor. They must miss her.'

'I'm no substitute for Helen. She did so much work on the farm, didn't she? Now that I'm leaving home for a while, you won't have my help will you, Mum? With you and dad working at the hospital and Jonathan working with the London Fire Brigade, it's not a quiet life, is it?'

'No, it's not, although your brother's not home much with the job he does. But yesterday was the start of the New Year and we've got to hope that this year will see the end of the war.'

'I wish I could be as optimistic as you, Mum.'

'You're young, Emily, and you've a teaching career ahead of you, so look on the bright side, dear. Oh, and I'll telephone you every Saturday from the box at the end of our road.'

Suddenly the engine let out a huge cloud of steam and the guard started walking along the platform banging all the doors shut. Emily hugged her mother and climbed on the train. She went to sit in the place she had reserved and looked out of the window. The guard closed the door and blew his whistle.

Mother and daughter looked at each other through the rather grubby window, each trying to force a smile and not upset the other.

Her mother waved and Emily put her fingers to her lips as the train began to move slowly out of Waterloo Station.

Emily looked blankly out of the window. The train jolted over the points and started to gather speed as it rumbled and jerked its way through the drab scene of damaged buildings and bomb sites. She closed her eyes as if to shut out the view, but could only see another scene of destruction, a scene which wouldn't leave her. She clenched her fists and forced her eyes open and looked at the floor of the compartment and then at a colourful picture on the wall above the seats opposite her. The sun was shining there and the sea was blue. Seagulls soared above the cliffs, and the grass was the greenest green. Happy children played on the beach and a boy was flying his kite. Families walked along the esplanade and an old couple were sitting on a bench enjoying their ice creams. It was a perfect scene. There were no bombs falling and everyone was happy and safe. She wanted to be there. She wanted her family to be there and all those children that she had wanted to protect and keep from harm. She closed her eyes and forced herself to see only that picture in her mind. The noise the train made as it picked up speed was rhythmic and comforting and she leaned back against the headrest and let the sound wash over her.

'Tickets please, Miss,' a voice called out to her. Emily sat up and brushed her wavy brown hair out of her eyes.

'Oh sorry,' she said, reaching for her bag and finding her ticket. 'I don't usually fall asleep like that.'

'Good for you, Miss. Make the most of it. There are soldiers further down the train and they're a noisy lot. Still, it's good to see our boys having a laugh.' The conductor handed her ticket back to her and smiled. 'We've got to find something to laugh at, Miss, but it's not easy, is it?'

'Thank you. You're right. We've got to find something to laugh at.'

The man left the carriage, whistling tunelessly as he moved on along the corridor.

Emily took out the sandwiches that her mother

had prepared for her. Spam. Oh well.

'They'll fill a hole,' is what her mother always said. Emily was glad of them and ate them while she looked out of the window. Green fields and trees swept by and the sun came out and shone on them, just like in the picture on the wall opposite her. Suddenly she felt tearful and tired. The train was slowing down and was approaching a station: Andover. Emily put away her sandwiches and took out a flask of tea. She could pour herself a drink without spilling it now that the train had stopped. The platform looked busy and people, many of them soldiers started to board the train. The door to Emily's compartment opened and a woman and a little boy of about eight climbed on and sat down opposite her. The woman smiled at Emily.

'It's busier than I thought it would be but we're not going far, just to see my mother at Exeter. I said to her, "You should come and live with us now that Dad's passed on," but she won't have it, and on top of that Exeter has been getting bombed. I told her, I did, that she'd be safer with us. She said, "No, you're nearer to London." "That's nothing to do with it, Mother", I said. "There's nothing the Jerries want to bomb in the little village where we live." Anyway, she won't have it, so we go and see her now and then don't we, Peter? Get your feet off the seat, dear. Here's your comic.'

The woman came up for air and Emily smiled at her and said conversationally, 'We're living in difficult times.'

'Oh, I know. Why, when Peter and me were in Exeter last, we saw what the bombing had done all around Paris Street and the Cathedral. Whole houses razed to the ground and rubble everywhere but the Cathedral was hardly hit at all, was it, Peter? But the blast and the fires, there must have been lots of lives lost.'

Emily swallowed the last of her tea and put her flask away while the woman droned on about the damage and carnage she had seen. Emily felt beads of perspiration starting to break out on her brow. She was beginning to feel nauseous and started to take short breaths. She looked at the floor of the carriage hoping that she wouldn't pass out. Suddenly, the woman switched her attention to her son.

'Why are you fidgeting like that, Peter? Did you go to the lav like I told you to before we left?'

The boy whispered something in her ear and passed her his comic.

'Come on then, we'll have to go down the corridor and find one.' She yanked him out of his seat and they left the compartment hurriedly, the woman closing the door behind her.

Emily put her hand to her mouth. She took deep

breaths, reached for her handkerchief and wiped her brow. She closed her eyes and sat very still trying to find comfort in the train's motion as it sped on westwards. Gradually, the feeling of overwhelming panic subsided.

It was nearly an hour before the woman and her son returned to the compartment.

'Sorry to leave you, dear, but we got talking to some of them soldiers down the train and one of them was so clever with showing Peter all sorts of card tricks, wasn't he, Peter? What a laugh! I said to him, "You should be on the stage." And do you know what he said?

"I was," he said. "I'm a magician and conjuror and do card tricks." But he was called up, see. So, I said to him – ' The woman started laughing while the little boy looked on with a serious expression on his face.

'I said, "If you're a magician, perhaps you can make Hitler disappear." "I'll do me best," was what he said. We all laughed, didn't we, Peter?'

Emily looked at the little boy. 'Did you learn any card tricks, Peter?'

He looked at her with his big blue eyes. 'Just one,' he answered quietly.

'Well done,' Emily smiled back at him.

The train was starting to slow down and the woman looked out of the window.

'Ooh look!' she said. 'We're just coming into Exeter. Doesn't the time go when you've got someone to talk with?'

'Exeter Central,' the guard shouted as the train stopped and people got out.

'Goodbye dear,' the woman said as she picked up her bags and nudged her son and nodded in the direction of Emily.

'Goodbye,' Peter said dutifully but with a shy smile.

'Bye, Peter,' replied Emily and waved as the couple stepped down onto the platform.

The train moved off, stopping shortly afterwards at Exeter St. David's before heading in the direction of North Devon. Emily left the carriage and went to find the toilet.

In about an hour she would arrive at Barnstaple. As she made her way along the corridor, she could see that there were not very many people left on the train. Exeter and Plymouth and their surrounding areas were so much more populated than North Devon. Maybe that's why her family liked it so much. The farm that her Uncle Fred and her Auntie Barbara worked had come down to them from her uncle's side of the family and had been part of family life for generations. Uncle Fred was a real softie and didn't like to see any animal go to market but Auntie Barbara was more like her sister,

Emily's mother, practical and tough when she had to be. Emily returned to her carriage, and sat and looked out of the window. The early afternoon sunlight shone on the rich green pasture land as the train ran parallel to the River Taw, crossing it now and then and giving picture postcard views of the landscape. Emily knew that there might be several stops before Barnstaple at tiny stations where one or two people would get off, but at this time of day, few people or none would get on.

Suddenly she saw a flash of blueish green over the river. A kingfisher. What a treat! She suddenly thought how good it was to be reminded that there was beauty still outside of all the dreadful and tragic things she and so many had witnessed. She started to feel tearful again but forced herself to gather her things together and set her mind on looking out of the window and recognising the familiar views from the train that had so entranced her and her brother when they came with their parents to stay at the farm before the war. At last, the train pulled into Barnstaple Junction and Emily got off, carrying her suitcase and her violin. She looked towards the exit and immediately spotted her Auntie Barbara, who was waving frantically.

'Hello, Emily. Let me take that violin. How lovely to see you.'

They hugged each other and walked towards

the exit. The train let out a big blast of steam and started on its way to Ilfracombe, the final stop.

'Hello, Auntie. Thank you for coming to meet me.'

'Of course, I'd come to meet you, dear. I can drive now. The car is outside and we should be home in the daylight. I don't drive in the dark.'

'I didn't know you could drive, Auntie. When did you learn?'

'Last week, dear.'

They reached the car, parked near the entrance to the station and put the luggage on the back seat.

'Last week? Emily was surprised. 'Where did you practise?'

'Oh, just up and down the entrance to the farm and round the field a bit. I only hit a few things. Your uncle will leave stuff about so what does he expect?'

Barbara started the car up and drove away from the station, over the Long Bridge and across the Square towards the Newport part of Barnstaple and on towards the villages of Landkey and Swimbridge.

Emily found the journey a bit nerve-wracking. Her auntie drove very fast and as the roads became narrower, didn't slow up to allow for any oncoming traffic.

'We want to reach home before dark, Emily, and

there's never many vehicles around here.'

Between Landkey and Swimbridge, Barbara suddenly turned left onto a narrow road which Emily remembered that eventually led to the village of West Buckland. The temperature was dropping and Emily thought that it must be near to freezing as her aunt put her foot down hard on the accelerator resulting in a roar of protest from the little Austin Seven as it battled up the long, steep hill towards the village. The light was beginning to fade as the vehicle let out some screams of pain as her aunt wrenched the gear stick into first, while appearing to jump twice onto the clutch. Auntie Barbara, however, was unrelenting and ruthless in her expectations of what she thought the car's performance should be. They reached the top of the hill where the road widened and as Auntie Barbara turned left, a tractor came towards them turning right from the village to go down the hill they had just come up. Emily shut her eyes and gripped her knees as the tractor missed them by inches and went straight into the hedge on the corner to avoid hitting them. It was lucky that he was driving so slowly, Emily thought as she lurched forward as a result of her aunt swerving and stopping in a conveniently placed gateway.

'These farmers think they own the road, Emily. Your Uncle Fred's the same. Just because they're driving something bigger than the rest of us they think they can do as they like.'

She backed onto the road and turned left at the corner and drove on up to the village without looking at the driver of the tractor who was backing away from the hedge and shaking his head in disbelief.

'Only a few miles now to our farm, dear. You'll be glad to get there and warm up. Uncle Fred will be milking, but when he's finished we'll have our supper together.'

'It will be good to see him, Aunt. Oh, and I have a little present that Mum knitted for each of you. Some mittens. She said it was no good trying to send you any food because you'd have more than she has, what with the rationing.'

'That's good of Lydia to think of us. I only wish she and Paul and Jonathan were down here safe from all the bombing. Still, with your mum and dad working at the hospital and your brother working with the Fire Brigade, they're doing their bit for the war effort. And you, Emily, you were – '

'I do want to help you both where I can.' Emily cut in. 'I don't want to give you more work than you've already got.'

'The main thing is for you to have a rest and – '

'Oh look, here's the entrance to the farm, Auntie, and I can see the light on in the milking parlour in the distance.'

Barbara drove right up to the farmhouse and stopped the car suddenly. They both got out and carried the luggage into the hall and walked on into the warm farmhouse kitchen.

'The first thing for us, Emily, is a cup of tea,' said Barbara as she took off her coat and threw it on the sofa by the Aga. 'You know where the toilet is and you know how I feel about living in the country. I won't go without a few home comforts so after you've had a drink, if you want a bath, the water will be hot and you know where the bathroom is upstairs. Your bedroom is right next to it.'

'Thank you so much, Auntie. Let me hang your coat up for you in the hall while you make the tea.' Emily returned to the kitchen and went to sit on the settee. She looked at what appeared to be a large cream rug in front of the Aga near her feet. Suddenly the rug raised its head and let out a 'Baa' which made Emily jump and fall back against the cushions.

'Oh, I didn't expect that! It's a sheep in here.'

'That's your uncle's idea. He'd have all the animals in here if he could, probably sitting up at the kitchen table eating supper with us. You know what he's like, Emily.'

The outside door opened and Uncle Fred could be heard taking off his boots and hanging up his outdoor clothes. He came into the kitchen and hurried over to his niece.

'Hello, Emily. It is good to see you. Look, Spot knows you. He remembers you from when you used to come to us with your family before the war. That dog will be glad to have someone other than me to make a fuss of him.'

'It's lovely to see you and Auntie Barbara again and so kind of you to have me come and stay.' Emily hugged her uncle and patted Spot.

'We've been looking forward to it haven't we, Babs?'

'We have, Fred. Now go and get washed and supper will be ready soon.'

'Just one thing, Emily,' her uncle said, looking serious. 'I'm glad to see you looking unharmed.'

Emily felt herself stiffen and hoped he wasn't going to start talking about the trouble she'd had. She looked up at her uncle and waited for him to continue.

His face was very serious as he looked at her and then at his wife. 'It's not many folks that have survived a ride in the car with Babs!' He smiled and winked at her.

Chapter 2

Emily awoke to the sound of muffled voices coming up from downstairs. What time was it? She sat up in bed and looked at the clock on the bedside table. Half past ten? She couldn't have slept so long, and without even waking up in the night and going over and over in her mind all the things that might have been different. She got out of bed and walked across the wooden floor which was warm to her bare feet, the heat permeating up from the Aga in the kitchen below her bedroom. Yes, of course, she had had a hot bath before going to bed at about nine o'clock and after laying her head on the pillow and pulling the blankets and eiderdown up above her neck, couldn't remember anything else. She hurried into the bathroom and got ready to go downstairs and apologise to her aunt for being such a 'lie-a-bed.'

Emily stood at the bottom of the stairs, outside the kitchen door and listened to the conversation from within.

'Well,' a voice was saying, ' 'twas bitter cold when I went up to the shippon to do the milkin' 'smornin' and I didn't turn the cows out after, just let 'em bide there with some feed. I don't like the look of the weather, Fred.'

'It was very icy first thing, Stan, but I fancy it's starting to warm up a bit now. How did you manage with your bike on the road coming up to West Buckland?'

'I walks a lot of the way 'cos 'tis so steep but I was slippin' an' slidin' about an' fell in the 'edge once. I collected the post an' got on with deliverin' it. Didn't stop chattin' much.'

'Here's your tea, Fred,' Barbara said, 'and I've made some pasties for us for later. They're just out of the oven if you want one, Stan.'

'That's like asking a donkey if he likes carrots, isn't it, Stan?' Fred commented, passing their postman a plate and the jar of chutney to go with the hot pasty.

'Proper, Barbara, they'm proper!'

There was a pause while Emily's aunt and uncle gave their visitor a chance to enjoy his treat. Emily knocked at the kitchen door and opened it slowly.

'Am I disturbing you, Aunt?' she asked peeping her head around the door. 'I'm sorry that I'm so late getting up. I never sleep like that at home.'

'Come in, dear,' her aunt said. 'Come and say "Hello" to our friend, Stan. Late? No. You're here to have a rest, so get up when you like. I'll cook you a fried egg and bacon in a minute.'

Emily walked into the kitchen and joined the others seated around the table.

'Hello,' she said, looking at the postman. 'Good morning, Uncle.' Aunt Barbara poured her niece a cup of tea and passed it to her.

'I think I knows this young lady,' Stan said. 'Only you was little when you was 'ere last. I think I remembers you 'ad a brother.'

'Yes, Mr – ' Emily paused but was quickly prompted by the visitor.

'Stan, please.'

'Yes, Stan, we used to come before the war with our Mum and Dad and stay on the farm here.'

'Babs and Emily's mother are sisters, Stan,' Fred said.

'That's it. I remembers now.' Stan pushed his plate away. 'That was bootiful, Barbara. Prize winnin' pasty, 'specially with the chutney. Lil made a lot of chutney last summer. Our two evacuees 'elped with the pickin' an' the peelin' of all they runner beans. 'Twas like a factory.'

'You still have Jimmy and Danny then, Stan, only some evacuees have gone back home?'

'Us 'ave still got 'em and us'll miss 'em terrible when they do go back 'ome. They'm like our own boys and a great 'elp on my small 'oldin'.

'Stan's job as postman for West and East Buckland and all the outlying houses and farms is a part-time one, Emily,' auntie Barbara explained.

'But you've probably done half a day's work

before you set off this morning, eh, Stan?' Fred commented.

'True, Fred, but us wouldn't 'ave it any other way, would us? But I'd better be gettin' on now. I meant to ask 'ee 'ow that poorly sheep be.'

'Doing much better, Stan, since I've had her indoors for a bit. She's in the barn now. In fact, I've got 'em all inside there since I heard the forecast.'

Emily sneaked a look at her aunt who was sighing and tutting her disapproval.

'I think we should rename this farm and call it "Animal Hotel," ' she said, but neither of the men was listening. They were already moving towards the door and preparing to go outside.

'Thank you, Barbara, I be spoilt as usual. Emily, when the weather's better get your aunt to drive 'ee down to visit us at Sunnybank one afternoon. Lil gets terrible lonely and 'er would love to see 'ee.'

'That would be very nice. Thank you, Stan.'

Fred was putting on his boots and several layers of outdoor clothes and Stan was covering his uniform with his cape and preparing to set off. Barbara put some bacon in a pan and cracked an egg alongside it. She lifted the lid on the Aga and placed the pan on the hotplate from where a comforting sizzling sound was immediately emitted. Emily breathed in the unfamiliar smell and closed her eyes in anticipation. They could hear the men outside saying their goodbyes.

'Look at the sky there, Stan. Nearly black and the wind has dropped too.'

'I don't like the look of it, Fred. Us be goin' to get snow. I just 'opes I can get me round done an' get back 'ome afore it comes down.' He got on his bike and cycled off unsteadily along the gutted driveway from the farm.

'What a lovely breakfast, Auntie. Thank you but you don't have to feed me like that every day.'

'No but it's a treat now and then, isn't it, and you need a bit of spoiling.'

'I want to help where I can. Please let me help.' Emily put down her knife and fork and took another piece of her aunt's homemade bread and spread some plum jam on it.

'You can help but I want you to have a week of complete rest first. Give yourself a chance to relax and then we'll take advantage of your offers of help.'

Aunt Barbara smiled and came over and placed her hand on Emily's shoulder.

'I promised your mother that we'd look after you, so there's no use arguing with that, is there?'

'I can see that you're all ganging up on me so I suppose you must be right, Auntie. There's no use arguing with that.'

Chapter 3

Lil **looked out** of the window at the gently falling snowflakes. The wind had dropped, the sky had darkened and even at midday she wondered about lighting the tilly lamps. Suddenly, the kitchen door was flung open and Jimmy and Danny rushed in, full of excitement.

'Look, Aunt. It's layin', ain't it, Dan?' Jimmy looked at his younger brother for confirmation.

'It's ever so pretty, too.' Danny always had to see the artistic side of things and stared out of the kitchen window in wonderment.

Lil shook her head and sighed. 'It's all very well on Christmas cards, boys, but when there be animals to feed and cows to milk, 'tis another matter. I be wonderin' about Uncle and 'ow 'e's getting' on with 'is post round. 'Tis never as busy on a Saturday an' there won't be much post just after New Year but if the snow lays too thick 'e'll 'ave to leave 'is bike an' walk back 'ome. 'Alf past twelve is 'is usual time for gettin' back.' She went to stir the stew and check the rice pudding in the oven.

'If he can't get back, Aunt,' Jimmy said, pausing. 'I mean, if he can't get back in time to feed the animals and do 'is usual jobs, me an' Dan can 'elp out. That's right ain't it, Dan?'

Danny nodded enthusiastically and Lil smiled. The boys had come on well in the nine months or so that they had come to them as evacuees at Sunnybank. The younger one especially had suffered badly with his nerves from all the bombing near their home in London, and as a result of shock was so badly affected that he couldn't speak for some time. He had gradually grown in confidence and enjoyed the peace and tranquillity of the countryside. Yes, they had settled well and loved to help with the never-ending outside work. And they looked up to Stan and did all they could to please him. He was their hero and he called them his 'little helpers'.

Lil looked at the clock and made a decision. She pointed out of the window at Bruce, their sheepdog, who was always alert at this time of the morning, and waiting on the grass outside of his kennel to welcome Stan back from his post round just before twelve thirty every day except Sunday.

'Look boys, Bruce bain't standin' lookin' up towards West Buckland like 'e usually do. 'E knows uncle won't be comin' down the road on 'is bike. Us'll go ahead an' 'ave our dinner an' then us 'ad better wrap up an' go outside an' feed the chickens an' the pigs.'

Jimmy and Danny went to the scullery to wash their hands and fetch the cutlery. Danny moved the wooden handle over the sink to pump the water up from the well. He loved to do that and was always fascinated by the fact that nothing happened for a few seconds and then after some strange, gurgling sounds, the water would come gushing out.

'This water's really cold today, Aunt,' Jimmy frowned holding his hands under the pump and then changing places with his brother to do the pumping so that Danny could wash his hands.

'Yes, an' us'll 'ave to wrap up warm when us goes outside after us ave 'ad our dinner. Pass me they plates please, Jimmy, and that big one there for uncle for when 'e does get 'ome. I'll keep 'is 'ot. Mind you, 'e'll most likely 'ave been fed over at Fred and Barbara's farm, I wouldn't wonder.'

After dinner they cleared the table and went out into the hall, dressed themselves in warm clothes and put on their wellingtons.

Lil sighed. She would have loved to have flopped out in a chair by the fireside and closed her eyes for a few minutes. That would be a treat but a rare one living in a Devon longhouse with no mains of any sort. Hard work. That's what it was but she had never known any different so just had to get on with it.

'Hats, scarves and mittens, boys. Us'll 'ave to go to the barn to get the feed.'

'No, Aunt, 'cos Uncle took a lot of it and put it in the small shed near the shippon. He said he thought the weather was going to turn nasty and we must think ahead, didn't he, Dan?'

'That's right. He's always doing things like that,' Danny answered in admiration of their hero.

They went down the front steps which were already covered in about three inches of snow, and walked towards the henhouse, heads bent against the steadily falling huge, white, fluffy snowflakes. After collecting feed from the shed, they fed the hens, picked up a few eggs and trudged on to the pigsty. The boys were fond of Pixie and Poppet and had been allowed to name them when Stan had bought them as tiny piglets. It had taken some time for the boys to accept that although all the animals were loved and cared for, they were eventually destined for the dinner plate. They had never really understood how food reached the table until they had settled to living in the country.

'I'm going to check on the cows. You comin', Dan?'

'I have to see that Madam is comfortable, Jim. Buttercup and Daisy will be all right but you know how Madam gets worried,' Danny replied. He saw Madam as his own cow and they had come through hard times together which had forged a strange bond between them. The animal would sometimes kick out but never when Danny was nearby.

'Aunt, If Uncle doesn't get back in a few hours, I'll have to milk them,' Jimmy said importantly.

He'd had lessons back in the Summer and loved to exercise his fairly newfound skills.

'And I'll help, Aunt,' added Danny. 'It's a two-man job really.'

'Well us may be glad of that, boys. Us'll see whether uncle makes it 'ome first though. I be goin' on back with these few eggs an' I'll leave 'ee to do what you knows uncle would want 'ee to.'

'Right, Aunt, but we may have a little snow fight before we get back.' Jimmy's eyes glistened.

'Yes, and we may build a snowman too,' Danny added.

'Boys, bring in a few more logs when you get back, please. There be some in the shed at the side of the 'ouse.'

Lil waved and walked carefully back to the farmhouse while the boys went into the shippon to check on the cows.

Stan was glad that he had brought his waterproof cape and had put it on before saying goodbye to Fred. He had a few more outlying farms to deliver to, mostly letters, what looked like late Christmas cards and a small parcel. It was getting impossible to ride his bike. He would just have to push it. It was considerably warmer now that it was snowing and the wind had dropped. With the effort of striding out and pushing his bike, and the fuel from the delicious pasty that Barbara had given him, he wasn't cold. The snow was lying in the lanes, on the hedges and the branches of the trees. It looked beautiful and he drank in the scene as he trudged along. Who'd want to work in the town or the city, he thought, where they'd be shut up indoors all day? That would be like being in prison. His life was the outdoors, whatever the weather threw at him. Making his way back through West Buckland on the road, or what he could see of it, Stan realised that he could no longer push his bike and certainly couldn't carry it all the way back to Sunnybank about three miles away. He had to call at West Buckland School, a public school for boys just outside the village, and surrounded by its own magnificent grounds. There was some post to drop off at the office anyway and he would ask permission to leave his bike in the gardeners' shed. Most of the boys had gone home for the Christmas holiday and would be returning soon. Some boys had to stay at the school if their homes were overseas. It was those boys who were out on the front drive having a snowball fight. One snowball caught Stan soundly on his shoulder.

'Sorry, Postie,' shouted a boy of about eleven years old, who clearly wasn't sorry at all.

'Good shot, young un,' Stan shouted back, intending to return the compliment when he had parked his bike. Stan went to the office but, being Saturday, there was no secretary there. The caretaker was in the corridor nearby, talking to the Senior Master. They all greeted each other and Stan was told that of course he could leave his bike and collect it when he was able to resume his postal duties, hopefully the following week.

'I see you got a direct hit, Stan,' commented the Senior Master. 'I'll reprimand those boys and bring them in to do some work in the Library.'

'No, Sir.' Stan replied. 'Please don't do that. I may just get a shot in at 'em on me way out. Boys will be boys, won't 'em?'

'That's true, Stan. They couldn't go home at Christmas so this snow is helping to make up for what they've missed.'

'Mind how you go, Stan,' Bob, the caretaker said as Stan handed over the post to the Senior Master and waved goodbye. After leaving his bike at the gardeners' shed, and firing a few snowballs at the group of boys, he trudged down the drive and back onto the road.

It was getting towards two thirty, and although he had emptied his post bag, it would take well over an hour to reach home and the snow was beginning to fall faster.

Back at Sunnybank, Lil and the boys had shaken the snow from their outer clothes and banged it from their boots. It was almost dark by the time they heard the sound of Bruce's barking heralding the return of Stan, who appeared at the kitchen door white with the glistening snowflakes falling from his cape and covering his cap.

'Oh, my goodness, Stan. If you'm wanting to play Father Christmas, you'm over a week too late. Don't come in yer with they wet clothes. I'll get a 'ot drink while you'm changin'.

Stan stepped into the hall and began to remove his wet clothes and shake them outside the front door. Bruce slunk in past him and hid under the wooden bench which was fixed to the wall and ran on two sides of the long kitchen table. Jimmy winked at Danny and they both smiled, knowing that Aunt Lil didn't allow the dog into the kitchen. Uncle always pretended not to notice that the old dog had come indoors and ignored his wife's exasperation when it did.

'I'd best change out of this uniform and go and feed the animals and milk the cows,' Stan sighed. 'I should 'ave 'ad skis to get 'ome,' he added. ' 'Tis thick on the ground now, Maid.' Stan started up the stairs.

'We've all fed the chickens and the pigs, Uncle,' Danny shouted, with pride.

'And we've milked the cows and fed them,' Jimmy added, pulling himself to his full ten-year-old height as if to stress his senior management role.

'The boys 'ave been wonderful, Stan. Us 'ave managed it together but you've taught 'em well.'

'What about Madam?' Stan asked doubtfully.

'Good as gold, Stan. No trouble at all, was 'er, boys? Now stop fussin' an' go and change an' then come an' eat your dinner for tea. 'An' yes, us 'ave managed to sort out the milk and some be in the churn for collectin' in the mornin'. Us 'ad a job wheelin' it down the lane, in the barrow, an' us don't know if the milk lorry can get 'ere in the mornin' anyway.'

Stan smiled at the boys in admiration. 'Well done, Jimmy! Well done, Danny! After I've 'ad somethin' to eat, I'll walk up round the shippon to check all the animals be settled for the night. I know you be city boys but there bain't many your age round yer could 'ave done what you've done today.' Stan nodded his approval and went upstairs to change out of his uniform.

Jimmy and Danny looked at each other, their eyes glowing with pride.

'Sit down and 'ave tea, boys, while uncle 'as 'is dinner.' Lil carried in bread and homemade cakes and sat at the table. 'You should be goin' back to school in a few days but 'tis snowing 'ard and I don't think the bus will be able to get through to pick 'ee up.'

'That's a shame, Aunt,' Jimmy commented with a straight face.

Stan returned to the kitchen, sat at his place at the head of the table and began to eat his stew. 'Terrible t'would be if 'em can't get to school.' Stan said with a wink at the boys. 'Whatever would 'em do yer all day?'

'There's plenty to do here, Uncle.' Danny said.

'I hope it snows a lot more,' Jimmy added.

Lil groaned. 'You go and play with one of your games now you two.'

'Snakes and ladders,' Jimmy shouted and they left the table and carried their plates into the scullery.

'You'm tired out, Stan. Did 'ee walk back, an' what 'ave 'ee done with your bike?'

'I've left it up at the "big" school. The Senior Master said I could leave it in the gardeners' shed. The walk 'ome was 'ard work. 'Tis layin' thick now, a good six inches.'

Lil passed her husband the dish containing the rest of the rice pudding. 'Eat that up from the bakin' dish, Stan, and save the washin' up.'

'Proper, Maid,' he smiled. 'Twas a good job I 'ad one of Barbara's pasties when I stopped there 'smornin'. That stoked me up for the walk 'ome.'

' 'Ow be they, Barbara and Fred, Stan? I 'aven't seen 'em for months.'

'They'm fine an' they've got their niece there

stayin' from London. Nice girl but 'er don't look quite right.'

'Oh, Emily 'er's called. An' there's a brother called Jonathan. I remember 'em from when they used to come with their parents an' stay at the Baxter's farm. 'Er's about twenty-two now an' a teacher. But what do 'ee mean by sayin' 'er don't look right?'

''Er talked to me friendly like, an' talked nice to 'er aunt and uncle but 'er looked like 'er mind was somewhere else. 'An' 'er face looked sad an' 'er skin was pale.'

'Livin' in London would make 'ee look pale, Stan, even without all they bombs droppin'.'

'Anyway, I told Barbara to drive 'er over one afternoon to see 'ee.'

'That would be lovely to 'ave a bit of comp'ny an' someone to talk to 'cos us 'avn't seen any volks over Christmas and New Year. It'll 'ave to be when the snow's gone though, won't it? And did 'ee say that Barbara can drive now, Stan?'

'Fred said 'er learned last week when 'e'd gone off in 'is tractor to get a part for it over at George's at Landkey. By the time 'e got back 'er could drive, or 'er said 'er could.' Stan finished the rice pudding, scraping the dish clean. 'Mind you, Fred said that when 'e got back from Landkey, one of the old 'en 'ouses 'ad been knocked over, an' there was a milk churn with a bit of a dent in un.'

'Oh. Stan, no wonder I don't want to drive a car.' Lil shook her head determinedly. 'Whatever did Fred say?'

'E wasn't too bothered, Lil. 'E said 'e was just glad 'er didn't drive into any of 'is animals.'

Chapter 4

Still. **So still** and silent. Nothing was moving. No-one was moving except her, in a slow-motion sort of way through the scene of devastation. Everything was grey. The sky was grey and the buildings were grey. The clothes the people were wearing were grey and the dust in the air was grey and choking. She struggled forward, straining to clamber over the piles of stone and rubble. Up, up she climbed in a cumbersome manner, slipping and sliding back and making hardly any progress towards the many pairs of little hands waving desperately at her from a parapet high above, where the sky was blue. No matter how hard she tried to go higher, she kept slipping backwards, until she saw an iron bar sticking out of a block of concrete. She gripped it tightly, pulling herself up. On and up she climbed, over ever bigger boulders and rocks, like you'd see at the beach. And still the little hands were waving but she wasn't getting any closer to them. Suddenly she saw a piece of torn cloth poking out from a crack in the rocks and flapping in the wind. She had to reach it. She was tiring and could climb no higher. In a final effort she stretched out her right hand towards the fabric and grasped it. Clinging to the sheer rock-face with her left hand she opened her right hand and saw instead a child's shoe. It was a black shoe and the buckle was broken. She closed her eyes and fell backwards, clawing at the smoking air and dropping the shoe. Down, down she went into the grey nowhere of despair.

Emily opened her eyes and sat up in bed. She was hot and breathless and the bedclothes were on the floor. She got out of bed and stood by the window. She pulled back one of the curtains and looked out on the silent scene, snow lying thick and glistening in the moonlight. She slowed her breathing and wiped her brow with the back of her hand. The wintry scene was as still as the scene in her dream but it held no threat and no fear. It wasn't asking anything of her. She didn't have to do anything, just look at it. How many times had she dreamt the same dream? Would she never be free of it? She picked up her blankets and eiderdown off the floor and remade the bed. She took a drink from the glass of water on the bedside table and closed the curtains.

Auntie Barbara passed Emily a cup of tea as the outside door opened and Uncle Fred came in and joined them at the table.

'I'm ready for elevenses today, Babs,' he said.

'Fred, have you stamped the snow off your

boots outside the front door?'

'Yes, dear. I knew you were going to ask me that, and I shook my coat, too.' He looked at his niece. 'You see, Emily, I'm well trained.'

'It's not snowing now, Uncle, is it?'

'No, and I don't think we'll get any more.'

'It makes much more work for you with all those animals inside. I do want to help, Uncle.'

'I've told Emily that she is not to do anything until she's had a week's rest. You can read or knit or play your violin if you like but you are not to do any work. I promised your Mum we'd look after you and she'll be checking up on us.'

Emily smiled. 'Yes, she said she'd be phoning every Saturday evening.'

Fred leaned forward and took one of the cakes his wife had put cooling on the cake rack. 'I'm worried about that sheep we had in here yesterday. I thought she was on the mend but I think I'll have to call out the vet if she doesn't pick up soon.'

'It won't be easy driving here in this, Fred,' his wife commented, moving the cake rack closer to Emily, 'and I'm sure we won't see Stan for a few days.'

'How did he manage to get home with his bike?' Emily asked. 'He couldn't have ridden it.'

'He'd have left it somewhere on the way back to pick up another day, Emily. I'm just wondering if our workers will get here today, Babs.'

'It's all a bit hit and miss with farm help now that we don't have our daughter helping us.' Barbara gathered up the cups and put them in the sink.

'Helen always wanted to work on the farm and could do the work of most men,' Fred remarked. 'Farming was all she ever wanted to do, although she could have chosen other careers.'

'She loved science, especially biology and we thought she might have chosen nursing.' Barbara picked up a dish cloth and started washing the dishes. 'But the indoor life wasn't for her and when she left school she worked with her dad on the farm here, as happy as Larry.'

'Then she met Donald at a dance in South Molton and that was that. A year later they were married and now she's living near Exford on the farm Don runs with his father. They have a lovely cottage there and all work the farm together.'

'Sheep farming mainly and beef cattle too,' Fred added.

'You must miss her,' Emily commented, 'but she's not too far away.'

'She's been a wonderful daughter and a wonderful worker, helping Fred with the farm.'

'Of course, we miss her. She was always positive and optimistic in her outlook. There are ups and downs in farming but she got stuck in and well, – '

Fred stopped and sighed deeply, and stared at the kitchen tablecloth.

Auntie Barbara looked at her niece and smiled. 'We have two Land Army girls that we share with our neighbour's farm, Emily. They are great workers but they're busy dashing between the two farms and this morning what with the weather, they will be slowed up. I was expecting one of them earlier to help with the milking but she didn't turn up.'

Suddenly, the telephone rang. Emily wasn't used to the sound. They didn't have a telephone at home and she didn't know anyone who did apart from her grandparents, who had one for the shop.

Fred stood up and went across and lifted the receiver. 'Fred Baxter speaking. Oh, I see. I wondered why she didn't turn up. No, of course not. Well, when she's better. You'll send the other girl to help with the milking tonight. Fair enough. Thanks, Gordon.' He replaced the receiver and looked at his wife.

'Is she ill, Fred?' Barbara asked.

'Apparently, the two girls went with a group of others to a Social Evening in Swimbridge one night last week and missed their lift home. They ended up walking all the way back and getting cold and soaked.'

'They're a tough pair but that wasn't very sensible, was it?'

'She's quite poorly, in bed at the moment,' Fred said.

'Do the two Land Army girls live at the farm next to yours, Uncle?'

'Yes, Emily. They live at Buckland Farm. They are friends and wanted to stay together so Gordon and his wife Dorothy were happy to let them live in at their farm.'

'It's very good of them to offer that but the girls are on hand to help out more there than they could do here. I hope you're not going to overdo it, Fred.' Barbara took some potatoes out of the larder and began peeling them.

'No, don't keep worrying, Babs. By the way, I've been meaning to ask you something. Do you know how the old henhouse got knocked over and broken? I know we weren't using it and I'd hoped to find time to do some repairs to it. It looks quite pretty now that there's a covering of snow on it.' He winked at Emily.

'Fred, that henhouse has been falling apart for months. I don't know what you're fussing about.' Barbara turned on the tap and swished the potatoes under it with considerable vigour.

'Well, dear I thought you'd given up on a henhouse and prepared us some firewood.' He left the kitchen, hurriedly closing the door behind him just as Barbara picked up a potato and threw it across the room.

'Now Emily. You're looking tired. Did you sleep all right?'

'Well, Auntie, I was awake some of the time. It is very quiet here and I'm not used to it, I suppose.'

'You were warm enough weren't you, dear?'

'Oh, yes and it's a lovely bed and a lovely room too. Thank you so much.' Emily looked down.

Barbara moved towards the sofa and sat down. 'Come and sit here by me, Emily.' She patted the worn sofa and shook one of the cushions.

Emily went and sat next to her aunt.

'Can you tell me how you are, Emily? Are you ready to talk about it, because I will be happy to listen when you are, dear?' She smiled gently at her niece.

'Not yet, Auntie. Not just yet, but thank you anyway.' Emily looked down at the rug where the sheep had been sleeping a few days earlier.

Barbara jumped up. 'Well, I'm not going to press you. Tell me what you want, when you want. Meanwhile, how about some exciting reading?'

'What would that be, Auntie?'

Barbara picked up a magazine lying on a low table.

'The "Farmers Weekly", dear. It's absolutely riveting!'

They both laughed.

Chapter 5

A few days passed, the weather turned warmer and the last signs of the snow melted away, just leaving a few white blobs here and there in dark corners of the yard where the sun never shone. Emily had gone for a short walk along the lane leading from the shippon to the henhouses. Barbara decided she would clean the brasses so she laid an old sheet on the kitchen table, collected some vests which her husband had worn to shreds, picked up the Brasso from the cupboard and reached up to the mantelpiece to take down the many items left to them when Fred's parents moved out. Fred loved the various brass animals and other farm objects, having grown up with them without having had to clean them, but Barbara wasn't fond of ornaments unless they served a useful purpose, which, in her opinion, these certainly didn't. She sighed and started on the task. She smiled as she started rubbing away at a horse pulling a cart, thinking of the telephone call her sister had made to them on Saturday evening. Lydia had asked if they were snowed in and trapped on the farm, away from all civilisation. Barbara had told her that if they were trapped, at least they would have enough food to keep them going for a good while. How were they doing for food in Lewisham, she had wondered? Having her niece come to stay found Barbara thinking back to the years she spent growing up in Lewisham in the home she had shared with her sister and their parents. Their father, Thomas Hicks, ran a grocery business and he and their mother Olive worked it successfully together. Dad's eyesight was poor, which is what kept him out of the first war although being a Quaker, a Member of the Society of Friends, taking up arms would have been an issue for him. He was a hard worker and a life-long member of the Liberal party. If there were banners to be made or carried on a protest march, dad was the one to do it. He didn't do any shouting, just protested quietly by his presence; he was tall and striking looking so didn't have to shout to draw attention to himself or his banner. Mum was more of a shouter, and soon had something to say if she thought things were unfair. Although they were better off than most of the neighbours in their area, they kept an eye open for the underdog and that social awareness was passed on to their daughters. Barbara helped her parents in the shop and worked part-time as a librarian, being an avid reader, and Lydia trained as a nurse. The two sisters attended Friends' Meetings occasionally but their parents were regular attenders and committed Members.

In 1921 Lydia met and married a quiet young

man named Paul Ward, who was working as a porter at the hospital where she was training. Having spent time as a young patient in the same hospital, Paul had a burning ambition to train as a nurse, a profession occupied almost entirely by women. They settled happily together in the same borough as the hospital in which they worked, being of like minds with so many issues. Emily was born in 1922 followed two years later by her brother Jonathan.

Barbara's romance began quite differently. She was on a day out in London with some of her friends. 'Going up West,' they used to call it. At the time she thought it was the height of glamour as they jumped on and off buses and even shared a taxi once when they went to see a show. Fred Baxter had taken a short break from the farm work he shared with his father and travelled by train from North Devon to London to see the sights. Barbara saw him standing by the lion statues at Trafalgar Square. He seemed lost and she left her friends to go and ask him if he was looking for something.

'Just a way out,' he'd said. She didn't know what he meant at first. He smiled at her, and all the hubbub he wasn't used to, the crowds and noise, faded away. She was standing in front of him, alone and pretty, with a kind expression in her dark eyes.

'Can you show me the way out?' he'd asked. She'd looked at him and seen a strong, handsome man, completely at odds with his surroundings. Suddenly it didn't seem a strange question to Barbara and she'd answered him without even thinking about it.

'Yes. Let's go to St. James's Park. It's quiet and peaceful there.' That was the start of their relationship. They married in 1922 and she moved from her London life of business and bustle to a country life of business and quiet. She took to it immediately, even though Lydia had expressed her doubts.

'It'll be like moving back into the Victorian Age, Babs,' she'd said. 'There'll be outside lavs and no electricity and lots of mud and cow pats everywhere. You'll never stick it. Look how you've always liked to follow fashion. It's no good parading the latest outfit before a herd of cows, is it?' But Barbara loved farm life. She and Fred settled in a rented cottage in West Buckland, about half a mile from the farm Fred worked with his father. Their daughter Helen was born in 1923. The years passed and in 1939, shortly before the start of the war, Fred's parents decided to retire and move out of the farmhouse. They bought a bungalow in South Molton where Albert Baxter could potter in the garden, as much as his increasingly arthritic hips would allow him, and Ada Baxter could enjoy a more social life, walking to the shops and joining the local Choral Society and Women's Institute, activities for which unending farm duties never seemed to allow time. Fred's dad helped out with the lighter duties on the farm occasionally but by the time war had broken out, young Helen had finished school and worked alongside her father doing what she'd wanted to do from her early childhood. She was a clever girl but her heart was set on a farming life and, just like her mother, when her mind was made up, there was no changing it, which proved to be a salvation to the family, as many young men who might have become farm labourers were called up to serve their country. Barbara smiled to herself when she remembered the three of them moving into the farmhouse. Yes. Lydia had been right about the amenities there. How had her mother-in- law put up with it? The family had come to a fair monetary arrangement so the farm was passed on to her and Fred.

'Right, Fred,' she'd said. 'I want an inside lavatory and a bathroom and a telephone. We both work hard so I don't see why we can't join the Twentieth Century.' Fred had agreed and the farm was modernised, adding an up to date milking parlour, and a nearly new but second-hand tractor. Barbara remembered the excitement of seeing the changes they'd made. It was lovely to be able to talk to her sister and brother-in-law on the phone now and then, although it was easier to talk to Mum and

Dad as they had their own phone at their shop; but when Lydia used the telephone box near her home, the call had to be short and was often interrupted by the pips sounding.

Barbara stood up and lifted the horse brasses from their hooks on the wall either side of the fireplace. She smiled as she looked back on the once happy day-to-day pattern of family life which had later become increasingly overshadowed by the threat of war. The country had been preparing for the worst for several years. Even in Germany its own government was a threat to Jewish families. Terrible things were happening to them, and Thomas and Olive Hicks felt that they could not stand by and be witness to such evil. They became part of the Kindertransport movement in 1939 which rescued Jewish children from Germany and Poland and brought them to England where they were fostered, or in the case of the older children, given accommodation in hostels. Mostly, the work offered to the older youngsters was of a domestic nature or in agriculture. Isaac, who was sixteen when he arrived at Liverpool Street Station with hundreds of other young people, was offered work in the family's shop which slotted in well as business was brisk. Although many groceries were rationed or unavailable, there was no rationing on vegetables, and people made up their meals with more of them as meat was in very short supply.

Barbara had listened to her parents talking about Isaac. He had arrived speaking no English and had spent most of his time talking with young Emily who was learning French and German at school. Her German improved considerably and she had planned to concentrate on music and languages, while training as a teacher. Isaac's English also improved although it was peppered with rather bizarre phrases such as 'Right, Mate,' and 'Can you Adam and Eve it?'

The sound of a motorcar penetrated Barbara's thoughts as she began to replace the gleaming ornaments on and at the side of the mantelpiece. She gathered up the cloths and the tin of Brasso and looked out of the window to see Daniel Smith stepping out of his car. The vet. She'd better tidy up and wash her hands. She'd take him a mug of coffee later. She ran the hot tap and soaped her hands under it. Fred was outside greeting Daniel. Not that Fred or anyone could get much out of Daniel in return. Not since that terrible tragedy. He was a changed man and seemed older and distant, although he was only in his late twenties. Barbara sighed. Changes, always changes. She and Fred hadn't expected Helen to meet her young farmer so early in her life but they were the perfect match for one another. Helen was not only a loss as a cheerful and loving daughter but an able help on the farm. Barbara frowned. Fred looked so tired these days, and no wonder. He was working too hard.

Such is the pattern of life; growing up and growing old and moving on. Wartime families, whether in the country or the cities, had to adapt and be resilient.

The kettle was on the boil so Barbara made coffee, or what posed as it in wartime and took some homemade biscuits out of the tin in the larder and put them on a plate. She wondered where Emily was.

Her young niece had wanted to know how her brother was when she'd spoken with her mother on the phone on Saturday. They'd always been close, best friends as children. If there was football in the street, Emily joined in and woe betide anyone who said she couldn't play because she was a girl. Jonathan was taller and tougher looking than all of the boys of his age, and some older. In fact, he was like their dad in build. What Jonathan said went with their playmates and if he said that Emily could join in the football games, that was the end of the matter. She had a good ball sense and was better than most of the boys so they all wanted her on their team. Jonathan was a gentle giant and didn't throw his weight about, and was well-liked in the Fire Brigade. which may have kept him out of the services but certainly had not kept him out of danger. She gritted her teeth as she thought of what he must have been dealing with during the Blitz. No wonder Emily was as she was.

Barbara loaded the tray, left the house and walked towards the sheep shed. Fred hadn't given up on the poorly sheep and Daniel had come to look at it.

'Tea up,' Barbara called as she walked into the shed. 'Or should I say, coffee?' She put down the tray on a bale of straw and looked across the shed at the huddle of people around a prostrate sheep.

'Hello, Daniel. Oh, there you are, Emily. I was wondering where you were.'

'She's been helping me, Babs, haven't you, Ems?'

'Not overdoing it, I hope.' Barbara glared at her husband.

'Good morning, Mrs Baxter.' Daniel Smith looked up politely and took the mug of coffee with a quiet 'Thank you.'

'So, can you see any hope, Daniel?' asked Fred, indicating the sheep while Barbara looked closely at Emily's pale face.

'Time will tell, Fred, but I'll do my best,' he answered.

Chapter 6

Emily came into the kitchen carrying a basket of eggs.

'Thank you, dear,' her aunt said as she took them, wiped them and put them on a deep bowl in the larder. 'Has Daniel left? I don't suppose he said much.'

'Yes, Aunt, he drove off about five minutes ago.'

Barbara finished peeling the potatoes, placed them in a saucepan of boiling water and put them on the hotplate on the Aga. She took the leftovers from Sunday's joint from the larder and started to carve it. 'You've just missed Stan. He brought a letter addressed to you but I don't recognise the writing. It looks unusual.' She pointed to the dresser and Emily picked up the letter and smiled. 'It's from my friend, Isaac and it'll be in German. He has a different style of writing from us and writes the address in a different order, with the county before the village.'

'It reached you, Emily. That's the main thing and Stan would have recognised your name anyway.' Barbara looked closely at her niece. 'I'm glad to see that you've got some colour in your cheeks today. A little walk each morning is good for you.'

'Uncle showed me how to feed the chickens and he's going to show me how to clean them out and look after them, Auntie.' Emily tore open the envelope.

'Oh, he is, is he? I don't think you – '

'Please, Auntie. I want to help somehow and uncle said he knew you wouldn't approve but perhaps a regular task would allow me to focus on something else. It would be good for me and I really want to do it and – ' she paused. 'Uncle is teaching me all their names.'

Barbara shook her head and smiled. 'Yes, I'll bet he is. All right, then, but don't do too much too soon. I'll make you a hot drink while you read your letter.'

'Thank you, Auntie.' Emily took the letter from the envelope and read it.

Isaac was fine, Emily's grandparents were so kind to him, they were all busy in the shop but couldn't get much fruit to sell. When they had oranges, they had to go to pregnant women. Joe, the delivery boy fell off his bike but was not hurt badly. He was free-wheeling downhill with his feet on the handlebars and lost his balance. Isaac wrote that there was still no news of his parents in Munich. He kept thinking about his grandparents who had had a farm in Bavaria. He described some of the happy times he had there and still yearned for those bygone days in the countryside.

When Emily has time to write, could she please tell him about the farm where she was living? It was signed, Your friend, Isaac.

Emily put the letter back in the envelope and smiled. He was such a kind young man. How terrible not to have any idea of the whereabouts of his family. She swallowed and closed her eyes, as the memories of some of the horrific things she had seen came back to her. Suddenly, her mood was broken by the telephone ringing.

Her aunt picked up the receiver. 'Hello. Barbara Baxter speaking. Yes, I'll tell him. The one who was ill is a little better and can come this afternoon to help with the milking, but not tomorrow morning or evening. No, if the other girl has caught it. She's coughing a lot. I hope it's not gone on her chest. Yes, of course, she'll be out of action for a while. I'll tell Fred and he'll phone you in a day or so. Thanks, Gordon. Goodbye.' Barbara Baxter looked up at the ceiling and sighed. 'There are only twenty-four hours in a day but your uncle seems to be working most of them, Emily.' The door opened and Fred Baxter came in and walked across to the sink to wash his hands.

'I heard Babs. So, the other girl is ill now?' Barbara nodded and took three dinner plates from the shelf and placed them on the table.

'I'd better get on with preparing the dinner. I meant to tell you, Emily that Stan said that his wife wondered if we would be free to drive over to Sunnybank this afternoon. The weather is kind and perhaps it would take our minds off things. What do you think? Are you happy with that?'

'It would mean being driven by the wrecker of henhouses, Emily, if you can put up with a bit of rally driving.'

'I'm grateful for the invitation, Uncle,' Emily smiled nervously, remembering her experience as a passenger on the day of her arrival.

'Fred, do you want some dinner? It's just mashed potatoes, cold meat and pickles today. I've been busy cleaning the brass.' She looked pointedly at her husband and then at the shining objects on the wall and the mantelpiece.

'Oh, they look lovely, Babs. I was thinking about getting a few more to go on the dresser.'

'Don't you dare, Fred.' She looked at him quietly, paused and said, 'I think we should try to get our own Land Army girl and have her living in here.'

'I'll manage, Babs.' He sat at the table, sighed, and opened a copy of Farmers Weekly and turned the pages distractedly without reading anything.

'You'll have to have more help, Fred, there's no denying it.' Barbara started to serve out the dinner while Emily laid the table. The meal proceeded without the usual banter.

'We'll be off to Sunnybank then, Fred,' Barbara said as her husband left the table to prepare for the afternoon's work.

'Babs, don't drive up to their garage or you'll have to back down. There's no place to turn up there. Leave the car outside the gate on the grass verge at the bottom.'

'You think I can't reverse, don't you, Fred?'

Emily could tell that her uncle's advice was interpreted as a challenge by his wife.

'Well, I'm only just saying, it would be better to walk up to the cottage. That's what I would do.' He waved at Emily and crossed his fingers as his wife turned her back to start clearing the table.

At about two o'clock Barbara and Emily set off in the car for the short journey to Sunnybank. Emily sat in the front, holding onto the sides of her seat as Auntie Barbara forced the car into action and shot off from the farmyard and through the entrance gate and onto the road leading to West Buckland. Fortunately, they didn't see another vehicle until they were driving down the hill towards their destination. Ahead of them and coming up the hill there was a delivery van. The road, like most roads in the area only allowed single traffic but fortunately, the two vehicles met one another at a place where there was a wide green pull-in leading to a gate. Auntie Barbara didn't consider turning in there and while Emily closed her eyes and gripped the sides of her seat, the oncoming van pulled into the grass verge at the last moment.

'Hmm!' Barbara frowned and drove on, turning right at the bottom of the hill into the wide area by the roadside where Fred had told her to park. She stopped the car and got out to open the gate so that she could drive up the stony lane and leave the car by Stan's make-shift garage.

'Auntie!' Emily called out to her. 'Look, there's a van already parked up there.'

Barbara returned to the car and took a basket from the back seat. They both started to walk up the steep narrow path to the house. A gaggle of geese came towards them, bending their heads and looking and sounding aggressive. Barbara handed the basket to Emily and ran at the geese, shouting and waving her arms. They beat a hasty retreat, quickly aware of who was boss. Walking on up to the homemade garage Barbara inspected the van parked there. 'Oh, it's the baker's van, Emily.'

'You've parked in a good spot, Auntie,' Emily said, relieved that Auntie Barbara wouldn't be testing fate by having to reverse down to the road later.

They reached the top of the lane, turned a corner and went up the steps and knocked on the front door of the Devon longhouse.

Chapter 7

Stan opened the front door and ushered the visitors into the hall.

'Come in. Lil will be so pleased to see 'ee. Us 'ave got our friend, Maggie yer too.' He smiled at Barbara and Emily, took their coats and hung them on the hooks in the hall. 'Go on in. Lil 'as just made a pot of tea.'

The two visitors went into the kitchen. Emily immediately connected with the cosiness of the room as the feeling of familiarity and comfort came flooding back to her from visits she had enjoyed many years ago with her parents and brother. A slim, brown-haired woman came towards them, smiling and holding out her arms in welcome. 'Do you remember me, Emily? I remember you but you was much younger. But you'm just as pretty as when us saw 'ee last, all they years ago before the war. Hello Barbara. 'Tis good to see 'ee. Us is neighbours but us never gets to meet much, do us?' Lil directed the visitors to the long wooden seat under the window. Emily recalled that it was attached to the wall on two sides with the large, rectangular table taking up much of the room and wooden dining chairs set at it on its other two sides.

'It's lovely to see you, Lil. You're right. We don't see each other often enough. There's always so much to do on a farm, outdoors and in.' Barbara smiled and took a cup of tea that Lil had poured for her.

'Now this be my friend, Margaret Partridge.' Lil indicated Margaret who was sitting in an armchair by the range.

Margaret stood up and walked across the room and sat on one of the chairs at the table. 'Hello, Barbara. Hello, Emily. You'll have seen the bread van parked by the garage. Sorry if I have stopped you driving up part way from the bottom of the lane. Sunnybank is the end of my round and I am always spoiled when I call here. I'm given a lovely dinner.'

'Of course, us gives 'ee dinner, Margaret. 'Er works much too 'ard in that bakery, don't 'er, Stan?'

Stan had seated himself on the narrow part of the wooden bench, facing the door to the hall and the place from where he could look out of the kitchen window down towards the road leading to Swimbridge.

''Er's cookin' in the bake'ouse, or servin' in the shop, or drivin' the van all over North Devon. Jill of all trades, bain't 'ee Maggie?'

'You exaggerate, Stan.' Margaret shook her head and smiled at him.

Lil passed a cup of tea to Emily. 'Do you remember comin' yer, Emily?'

'Yes Mrs Webber, and I remember seeing the animals and especially the little goslings.'

'Call me Lil, please Emily, or Aunt Lil, if you like.'

'Didn't 'ee fall in the stream at the bottom of the field, Emily?' Stan asked.

'Yes, I did. I certainly remember that. It was Spring and the primroses were lovely and there was a big clump of them on the other side of the stream, and I thought I could just reach them if I balanced on a big stone in the middle.' Emily closed her eyes and smiled. The room was silent apart from a log spitting as it burned unsteadily in the range. She opened her eyes wide and said, 'But the stone wobbled and I lost my balance and fell in. The water wasn't deep but it was cold and I was soaked. Jonathan was there and he pulled me out.'

'And 'e brought you back up 'ere to me,' Lil added. 'Your mum and dad dried 'ee as best 'em could and then Stan drove 'ee all back to your Auntie Barbara's.'

'What a nuisance, I was,' Emily's face was lit up with the memories of those happy childhood days.

The room was quiet and Barbara held her breath as she looked at the transformation on the face of her niece as she relived those carefree times.

Stan stood up. ' 'appy days,' he nodded, 'but I must be gettin' on. I want to spread some more muck on the vegetable patch while us 'ave got a bit of dry weather. I'll see 'ee all later.'

He left the room as Lil shouted out to him. 'Stan, us'll ave our proper tea early cos I 'spect Barbara won't want to drive back in the dark, will 'ee, dear?'

The front door banged shut and the ladies looked at each other.

' 'ow's Fred, Barbara?' Lil enquired.

'Overworked, Lil. The Land Army girls are very able but sharing them with our neighbour's farm doesn't really work. One of them caught a chill and got better but not before she had passed it on to the other one! They've been quite poorly with bad coughs.'

'It's a dairy farm you have, isn't it, Barbara?' Margaret asked.

'Yes, Margaret, but we have sheep too, and now that our daughter has married and is running a farm on Exmoor with her husband and father-in-law, there's too much work for Fred, really.'

'Are you staying long with your aunt and uncle, Emily?' Margaret smiled at the young woman. 'Lil told me that you live in London.'

Suddenly Emily found herself tongue-tied. She looked at her aunt with a worried expression, as she attempted to form a reply.

'I – I – I'm not sure.'

'Emily witnessed a terrible bombing as she was going to work in London, didn't you, Emily? My sister Lydia thought it would be a change for her to come and stay with us for a while to get over it.' Barbara looked at Lil and then at Margaret. 'Do you live in Barnstaple, Margaret?' Barbara thought it would be a good idea to divert the conversation.

'Yes, I do. My husband, Jack works at Hopgoods Garage, I work at the bakery in the town and we have two children, Diana and Mary. Diana is eight and Mary is three. We did have an evacuee but she returned to her home in London just after Christmas.'

'You have been busy, then.' Barbara smiled.

'Yes, but I couldn't manage without the help of my mother and father. They live in the next street and help out with the children.'

'That reminds me, Lil, how are your evacuees doing, Jimmy and Danny?'

'Oh, they'm good boys, and 'ave come on wonderful since us 'ad 'em. They'll be back from school soon, starvin' as usual. I think I'd best get us somethin' to eat afore they gets 'ere.' Lil gathered the cups and saucers onto a tray to carry into the scullery.

Barbara stood up to help.

'No, Barbara, stay and talk to Margaret. 'Er'll

'ave to go soon.'

'Yes, Lil. Before I leave, let me have that skirt you wanted me to alter.'

'It's on the dresser, Margaret. Thank you. The 'em's come undone and you know I be useless with sewin'.' Lil went into the scullery to fetch scones, their own clotted cream and homemade jam.

Margaret folded the skirt and put it into her bag. She picked up her bread basket and leather shoulder bag containing the day's takings for the sales she had made during her round.

'If you are in town, come and call on us, Barbara, and bring Emily, of course. I don't work every day but I usually know a week or two ahead which days I have off and which days I only work half a day.'

'That would be lovely, Margaret. I don't come into town very often but sometimes Fred goes to the Cattle Market on a Friday. We could come in with him, couldn't we, Emily? I'll write down my phone number and we could arrange something.'

'We don't have a phone, Barbara, but I think Bert would allow me to phone you from work.'

Barbara opened her bag, took out a note book and pencil and hastily scribbled down the phone number for the farm, tore out a page and handed it to Margaret.

Lil came into the kitchen with a tray laden with scones, cream, jam and crockery. 'I'll fetch the teapot and the milk and us'll 'ave our proper tea. The jam's not quite like it should be,'cos I've used 'oney instead of sugar, what with the rationin'.' She placed the tray on the table and Barbara and Emily set out the tea things. 'Us 'ave only got two 'ives 'cos Stan's got quite enough to do what with 'is post round as well as runnin' this small 'oldin' but the bees 'ave 'elped out with the war effort.'

They all laughed as the door from the hall opened and Stan came into the kitchen with his beloved dog, Bruce, close at his heels. Unnoticed by Lil, Bruce slunk silently under the table to sit at Stan's feet as his master sat at the head of the table.

'Stan, you can smell the teapot. Margaret, are you goin' now or do 'ee want some tea first?'

'No thank you, Lil. I must be off. Thank you for the lovely dinner, as always. I've left your order on the dresser and taken the money you put on the saucer. Is that right?'

'Yes, that's what it was there for, Margaret. Us'll see 'ee in a week, or maybe this Friday.'

'I'm not sure yet, Lil. It may be Maurice doing the delivery if Bert wants me in the bakehouse.'

'There'll be a dinner for whoever 'tis,' Lil replied, waving at her friend as Margaret left the room.

'Bye, everyone,' Margaret smiled as she closed the door and made her way down to the van.

Barbara stood up and looked out of the window.

'Will Margaret be able to pass my car at the bottom of the drive? I think it's wide enough, Stan.'

'Yes, 'er'll get by. 'Er's a good driver.'

'Please take a scone, Emily.' Lil pushed the plate towards her.

'That reminds me, I have a little something for you, Lil.' Barbara reached down for her bag and took out a package wrapped in brown paper and handed it across the table to Lil.

'Oh, 'ow lovely.' Lil took the parcel and lifted out a large jar of blackcurrant jam. 'That's very kind of 'ee, Barbara.' Stan nodded his approval as he spread a dollop of cream on his scone and topped it with some of their own jam. 'Us 'ave got some blackcurrant bushes but us didn't do well with 'em this yer. The weather was either too 'ot or too wet, so well done you and Fred.'

'Win some, lose some with gardening, isn't it, Stan?' Barbara smiled. 'There's just too much to do to get everything right, but Emily is going to help Fred with the hens, aren't you, dear?'

Emily had been listening to the gentle conversation and relaxing in the homeliness of the cosy kitchen. 'Yes, I want to learn about that, and maybe I can help somewhere else on the farm, too,' she replied with a little smile.

They finished their tea and Barbara stood up and started to help clear away the dishes. 'We must go soon, Lil, as I don't drive in the dark, and it gets dark so early, doesn't it?'

'No, dear. You leave they dishes to me. I think you'm very brave to drive in the daylight, Barbara. I wouldn't want to drive at all.'

Emily couldn't help thinking that **she** was very brave to be driven by her auntie, but sat quietly and looked at Stan, who raised his eyebrows and took another bite from his scone.

They said their thanks and goodbyes and agreed that they mustn't leave it too long before seeing one another.

Aunt and niece walked down the path and through the gate at the bottom to the car. Barbara started it up and backed out rather erratically onto the road, pulling away in the direction of West Buckland, just as the bus stopped at Sunnybank to drop off Jimmy and Danny from their day at Filleigh School.

The ride back to the farm was fortunately without incident and they got out of the car, cold and shivering, and hurried into the farmhouse.

Chapter 8

It had started like all the dreams she had had before. She was the only one moving through the rubble and destruction. All the grey figures were frozen in time against a grey background of bombed buildings showing through the grey, dusty air. She had climbed over the bricks and upturned paving slabs and clawed and pulled her way upwards past bodies lying at strange angles, and hands and feet poking out through gaps between the shattered concrete. She had reached the top of a row of steps leading to a front door which stood alone with no building on either side of it. It was bright green and freshly painted. She reached forward and opened it, and unexpectedly, lots of hens flew out, flapping and brushing against her face. She waved them away with her two hands, blowing at the feathers that weren't there. Suddenly, she awoke and sat up in bed. Where were the pairs of little hands, Emily asked herself? They were always there in her dream, waving at her and reaching for her. Where were they?

She looked at the clock. It was nearly eight. She got out of bed and looked in the mirror. No, she wasn't sweating and her breathing seemed normal.

Strange. She looked out of the bedroom window and saw her uncle crossing the yard carrying a fork-full of hay. She washed, dressed and went downstairs.

The weather was dry, and after breakfast Emily went to attend to the hens. She was learning a lot and knew all of their names, some unlike any name she had ever heard, but which had been given to them by Uncle Fred and fitted their personality perfectly. She thought hens were just hens but soon realised that they were all different, just like people. She let them out to forage in the yard.

At about eleven o'clock she went indoors, and was joined shortly afterwards by her uncle. They sat on the sofa, and Barbara brought them a mug of tea and placed it on the small table in front of them.

'You've just missed Stan. He came earlier than usual and wanted to get on but sends his regards. I'll fetch some little coconut cakes and then I'll sit alongside you for ten minutes.'

Barbara took three cakes from the cake tin, and placed them on the low table alongside her own mug of tea. She flopped down onto the spare seat on the sofa next to the others and suddenly there was a loud crack. The seat gave way under her. She screamed and went down like the lower half of a see-saw. Emily and Fred looked down at Barbara, crawling about on the floor and scrambling amongst the cushions. She sighed loudly and stood up.

'Are you all right, Auntie?' Emily stood up and went to help her aunt.

'Too much weight, Emily,' Fred chuckled but suddenly his end of the sofa collapsed under him, and went down with a splintering crash as he landed with his legs in the air.

'You were saying, Fred?' Barbara shouted as her husband struggled to his feet still holding his tea mug, the contents having been emptied onto his pullover.

Barbara and Emily cleared up the spilled tea and they all they all brushed themselves down and went and sat at the kitchen table.

'Right! That's it!' Barbara declared.

'What's it, Babs? Don't worry about the sofa. I'll soon put a few screws in that and it'll be as good as new.'

'As good as new? A few screws in it? I know where the screws will be coming from, Fred. You must have some loose ones to spare. That sofa has reached the end of its days. Emily, I had a phone call from Margaret. She said she has Friday afternoon off and asked us if we would like to go to her house and see her. You can drop us in town on Friday morning, Fred. You said you were going to the Cattle Market and we'll go to Padfields and see about a new sofa.'

'But I can repair it, Babs, and my parents used it for years. It was a good quality one. In any case, you'll only be able to buy a utility piece of furniture and that won't be much good.'

'I've heard that Mr Hooper in Padfields buys good second-hand furniture so it won't be wartime utility stuff.'

Emily sat quietly and looked at the pattern on her china mug. It was a pretty landscape with cows grazing peacefully in a sunlit meadow.

'Second-hand? It won't be any better than our sofa when I've mended it.'

'Now, Fred,' Barbara took a deep breath and looked at her husband determinedly. 'Second-hand it may be but how many generations of bums have sat on that sofa?' She smiled patiently and waited for the answer.

'Well, um, there was Mum and Dad – '

'And you and your mates.'

'And then there was Gran and Granfer Baxter – '

'Yes, and they had it off a cousin, didn't they? All I can say is that a second-hand sofa off Mr Hooper at Padfields will be a lot better than a clapped out old fourth-hand relic that's laying in pieces on the kitchen floor.'

Fred could see that his wife's mind was made up so he got to his feet, shrugged his shoulders at

Emily and left the kitchen.

Barbara looked at Emily and they smiled at each other and both burst into laughter.

'We're going shopping on Friday, Emily.' Auntie Barbara nodded.

Chapter 9

'Are you ready then, you two?' Fred asked as he put on his coat and cap and opened the front door. Emily and Barbara came from the kitchen and took their coats from the coat rack in the hall.

'Yes, Fred, but I thought you'd be taking the truck, in case you buy anything at the cattle market.' Barbara picked up the basket in which she had put a flask of tea and a few sandwiches.

'No. I've got the car for you two to ride to Barnstaple in style. In any case, I'm only looking, I'm not buying. In fact, I'm thinking that without the extra help, I may have to cut back.'

Emily got into the back of the car and Barbara sat in the front next to her husband, and placed her basket on her lap. 'Cut back? What do you mean, Fred? Get rid of the sheep, maybe? It's not a bad idea. With the milking herd, the pigs and everything else, – '

Fred started the car and drove from the farm onto the road. 'I don't know about "get rid of", Barbara. Just not "get more of" is what I meant.' His wife turned her head to look at Emily sitting quietly in the back of the car and raised her eyebrows.

'What about you, Emily? Are you planning to buy

anything in the great metropolis?' Fred handled the car with more respect than his wife, Emily thought.

'I don't think so, Uncle, but I would like to see the Pannier Market while we're in town.'

'And I'm going to Padfields.' Barbara pursed her lips and looked straight ahead as Fred drove sedately through West Buckland. Most of the journey to Barnstaple was in silence as Fred fondly contemplated the ancient family sofa, while his wife dreamt of finding something attractive and comfortable to replace it.

'Your Uncle Fred is going to pick us up at half past three at Margaret's house. She's told me where she lives and she'll be expecting us there at just after two. Now, Emily, do you want to come to Padfields with me?'

'Do you mind if I have a look around the town instead, Auntie? I want to see the Pannier Market and look at the Cattle Market too.'

'That's fine, dear. Why don't we meet by the mound in the Castle grounds? There are some seats there and we can sit and eat our sandwiches. It's not far from the Cattle Market and anyone will direct you there. It's not too cold and not raining either. Shall we say about quarter past one?'

'Yes, Auntie. I'll see you then.'

They waved to one another and Barbara set off resolutely in the direction of the furniture shop at the far end of Boutport Street.

Having been dropped off at The Square, Emily followed her aunt at a distance, stopping to look in the windows of some of the shops in the High Street. There were lots of people in the town for market day, which Emily guessed must be the busiest day of the week. She had to keep getting off the pavement and walking in the road as she made her way up the street, passing what appeared to be some very popular shops, by the number of people queueing outside of them. Bromleys was one. Was that the bakery where Margaret worked? Emily thought it wasn't but it looked inviting, and in spite of food rationing, there were plenty of people inside, and some were seated and drinking from china teacups. She continued up the street and looked in at a window displaying lovely rings, bracelets and necklaces. Garnish and Winkles. It had an old-worldly frontage showing black beams and white-washed walls. Emily crossed the road and walked up a narrow, cobbled lane which ran off the High street; Church Lane. It turned sharply to the left and was bordered on its right-hand side by a row of alms houses, at the end of which was a school with its name above the door, The Parish Church Infants' School. She stopped at the gate and looked through the bars at a small yard leading to the large, wooden door to the school.

Suddenly, there was a burst of children's laughter and shouting, indicating what Emily thought must be the start of playtime. She wished that she could see them playing but realised that perhaps the playground was on the far side of the building, or maybe the school didn't have a playground. Emily gripped the wrought iron bars of the gate and listened to the familiar carefree sounds of children chatting and laughing. She could picture them drinking their milk and enjoying their moments of morning playtime, even if it was spent indoors. That's how it should be, she thought. That's how it should have been for those children who will never know the joy of playing with their schoolfriends and growing up to have children of their own. Her eyes filled with tears as she listened to the shouts and laughter and she leaned her head against the bars of the gate and closed her eyes.

'Are you all right, dear?' Emily turned to see a young woman holding the hand of a little girl of about six years old.

'Oh, yes, thank you. I felt a bit dizzy for a moment, but I'm fine really.'

The woman smiled and came up to the gate. 'We're going into the school. Catherine had a tummy ache this morning and didn't want to go to school, but she's better now.' Emily stood to one side and the woman opened the gate and the couple walked through. The woman closed the gate and looked at Emily and winked, nodding her head towards the child and sighing. The child looked as if she had been crying. She looked at Emily out of her serious big brown eyes and pulled nervously on one of her pigtails.

'You've come at just the right time, Catherine,' Emily smiled. 'It's playtime, so hurry up. You don't want to miss it.' The little girl smiled back at her and the mother nodded her thanks. Emily waved goodbye and walked a few yards on to where the lane intersected a longer lane running to its right and left; Paternoster Lane. She turned to the left and looked towards The Parish Church of St. Peter's. There was a tall spire pointing into the cloudy sky but it appeared to be twisted. Emily stepped back and looked at it again. It's not perfect, she thought. She stood looking up at it and said aloud, 'It's not perfect, but nothing is perfect.' She turned and walked thoughtfully along Church Lane and came out onto Butchers' Row, where the Pannier Market could be seen leading off it on the opposite side of the road. Emily looked along Butchers' Row in both directions. Not all the shops were butchers' shops. There were fishmongers too. Meat is scarce and rationed, she thought, so if there are fish being caught locally it must provide a good alternative and supplement the diet. There were queues outside some of the shops and she crossed the road and entered the market. It was bustling and noisy and produce of all sorts was displayed on the stalls. There were vegetables in abundance and homemade items such as baskets, knitted and sewn garments and flowers. One or two stalls were selling unrationed fresh chicken and rabbits. It presented a colourful picture against the drabness of wartime. She spent nearly an hour wandering from stall to stall, then feeling suddenly tired, came out through Market Street onto Joy Street and found her way along it and back to the High Street. The Cattle Market, she thought. Yes. She should see that. She remembered having been taken there when she came to North Devon with her brother and her parents before the war. As a little girl, she'd been lifted up to see the animals in the pens. She'd liked the sheep especially but felt sorry for them, thinking that they looked as if they'd been squashed into too small a space. Emily could tell that she was getting near the Cattle Market by the noise the animals were making, and by the smell. There was a lot of shouting from men bidding to buy young cattle. It was too noisy for her so she turned and walked back to the High Street. She suddenly felt hungry and walked to the far end of the street and saw a queue outside a baker's shop. She joined the back of the queue and looked in the window. It was bright and stocked with buns and cakes and there was a pretty girl serving customers. She was laughing and joking with them and looked towards the window and smiled as she saw Emily. After a few minutes, Emily reached the front of the queue and stepped into the shop. At the same moment, a door at the back of the shop opened and Margaret walked behind the counter carrying a tray of scones. She looked at Emily and came to serve her. 'Oh good, Emily. It's lovely to see you. This is Doreen.'

'Hello, Mrs Partridge, I mean Margaret,' Emily replied shyly. 'Hello Doreen.'

Doreen came around to Emily's side of the counter and put her hand on Emily's shoulder. 'Hello, Emily. Maggie's been telling me all about you. You're going with your aunt to Maggie's house this afternoon, aren't you?' Doreen turned towards the display of cakes and buns in the window. 'Are you hungry? The buns are good but I can't say the same for some of the rest of the stuff.' She laughed and went back to the other side of the counter.

'You know what rationing's like, Emily, coming from London,' Margaret remarked. 'We can only do our best with the ingredients that we're allocated.'

A woman wearing what looked like a dead fox around her neck had just entered the shop and stood at the side of Emily.

'The buns are safe enough so I'll have two of them, please, when you've finished with this young lady.'

'Good morning, Mrs Gilbert. How are you today?' Doreen smiled at the customer. 'You hadn't decided what you want had you, Emily?'

'I'd like a bun too, please, but after you've served this lady.'

Doreen put two buns into a paper bag and handed it to the customer.

'Better than I was, dear.' Mrs Gilbert turned to Emily. 'It's my leg you see. It's sensitive to changes in the weather. It doesn't like it when the pressure drops on the barometer. It's very sensitive to the barometer. I have to keep it in the spare room.'

'Oh dear. I'm sorry,' Emily said. 'That must be difficult.'

'No, dear. Not my leg, I mean the barometer. Anyway, I must dash in case it rains.' She handed over the money and hurried from the shop just as Doreen started giggling. 'Poor old thing. She makes us laugh but she does have problems with her leg.'

Margaret picked up an empty tray and carried it through the door at the back of the shop to return it to the bakery.

'I'll be back in a moment Doreen, and I'll serve in the shop until one o'clock, when I'm off for the afternoon. Why don't you go for your dinner break a bit early and take Emily with you?' Emily handed over the money for the bun.

'I'm meeting Auntie at quarter past one in the Castle grounds, near the mound. I hope the rain holds off.' Doreen looked out of the front door of the shop. The rush of customers had dwindled and the sun was starting to come out.

'When Maggie comes back, we'll go out together,' Doreen said. 'That is, if you'd like some company, Emily?'

It was rare for Emily to spend time with people of her own age and she had warmed to this young woman immediately. 'I'd like that, Doreen. Thank you.'

'Ah, here's Maggie. Are you sure you don't mind if I go now with Emily, Maggie?'

'No. Just go while things have quietened down here. Why don't you take Emily out to the back yard and sit by the shed? It's not raining but it's more sheltered there.'

'Good idea. Follow me, Emily. We'll go through the bakehouse and out to the back. I have to pick up my coat and my pasty.'

Doreen took off her white cap and apron and the two young women went through the back door of the shop and on through the bakehouse to the back yard.

Chapter 10

'The weather's clearing up nicely now.' Doreen smiled and poured some tea from her Thermos into a mug and handed it to Emily.

'Are you sure, Doreen?'

'There's enough for both of us, so you're not robbing me,' Doreen bit into her pasty. 'Bert calls this a meat pasty but it's a case of find the meat. It's a potato pasty really and you can have half of it if you like.' She started to break the pasty in half.

'No, Doreen. That's very kind but I'm meeting Aunt Barbara soon and this bun will keep me going until I share the sandwiches she brought with her for us. Have you worked long in the bakery, Doreen?' Emily took a bite from her bun and sipped the hot tea.

'Since I left school. What do you do, Emily?'

'I'm a teacher but I haven't - I'm not - ' She stopped and looked at the ground. 'I'm taking a break from it. I couldn't - '

There was a short silence as Doreen looked at Emily sitting quietly on the bench next to her, and said, 'It's good to get away sometimes; do new things, meet new people. It's like getting a spring clean, that's what I think. I wish that I could get a spring clean. I haven't done anything with my life really. I like working in the shop, but I want to do more than that; learn more and try to catch up.' She sipped her tea and smiled at Emily. 'You've had an education, Emily. I had no ambition when I was at school. I didn't think that education was for the likes of me.'

'And now? What do you think now?' Emily wiped her mouth with her handkerchief and looked at the pretty young woman sitting next to her.

'And now, well now I feel I'm waking up. You see, I've met a lovely young soldier. He's keen on me but I can't think why. He's educated and interested in the sorts of things that I don't know anything about. But I love him and want to be more than just a girlfriend. Do you think it's too late to try to catch up and fill my empty head with things that are worth something, Emily?'

'It's never too late to learn things but life's not just about learning facts, is it? If he's nice, he'll like you for what you are, won't he? Is he a local boy?'

'No. he's an American. There are thousands of American soldiers stationed here in North Devon. I think they practise their shooting and stuff on our beaches. He's called Oliver. It's because of Maggie that I met him. She and her husband and eight-year-old daughter, Diana, were coming out of the pictures one day, and he walked up to them and offered the young one a banana. The grown-ups got talking and Maggie asked him to tea at her house. Then later he came into the shop with a banana for the other little girl, Mary. She's the younger one and missed out first time. He came back to the shop lots of times, buying buns and cakes. We got chatting and he asked me out. I've been going out with him for a few months now.'

Doreen paused and looked at her half-eaten pasty. 'He's different. I know he's clever, but he doesn't talk about himself. He's kind and interested in other people.' Doreen looked unseeingly at the clouds clearing to reveal some weak sunshine. 'He's too good for me, Emily.'

'Don't say that, Doreen. He sounds nice and I'm sure he wouldn't want you to think that.'

Doreen put the rest of her abandoned pasty in a paper bag and looked at Emily apologetically. 'I'm sorry, Emily. I've talked about myself and I'm sure you don't want to hear all that.'

'It's been nice sitting here with you, Doreen. I don't have any friends of my own age really and somehow, although we've only just met, it seems like we've known each other for ages.'

'That's how I feel, Emily. Will you come and meet me at the shop again soon? If you call around the same time you did today when I have an afternoon off, we can spend some time together. Or we could meet when I have a day off.'

'I'd like that, but wouldn't you want to see Oliver?'

'Well yes, but he mostly only has time off in the evenings. Is your aunt on the phone at the farm? I could contact you easily, as Bert won't mind if I telephone you from the shop as long as the call is "short and sweet", as he says.'

Emily smiled and opened her bag and took out a small notepad and pencil. She wrote down the farm phone number, tore the page out and handed it to Doreen. 'Thank you for spending time with me. It's been so good to meet you, but I must go now and find my aunt.'

'I'll telephone you soon, Emily, when I know what time off I have next week.' They both stood up and hugged one another. Doreen turned to go back into the bakehouse and Emily walked towards the Castle Grounds.

There was no sign of her aunt but it was not quite one o'clock. Emily looked up at what was called the 'Mound'. She saw a path winding up around it and decided to follow it. On walking through a heavily overgrown area dotted with trees, she reached the top and could see that at one time it would have afforded a reasonable look-out in all directions, especially at any unwelcome approaches coming from the river. Emily thought that there must have been a castle on the top at some time in the distant past but there was no sign of it as far as she could see. She'd like to have known more about it, but after wandering about looking for clues of a long-gone age, she checked her watch and made her way down to the lawned area and the seat where she was to meet her aunt. It was nearly half-past one. The sun had come out and the temperature was more conducive to eating a picnic outdoors and sitting on the bench which was perfectly dry.

What could have kept Aunt Barbara? Perhaps she was trying to decide on a new, or nearly new sofa. At that moment, she caught sight of her aunt hurrying towards her from the direction of the Cattle Market.

'Oh, Emily, I'm sorry I'm late. My watch has stopped, and I didn't realise it until I looked at the clock in the Pannier Market.' She sat down next to her niece and took out the sandwiches from her basket. How have you got on, dear?'

'I've had an interesting morning, Aunt, looking around the town and making a new friend.'

Barbara handed some sandwiches to Emily and undid the thermos flask and poured tea for them both.

'Well that's good. Tel me about it.'

'I found the bakers where Margaret works and she introduced me to her colleague. She's about my age and is called Doreen. She's so nice and wants us to meet soon and spend some time together. I gave her your telephone number. I hope that's all right, Aunt?'

'Of course, it is. You can invite her to come to visit you at the farm when she has some time off. I'm glad you've had a good morning.'

'How did you get on finding a sofa, Auntie?'

'Quite well. I didn't see one in the shop but Mr Hooper said that he is sure he can find us one of good quality as long as we realise that it would be second-hand. Some of the utility stuff I saw was nearly as bad as what collapsed under us recently. I told him about it and he had a good laugh! He will phone me when he has something suitable and sturdy enough to support us when we sit on it!'

'That's good, but I wonder what Uncle Fred will say about that, Auntie?' Aunt Barbara swallowed the last of her tea and took a deep breath.

'Whatever he says, that old sofa is not staying in the house one minute longer than it has to. Now, dear what time is it by your watch?'

'It's quarter to two, Auntie. Should we be going to Margaret's house now?' Barbara packed away the picnic, stood up and brushed down her coat.

'Yes, Emily we don't want to be late, do we?'

Chapter 11

‹It feels colder here, Emily,' Barbara said, pulling her scarf higher around her neck as they walked across the Long Bridge towards Sticklepath. Suddenly a train appeared from the direction in which they were walking and puffed across the iron bridge curving over the river Taw and on towards Barnstaple Town Station. It was a noisy but picturesque distraction and they stopped to watch its progress. At the end of the bridge, on their right, they passed a narrow entrance to a large cream-coloured brick building.

'Here's Shapland and Petter, the factory Margaret wrote down on the map she drew for us.' Barbara showed the sheet of note paper to Emily.

'Oh yes. Now we have to walk along Sticklepath Terrace and take the second turning on the right into Signal Terrace, Auntie.'

'Yes, and the house is a small terraced one down at the bottom of the street on the left.'

About five minutes later, they were standing at the front door of Margaret's house and ringing the doorbell. It was just after two o'clock by Emily's watch.

The door opened and Margaret welcomed them.

'Come in. out of the cold. The temperature is dropping again. I've just lit the fire in the kitchen.'

'It is so kind of you to ask us to call on you, especially as you can't have been home from work long.' Barbara smiled and she and Emily followed Margaret into the narrow hallway known as the passage and on through the second door on the right into the kitchen. A cheerful fire was burning in the grate and the guests were shown to the two armchairs either side of it.

'I'll make us all a cup of tea, if that's all right with you both. It's not often I have time to see people socially but Jack is at work and doesn't usually come home for dinner. Diana is at school and my youngest, Mary, has been taken by my mother to see the animals in the Cattle Market.' As Margaret started towards the scullery, Barbara stood up and looked apologetically at their host. 'Margaret, would you think it very rude of me if I leave you for a while? As we turned the corner at the top of the road, I noticed a watch-mender's shop. It's just that my watch stopped this morning and I am lost without it. Do you think I could get it repaired there?'

'Oh yes. The chap who owns the little shop is very good and always obliging. He's called Joe. You go and see if he can do anything this afternoon to get it going and Emily and I will be fine here.'

'Thank you, Margaret. It seems very impolite to leave as soon as we've arrived, but – '

'No, Barbara. See if he can sort it out while you have the chance. Emily, come out to the scullery with me while I'm making the tea and I'll introduce you to someone to keep you amused.'

Barbara left by the front door as Margaret and Emily went into the small scullery. In the corner there was a large cage placed on a high table. The occupant was a cockatoo sitting still and watchful on its perch.

'Oh! What a beautiful bird!' Emily smiled and walked up to the cage, her eyes gleaming in admiration, whereupon the creature sidled along its perch towards her and raised its yellow comb.

'Yes, he's taken to you straightaway, Emily.' Margaret filled the kettle and put it on the gas cooker. 'He likes the ladies, so you're quite safe. He's called "Cocky" and he was given to Jack by a sailor who called into the garage where Jack works.'

'Hello, Cocky. Do you talk?' Emily looked at Margaret. 'I've heard that some of them talk, as parrots do.'

'Oh, yes. He talks all right; and sings and dances too, usually at about six o'clock in the morning. Jack had no idea what he was letting us in for. "It'll be nice for the children to have an animal," he said, "and it's not as if we have to take it for a walk." No wonder the sailor wanted to get rid of him.'

Emily looked puzzled. 'But he's so friendly and looks really pretty.'

'Friendly with women, Emily.' Margaret poured the boiling water into the tea pot.

'Do you ever let him out of his cage?'

'Not often but he has escaped before. His beak is so strong that he has pulled the bars apart and squeezed through. We had to buy another cage with beak-proof bars. You see my broom handle?' Margaret lifted her sweeping brush from the corner of the room and showed it to Emily. 'I left it leaning against the side of the cage and he had a great time with it. He chewed as much of it as he could reach and we found a pile of sawdust on the floor outside his cage. That's why the handle is so thin at the top and thick at the bottom. He's on borrowed time, that's what I've told Jack.'

'Do the children like him?'

'Oh, yes. He's a bit of a character to them but his stay may be only temporary.' Margaret placed the teapot, milk jug and a pot containing a small amount of sugar on a tray with a few little cakes.

'Let's go and sit beside the fire, Emily. You can talk to that delinquent later.'

They sat and sipped their tea and Margaret put some more coal on the fire.

'How are you, Emily? I don't want to pry but I

know that you have suffered a shock and a sadness and have come to your family in the country to get away from it all. We are lucky here. We have our problems with this war, of course, but at least we have no bombs dropping on us.'

'I can't quite move on, and I find that as soon as I try to talk about my experience, I start to feel faint and breathless.'

'I wouldn't like you to think that your family has been talking about you, but Stan the postman knew that your aunt and uncle have been trying to help you and he told Lil about it one day when I happened to be at their house. It's good that you have got out of London for a while. A change is as good as a rest, as they say.'

'I've found it more difficult to talk about what happened with my family. They are so emotionally involved, whereas with people I don't know as well – ' Emily sighed apologetically and sipped her tea.

'Have a cake, Emily. I made them yesterday and have rescued them from being devoured by the family.'

'Thank you.' Emily took what looked like a little fruit cake and bit into it. 'It's delicious, Margaret. You are a good cook. Have you learned a lot at the bakery?'

'Oh, yes. I have. If I had the money, I'd love to open a tea shop. That's not likely to happen, but after the war, who knows? If we can win this war and recover our lives, those of us who've not lost them, that is, I think there will be big changes in the way we live.'

'Yes. It's the dreadful loss that I can't get over, Margaret. Young people's lives cut down before they've done anything. It's such a waste! If only I could change what happened that day.' Emily replaced her crockery on the tray and stared unseeingly into the fire.

'You will move on, dear, but you won't forget. Perhaps you will find other positive things to put into your life. After all, from what I've heard, you are a clever girl and have trained as a teacher. What age group were you teaching?'

'I trained to teach the younger age group but switched to teaching senior children.'

'Do you teach any particular subject?'

'Well, I was - '

The sound of the doorbell broke into their conversation.

'It's probably your aunt. I hope she's managed to get her watch repaired. Pour yourself another cup of tea, Emily, and I'll let her in.'

Emily didn't want any more tea so she sat back in the rather worn armchair and closed her eyes. She could hear distant voices coming from the front door but one of them was a man's voice. Suddenly the door from the passage opened and Margaret stepped into the kitchen followed by a tall, dark-haired, middle-aged man wearing a rather shabby raincoat and carrying a battered brief case. He had a vicar's collar around his neck and on seeing Emily, a friendly smile lit up his face.

'Oh, I'm sorry, Mrs Partridge. I see you have company. I've called at a very inconvenient moment for you. Would you like me to come back another time?'

'No, Reverend Langford. This is my young friend, Emily. She is from London and is staying with her aunt and uncle on their farm just outside West Buckland. Please sit down by the fire and I'll make a fresh pot of tea.'

'Thank you so much. Hello, Emily,' the vicar said, taking off his mac and draping it over the back of the armchair. He sat down opposite her and placed his brief case by his side.

'Hello, Reverend.' Emily wondered what his reason for calling on Margaret could be.

'You're from London, aren't you? Many of the youngsters evacuated here are from London, and some have been sent from cities in the Midlands. I'm the vicar of St. Paul's Church at the top of Sticklepath Hill. The Women's Union at our church and the local Women's Institute are working together to give a party for some of the evacuees in our area. I'm here to find out if Mrs Partridge will help to organise the food for the party.'

'Yes. Margaret is a good cook but she is so busy.'

'Ask a busy person!' The Reverend Langford laughed. 'That's what I always say.' The vicar had a jolly laugh and a loud one, and its ripple of merry sound travelled through the door to the scullery where it was heard by what Margaret called 'the delinquent'.

'What did you say?' A strangulated voice sounded loud and clear in response to the vicar's comment.

'Rubbish! You talk rubbish!' Emily was surprised at the volume and clarity of Cocky's comments. He was clearly in disagreement with the Reverend Langford. Emily opened her mouth to say something but nothing would come out.

'Cocky, stop it! Behave yourself or I'll cover you up.' Margaret spoke forcibly to the cockatoo and left the scullery, carrying a cup of tea into the kitchen for the vicar. She set it down on the table as the Reverend Langford stood up and walked past her, around the table, his eyes shining with excitement and anticipation.

'Is that a parrot, I hear Mrs Partridge? My Aunt Agatha had a cockatoo. It used to sit on my shoulder and loved me to walk it around the house. Please let me see it.'

'Well, Vicar, I'm not sure that – ' Margaret

hadn't fastened the door between the kitchen and the scullery and it suddenly swung open to reveal the off-stage voice sitting on its perch and swaying hypnotically from side to side.

The Reverend Langford's face lit up and he walked into the scullery, elated as he recalled those happy boyhood times with Auntie Agatha's cockatoo.

'What a beautiful specimen, Mrs Partridge. Look! You can see it knows I'm a fan. Male or female?' The vicar was at the cage coo-cooing to Cocky who looked as if he wouldn't hurt a fly.

'Male.' Margaret had followed the vicar into the scullery and was standing behind the visitor. Emily quietly tiptoed from her place by the fire and stood behind Margaret, sensing that all was not boding well.

'Male? My aunt's bird was female and was called Gertrude; Gertie for short. Ah, yes! You see? This bird would eat out of my hand.' The vicar continued to make coo-cooing sounds to Cocky. Margaret leaned her head back towards Emily and whispered, 'This bird would **eat** his hand if it had half the chance.'

'Can we get him out? I'm marvellous with animals. All the family tell me that.' The vicar started to open the door of the cage. 'Cocky, come and sit on Uncle's shoulder and we can walk around together.'

'I'm not sure if – ' Margaret stepped forward. 'I mean. I wouldn't do that, Vicar. It's not a good – ' The sound of her voice fell upon deaf ears as the Reverend Langford confidently took Cocky onto his outstretched hand and placed him on his right shoulder. 'There you are, Cocky. You and I are friends, aren't we?'

There was a mirror on the wall in the scullery which Jack used when he was shaving at the sink. The two looked at one another in the mirror, the vicar smiling confidently and the bird with its head on one side, looking undecided about the relationship.

Margaret had her hand to her mouth and was biting her knuckles.

She turned towards Emily and shook her head. Emily bit her lip in response.

Suddenly, a train could be heard in the distance approaching from the Junction Station and gradually picking up speed as it travelled towards the iron bridge, the track first passing close to the bottom of Signal Terrace, and within sight and sound of Margaret's house. Margaret looked in horror at Emily and shook her head. The custom was for the engine driver to let his whistle sound fortissimo as a sort of greeting as the train passed by.

'Vicar, shall we put him back in his cage?'

Margaret's plea came too late as an ear-splitting whistle from the train's engine rent the air.

Cocky responded by turning his head to the left and grasping the Reverend Langford's right earlobe with his beak.

The vicar let out a yell and tried to get hold of Cocky to rectify the situation, which resulted in Cocky intensifying his grip. They started to move around the little scullery in a sort of heathen dance with the Reverend Langford shouting out in desperation, 'Get the bloody thing off! Get the bloody thing off! The little bastard!'

Emily was amazed to hear such language coming from the mouth of a holy man and suddenly saw the farcical side of the situation. She started to giggle quietly. Meanwhile, Margaret had rushed to the sink and filled a jug with water which she promptly threw over Cocky, hitting the vicar at the same time but succeeding in getting the bird to release his beak on the now bloody earlobe. She grabbed the creature firmly and almost threw him back into the cage and shut the door. Finding a clean towel, she wet it and offered it to the Reverend Langford, who was leaning against the outside door trying to get his breath and regain his composure.

'I must apologise for my language, Mrs Partridge. It was such a shock. I had no idea that – '

'Language? What language? I didn't hear you

say anything, Vicar. The train whistle makes such a noise.' There was a sort of choking sound coming from Emily as she tried to control herself but suddenly she burst out laughing. She turned and staggered into the kitchen and sat in the armchair by the fire and put her hand over her mouth in an effort to stifle her giggles. The vicar dabbed at his ear and he and Margaret followed Emily into the kitchen and sat on the opposite side of the room from her. Her laughter became louder and more hysterical until suddenly, it turned into huge sobs, and tears flowed from her eyes and down her cheeks. Her breathing came in short gasps.

'I couldn't save them,' she groaned. 'Nobody could save them.'

Margaret and the Reverend Langford looked at one another as suddenly, the door opened and Barbara entered the kitchen. She went over to her niece and knelt beside her as the sobs subsided.

'Of course, you couldn't save them, Emily. No one could.' Barbara put her arm around her niece's shoulders and passed her a handkerchief. She looked at Margaret and the Reverend Langford and shook her head.

'It's time you cried, dear. And whatever has brought it on, is a good thing and not before time.' Emily closed her eyes and leant forward and put her head in her hands.

'I'm sorry,' she muttered. 'I should explain. I've made such an exhibition of myself. I'm sorry.' Her voice petered out and she sat still and silent.

'I'll explain, Emily. You just relax and you'll feel better soon.' Barbara moved to a chair at the dining room table and sat down. 'This goes back to almost a year ago when a bomb fell on a school in Catford in Lewisham, near where Emily and her family live. She had been invited to the school that afternoon to observe some lessons and meet the teachers. You were going to apply for a job there, weren't you, Emily?'

'Yes, I wanted to work with young children and had studied at Homerton College.' Emily dabbed her eyes and smiled tearfully at Margaret as she was handed a glass of water. 'I was to study further but teachers were needed in London so my course was cut short.'

'You wanted to work in your home area, didn't you, Emily?' Aunt Barbara asked quietly.

'Yes. That was why I was going to the school around lunch time that day.'

'Was that the school where the bomb fell, Emily?' The vicar leaned forward with a concerned look on his face.

'Yes. Sandhurst Road School.' Emily looked into the dying embers of the fire. No one moved to stoke it and no one spoke. 'I had just got off the bus and was walking towards the school. I must have been just a few minutes away from it when the bomb fell.' She closed her eyes. 'It was total devastation. There were clouds of smoke and dust, and screaming. I remember standing and looking at the scene. At first it was as if everything was frozen in time. Then crowds of people came, helping, digging and searching for their children. The scene is etched on my memory. A wasteland – and a waste!'

'What a terrible tragedy it was,' the vicar muttered.

Barbara shook her head and sighed. 'Yes. Thirty-six children and six teachers died and Emily witnessed it. January 29th, 1943 it was. The people of Lewisham, including my sister and of course, the families were grief-stricken.'

Margaret looked at Barbara. 'That was nearly a year ago, you said. Yes. I remember reading about it. And all this time, – ' She paused and looked at Emily thoughtfully.

Barbara read her thoughts, looked at her niece and said, 'You never once cried, did you, Emily? You just carried on.'

'I felt I had to pull myself together. Those teachers were lost and others had to step into their place. No. I never cried, but I did change my mind about what age group I was going to teach, which is why I switched to teaching senior children. I couldn't cope with seeing those innocent little faces every day.'

'And you found a school not far from where you live and started teaching until suddenly things caught up with you.' Barbara looked at her niece.

'Yes. I was coping but not feeling right; not feeling part of things and suddenly something happened to bring it all back. It was a Saturday, late afternoon around the middle of December last year. I was walking home from calling to see my grandparents at their shop. I often went there to help them at weekends. They work too hard. I have a friend, Isaac, who came over from Germany with the Kindertransport when he was sixteen. He works at my grandparents' grocery shop. He is a lovely person and has no living family that he knows about. He had that afternoon off and was planning to be at a local Social Club to play snooker with some friends when an unexploded bomb accidentally detonated in a nearby, bombed-out building. It was a big bomb. You could tell from the noise of the explosion. It was hidden underground and something must have set it off. I had just walked past the Social Club on my way home and ran back to find my friend. There wasn't much damage to the Club but most of the windows were blown out and some of the young people inside received cuts and bruises. There was no sign of Isaac and no news of him for several hours as people in the building and the surrounding area were accounted for. My mind went back to the moment that I was standing within sight of the bombed school last January. I was overcome by a feeling of helplessness and hopelessness. I thought, "No, not Isaac. He's suffered enough." Suddenly I couldn't get my breath and started gasping for air and sweating. I must have collapsed in the street. The next thing I knew was that someone was dabbing my forehead with a wet cloth. I was helped back to my home and on the Monday - '

Barbara smiled at her niece. 'My sister took you to the doctor, Emily, and you were advised to take time off work, and give yourself an opportunity to get away and rest. That's why you have come to stay with us at the farm for a while. A change and a rest. That's what the doctor ordered, didn't he?'

'I didn't like to let them down at the school but I knew I couldn't go on. Oh, and Isaac hadn't been at the Club after all. He had decided to visit an elderly Jewish gentleman who lives alone, to play a game of chess with him.'

'A lovely person, as you say, Emily.' The vicar nodded. 'I think you will get your strength back. It isn't always physical strength we need to cope with life.' The Reverend Langford stood up and reached for his coat and briefcase. 'It's mental strength too. But sometimes we have to allow ourselves to recover. After all, if you'd broken your leg, you wouldn't expect to be able to walk on it straightaway, would you? Give yourself time. Be kind to yourself and If you ever feel you would like to talk with me, please let Margaret know and we can arrange something.' He smiled and turned to Margaret. 'I'd come to ask you if you would help with organising the food for the evacuees' party later in February, Mrs Partridge, but this isn't the time. Thank you for the tea.' He paused. 'And the entertainment earlier.' Margaret smiled. 'I'll come to Evensong on Sunday, Vicar, and if you have time, I can discuss the catering with you then.'

'Wonderful. Goodbye, everyone. I'll see myself out.' He nodded and left the room.

'You haven't had a drink, Barbara,' Margaret remarked.

'No, but please don't worry. Fred will be here soon with the car to take us home, and your family will be back too.'

'It has been an eventful afternoon, hasn't it, Emily? But perhaps you will start to feel better and see a brighter future.'

'Thank you, Margaret. I'll try to be more positive.'

The doorbell rang.

'That will be Fred,' Barbara said. 'We'll be back in time for him to do the milking.'

They started to walk to the door when Margaret asked, 'Oh! What about your watch, Barbara?'

'Yes. Joe repaired it. I told him that Fred gave it to me two Christmases ago but I'd worn it in the barn recently when we were moving the hay about.

"It's dirty with dust and needs cleaning," Joe said. "There's no permanent damage and I'll soon have it as good as new." Isn't that wonderful?'

Margaret opened the front door and the two women waved and got into the car. Margaret waved back at them.

'Yes, it is.' She smiled thoughtfully. 'As good as new.'

Chapter 12

'**Another cup of** tea, Stan?' Barbara took his cup while Stan searched his bag for the post he'd brought for the Baxter household.

'Oh, yer 'tis, right down the bottom of me bag. Thank you, Barbara, and they little cakes was bootiful. Where's the Master of the 'ouse 'smornin', and the young maid, too?'

The door from the hall suddenly opened and Emily entered carrying a basket of four freshly gathered eggs.

'Good morning, Mr Webber, I mean, Stan.'

'You're looking much better today, Emily,' Barbara commented taking the basket, opening the larder door and placing it inside on the marble shelf.

'Fresh country air is what makes all the difference.' Stan sipped his tea loudly. 'Where's Fred, then, Emily? 'E always joins us for elevenses.'

'He's waiting for the vet to come from South Molton. One of the cows has caught her leg on some barbed wire and gashed it badly. Uncle has her in the shippon. He said he needs to find time to inspect the fencing as he wants to know where the barbed wire is broken away from the fence post.' Barbara shook her head, despairingly. 'There's so much to do on the farm here, Stan, and the Land girls can't be in two places at once. They live and work at our neighbour's farm, and one or other of them helps out here with Fred most days. Unfortunately, both girls have been struggling with bad coughs and colds, so haven't been able to do their usual work. Fred could do without an injured animal to cope with, on top of everything else.'

'The vet from South Molton be comin'? I 'ad 'im come to us last summer. Nice chap and knows 'is job but very quiet. Me and Lil could 'ardly get a word out of un, and us couldn't get 'im to come up to the 'ouse and 'ave a drink an' a bite to eat.' Emily sat at the table as her aunt poured her a cup of tea and offered her a cake from the cake tin.

Barbara shook her head. 'Daniel is a changed man since that tragedy happened.' She sat at the table between the others. No-one was risking a seat on the sofa, half of which looked almost useable, while the other half was piled up in pieces in the corner of the room.

'You probably know the story, Stan. You see, Emily, Daniel and his girlfriend had got engaged. They were very much in love and ideally suited to one another. She had studied to be a vet. She'd come from a farming family in Yorkshire and they'd met as students. It is rare for a woman to become a vet and Daniel said that she had to be better than most men to convince the authorities to allow her to be accepted on the course. They had wonderful plans. They hoped to start their own practice here in North Devon eventually, and she would concentrate on the small animal side of the business while he went out to the farms. It was their dream. Daniel told us all about it. He was so excited. They both qualified and got engaged. They even had the date set for the wedding, it was to be in June 1942, in Yorkshire, of course.'

Emily listened in silence and Stan looked steadfastly at the pattern on the tea cup. 'I only saw 'er once. 'Er was a very pretty maid, as I remember. But I can't think what 'er was called.'

'Angela. And she looked like an angel too; fair curly hair to her shoulders and smiling blue eyes. She had everything; brains and beauty. She was musical and played the clarinet. Daniel played the viola. Yes, they had so much in common.'

'What happened, Auntie?' Emily placed her cup in the saucer. The tea had become cold and she didn't feel like drinking it anyway, as she waited for what she knew must be a heart-breaking outcome to a wonderful relationship.

'Angela had moved into a small cottage next to the house where Dan was living in South Molton. They were planning to convert it into consultation and treatment rooms for the veterinary practice they were going to set up and had already taken out a loan to get them started. Everything was set for a wonderful future. Angela had a friend she'd known from her schooldays who was working in Exeter. The two young women had always planned to be bridesmaids at one another's weddings and both young women were marrying within a few months of one another. Angela went to stay with her friend in Exeter for a few days. They were looking for some material to make their wedding dresses and had saved their clothes coupons to do it. Of course, it was very much a make-do affair with rationing preventing anything too showy but they were going shopping to see what they could find. Daniel said they were very excited. Exeter had suffered some bomb damage in the early spring of 1942 but on the night of May 4th there was a big raid and great damage done to the city with many lives lost. Both young women were killed in that raid.'

'How terrible! What a waste!' Emily looked at her aunt. 'Whenever is this war going to end?'

' 'Tis no wonder Daniel be a changed man.' Stan sighed and walked towards the door. 'Us 'ave just got to 'elp each other an' see it through. But 'tis 'arder for some, Barbara. I'll see on Monday. Thanks for the tea an' cake.' He smiled weakly and walked out.

'No wonder Daniel is so quiet,' Emily murmured. 'Perhaps he just can't move on with all his dreams broken.'

'Moving on is easier said than done, isn't it, but it takes time and courage,' Barbara cleared the dishes from the table.

'I'm just going to pop upstairs. There's something I want to look for that Mum put into the bottom of my suitcase that I haven't taken out yet. I'll come and help you later, Auntie.'

'No hurry, Emily. Take your time.'

Emily pulled her suitcase out from under the bed and placed it on the eiderdown. She opened it and saw a large brown paper parcel tied with string. What had her mother put in it, hidden away at the bottom? She untied the string and took out a selection of various violin pieces that she had played at some time or other. What was there? Quite an assortment. A book of classical short pieces with the piano accompaniments. No wonder the case was heavy! Some individual pieces, Elgar, Schumann and, - what was this? 'Songs My Mother Taught Me' by Dvorak. An arrangement, but Emily had once had to play it over and over because it was a family favourite. She picked up the music and looked around the room for something to stand it on. She propped it up against the mirror on the dressing table and went to her violin case which was in the wardrobe. The floor of the bedroom was above the kitchen and the Aga made it warm to walk on without wearing anything on her feet. Not a good place to keep the violin, Emily had decided when she had first arrived. She put the case on the bed, took out the violin and checked the tuning. The D was out a bit but the other strings had held their pitch quite well. She had not played the instrument since shortly before that terrible day she had set out to visit Sandhurst Road School. She adjusted the tuning and played a few notes and a scale or two. The bedroom was quite warm, the day being mild, and she opened the window a little to let some air in. She sat down on the bedroom chair in front of the dressing table and looked at the music leaning precariously against the mirror. She started to play. The melancholy melody gently filled the air and floated out of the window. It wasn't too taxing technically to play, and she was glad she had chosen it as she knew that her technique would be very rusty after so long without having touched the instrument.

Outside, a car turned into the yard and Daniel Smith got out, picked up his bag and overall, and made his way towards the shippon. Emily decided to play the piece through again. She was more relaxed and became lost in the beauty of the melody. Down in the front yard, Daniel Smith stopped in his tracks and looked up at the window. He stood still until the piece ended and then walked on slowly.

Emily looked at the clock on the bedside table. She'd been in the bedroom over half an hour and so hurriedly put away her instrument and went downstairs to her aunt in the kitchen.

'Sorry, Auntie. I haven't helped you this morning. I thought I'd see what Mum had put at the bottom of my case.'

'Oh, but you have, Emily.   It's been lovely to hear you play. It was "Music While You Work," for me, only without putting the wireless on!'

Emily smiled. 'I haven't played for months and didn't want to bring my violin but Mum was insistent that I should have it here.'

'Well you know she's always right, don't you, Emily? Mums usually are, dear.'

'Yes. She said I just might want to play it when I feel better.'

Chapter 13

It was a bright, crisp start to the morning with the temperature just above freezing and the ground firm under foot. Emily had spent a dreamless night, woken early and refreshed, and left the house before breakfast without seeing her aunt or uncle. She decided to walk around the farm and look at the fences that her uncle had intended to inspect but had been unable to find the time to do so. He'd have to have more help from somewhere, but she thought that at least she could do some of the farm work if he'd teach her. She was learning a lot about keeping chickens, and had borrowed a book about the subject from the library in South Molton, and had just started to read the Farmers Weekly, which was far more interesting than she had first thought. It would take a good hour or more to walk the boundary of the farm but she had her wellingtons on and was well wrapped up against the cold wind that nearly always blew in the more exposed fields on the higher ground. She carried a stick which she had found in the umbrella rack in the hall, just in case she encountered any unfriendly cattle. After about half an hour, Emily reached a field which bordered a sheltered, deciduous wood, frequented sometimes by red deer, according to her uncle. She walked along the hedge and soon saw where the barbed wire had been torn from the fence post. It appeared to be a favourite crossing path by the creatures, which she knew could easily jump clear of most fences, but one of them must have missed its footing and become entangled. Emily hoped that it wasn't injured like the cow whose leg Daniel had stitched up the day before. There were some beautiful snowdrops along the hedge and some fresh, long green grass in the sunnier places. Perhaps that was what the cow was reaching for when it became injured. Making a mental note of where the fence was damaged, Emily continued her inspection of all the boundaries of the Baxter farm and made her way back to the farmhouse, ready for breakfast. Passing the shippon, she met her uncle coming from it.

'Hello, Emily,' he called. 'Where have you come from?'

'I woke up early, Uncle, and decided that I could be useful if I checked the boundary fences for damage.'

'You mean you've walked all round the farm at this time of the morning? Have you had breakfast yet?'

'No, but I don't expect you have either, Uncle.'

'Well, no, but Babs has been out to help me with

the milking early this morning and has gone indoors to make breakfast. Let's go and see what your aunt has cooked up for us. She'll be wondering where you are.'

'I can tell you about the fence that I found damaged, uncle. There's only one spot, as far as I could tell.'

'You've saved me time looking for it, Emily. That's a great help.'

'Now get this breakfast down you, Emily, and drink your tea while it's hot. We're going to use our bacon ration today and we're lucky to have our own eggs.' Barbara placed the plates on the table and cut more slices from the loaf. 'I had no idea that you were up and out trudging around the farm at such an early hour.'

'She's found the place where the barbed wire was hanging loose so I'll get up there and sort it out after breakfast. I don't like barbed wire attached to fences anyway and would replace the lot if I had the time and the money.' Fred Baxter reached for another slice of bread and smiled across the table at his niece.

'You're supposed to be here resting, Emily, not dashing all over the farm in the early morning. I promised my sister that we would look after you and – '

'But, Auntie, you are looking after me, and I do feel better. I don't know what came over me at Margaret's home, but I know that I can't change the past, and that I have to mourn it and move on.'

Barbara nodded. 'That's all you can do, dear. I explained to your uncle how you broke down and let it all out.'

Fred drained his mug of tea and looked thoughtfully at his niece.

'There's little sign of the bombing here in North Devon. That's not to say there's little sign of the war. Lots of evacuees are being cared for, the Land Army girls and the Women's Timber Corps are doing amazing work, hard physical work; and there's loss, loss of young men who will never return to this beautiful part of the world. Then there's all the young American soldiers, away from their homes and training on our beaches for who knows what? Whatever normal is, life isn't normal and will never be quite the same again. We just have to do our best and realise that so much is beyond our control.' Fred Baxter stood up and pushed his chair back. 'Beyond our control, Emily. We can only do our best and help each other when and where we can.'

'That's just it, Uncle. I am starting to feel better and I didn't have any bad dreams last night.' Barbara looked closely at her niece.

'That's good, but give yourself time to recover.'

'The thing is that I'm not paying you anything for my keep, Auntie, and look how much work there is for you and Uncle here with almost no help. So, I want to help on the farm. I want to learn to milk the cows.'

'Milk the cows?' Fred Baxter paused as he prepared to leave the kitchen.

'Why not? The Land Army girls had to learn the job, didn't they? If they can learn it, so can I. In any case, a lot of the time the girls can't always get here to help you out, Uncle. Once I know what I'm doing, it will be an extra hand on the farm. What do you think?'

'Well, it's a kind offer, but – '

'Good. Then we'll start the lessons tonight, Uncle. Oh, and by the way, I've been reading about keeping hens in a book I borrowed from the library. There are some new ideas, and I wanted to ask you what you thought when you have a moment.'

Barbara looked at her niece in astonishment. 'I don't know what your mother will have to say about this, I really don't.' She put down the teapot and looked out of the window in bewilderment.

'Well, that's stopped your aunt in her tracks for a while, Emily. It's not often she's lost for words.'

I'm off to look at that fence, then we'll go in the shippon and see how Daniel's patient is doing.'

Fred Baxter smiled to himself and left the kitchen as the phone rang.

Barbara shook herself out of her contemplation and picked up the receiver. 'Hello. Barbara Baxter speaking. Yes, oh, is she? That's good. So, she'll be here for milking tomorrow morning? As long as she is well enough. It's good of you to think of Fred, but are you sure she's recovered? Don't you want to give her another few days before she goes in the milking parlour early on a cold morning? So, it's not still on her chest, then? That's good. Fred will be glad of the help. Well, I know those girls are pretty tough, but they got soaked walking home from that night out in Swimbridge, didn't they? Were we ever young and foolish like that, Dorothy? Yes, I suppose we were. Goodbye Dorothy.'

'Is one of the Land Girls coming soon to help with the milking, Auntie?'

'Yes, one of them is coming tomorrow morning.'

'And I'm going to start to learn to milk this evening.'

Barbara saw the set of her niece's lips and decided not to make any further comment.

The phone rang again. 'Hello. Barbara Baxter speaking. Oh, Doreen. Doreen from the bakery. You'd like to speak to Emily? Yes. Of course. Here she is.' Barbara passed the receiver to her niece.

'Hello, Doreen. Yes, I know the shop is closed

on Wednesday afternoons. This Wednesday? Yes, I could meet you, and if the weather is dry, or if it's wet, we could go to the pictures. Yes, I'll meet you as you come out of the bakery. No, I mustn't be home too late because I like to help my uncle with the farm work. I'll get the bus and - oh, my aunt is just saying that she will meet me in the car at Swimbridge and we will be home before dark. One o'clock then outside the bakery. A pasty will be fine, Doreen. Yes, even a potato one! Yes. Goodbye.' Emily replaced the receiver and smiled at her aunt.

'That's lovely to have a friend, Emily. You need to spend time with people of your own age.' Barbara bent down and picked a newspaper from the magazine rack.

'Here we are. The local paper; The Journal.' Barbara opened it out and laid it on the kitchen table. 'Now we can see what's on at the two cinemas in Barnstaple.'

Chapter 14

‘The weather's not very nice, is it? Why don't we go to my house and eat our pasty? We can make a cup of tea and decide whether to go to the pictures for the matinee.’

‘Yes, Doreen, if you think your family won't mind me joining you in your home.’ Emily buttoned her coat up at the neck and pulled her hat down over her ears.

‘No, of course they won't. Mum's at work anyway. She works in Banburys and Dad's at work too. He's a mechanic at Hopgoods Garage. My sister, Christine is at school. Come on, we'll have the house to ourselves. Let's get out of this rain.’ The two young women hurried away from the bakery. Early closing on Wednesdays at one o'clock and the town was always very quiet, but it had turned out to be a dismal day, cold and wet. Emily followed her new friend to Boutport Street and into Vicarage Street. The rain came down even harder as Doreen hurried around the corner and into King Edward Street. Suddenly she had disappeared from view as Emily stumbled after her.

A door was opened onto the street and a long arm reached out and grabbed Emily. ‘Here I am,

Emily. Quick, come in here out of the rain.'

'I didn't realise you lived so close to where you work. You must be within five minutes, door to door.' The two young women took off their wet coats and hats and Doreen hung them up on the coat rack in the passage to dry off. Emily followed her friend into a room where a fire had been lit earlier but its embers were glowing dimly.

'I'll put on the kettle and bank up the fire once I tickle a bit of fresh life into it,' Doreen said cheerfully. 'Sit down in the armchair and I'll fetch some plates for our pasties. Bert says these are slightly better than his usual ones. He means there may even be some meat in them but I wouldn't get too excited.'

'Can I do anything, Doreen?'

'Follow me into the scullery and you can reach the cups, saucers and plates off the shelf while I make the tea. Bert's put two buns in that bag for us to have after the pasties. He's a kind man and a good cook.' She filled the kettle and put it on the gas stove. 'He's always complaining though, not for himself but because he can't obtain the ingredients he wants in order to turn out what he calls a decent standard of baking. Margaret says that they just have to do what they can with what they've got.'

Emily found a tray propped against the wall and laid out the crockery and food on it. 'She's a good cook, isn't she, Margaret, I mean?'

'Oh yes, and a very quick learner. I 'd like to be quick and bright like that.' Emily looked thoughtfully at Doreen and then carried the tray into the living room and set it down on the table. Doreen poured boiling water into the teapot, picked up a jug of milk and followed Emily. 'Sit here at the table, Emily, and I'll join you after I've coaxed some life into this fire. Mum banks it up and it usually lasts all day until we get home but we want it to wake up now. It's cold isn't it? Are you keen to go to the pictures?'

'I don't mind, Doreen; whatever you want to do.' Doreen cleared some spent ash and a few flames shot up encouragingly.

'Ah, there's life in it after all. I'll give it five minutes and then chuck some coal on.'

The two girls sat and ate their lunch and drank their tea and chatted happily when Doreen suddenly said, 'I'm not that keen on going to the pictures and it's not very welcoming outside.'

'No. My aunt looked to see what's on. There's "Sahara" with Humphrey Bogart. There was a sudden clap of thunder. Both girls looked at one another and laughed.

Doreen screwed up her nose. 'I don't think so, do you?'

Emily shook her head. 'No. I don't think so.'

Doreen lifted the tea pot. 'Let's have another cup of tea and I'll bank up the fire.'

The two friends sat comfortably either side of the fire and looked into its gradually rejuvenating embers. Doreen fidgeted and looked up at Emily. 'Do you mind if I ask you for some advice?'

'If you think there's anything that I can help you with, Doreen'

'Well, you know that I told you about my nice boyfriend, Oliver?'

'Yes. Are you seeing him this week?'

'On Saturday, yes. But it's about – I need some help, Emily. I told you that he's clever and I don't want him to get tired of me; I mean once he finds out that there isn't as much in my head as he thought there was.'

'Oh, Doreen!'

'No. I'm serious, Emily. I want to learn something, read and educate myself. Oliver's going to take me to a concert soon, if he can get off duty, that is. But I want to start reading and being able to talk about things with people; people like you and Oliver, who've had some sort of education. What do you think?'

'It's always good to read more. What sort of thing do you have in mind?'

'That was what I hoped you could come up with; you know, suggest something for me to read.'

'Oh, my goodness! Well, let me think what I like to read and go from there. Saying that, I haven't read anything much for the best part of a year, but I'll tell you about that in a minute. I know. What about "Pride and Prejudice?" Then there's "Jane Eyre."'

'I'll start right away this week. Margaret gets books from the library. Perhaps I could join.'

'Yes, ask her about it. She'll help you.'

'Yes, and when I've read those two, you and I could discuss them. That's if you don't mind and you have time.'

'Of course, I will talk about the books with you but I'll have to brush up on them again, I think. You know, don't you, Doreen, that I came to stay with my aunt and uncle on the farm to get away from London for a while. I've had a breakdown following witnessing a dreadful bombing last year at a school near my home. I couldn't rid myself of the feeling of guilt that I was still here and so many children and teachers were killed. I was just finishing my Teacher Training at the time and was about to call at the school to discuss taking up a job there when the tragedy occurred right in front of me. I was yards away from being a victim myself. After witnessing that, I changed my decision to teach young ones and opted to teach senior girls instead.'

'What were you teaching, Emily?'

'French and music; the violin was my instrument. I started teaching in the academic year of September 1944, but struggled through most of that first Autumn term until my nerves were so bad that I couldn't continue and the doctor signed me off and ordered a rest, which is why I'm at the farm.'

Doreen leaned forward and poked the fire disconsolately. 'But the tragedy that happened at the school was beyond your control, wasn't it?'

'That's what everyone kept telling me. But if I'd arrived five minutes earlier, I would probably have died too, but I would have been with the children.'

'So, you felt guilty for surviving. It's chance, isn't it, in this war? Who knows what is going to happen? It seems as if it is safe here but we don't know. We don't know what will happen to Oliver and all his mates far from their homes. Will they ever see their families again? We have to make the most of every minute. Do you feel better than you did when you came to North Devon from London?'

'Yes, I do. I used to dream the same terrible dream so often, and I haven't had it at all recently. It was while we were visiting Margaret at her house that something took place that tipped me over the edge. She was very kind, and since then I feel calmer. And I'm going to help my uncle with some of the jobs on the farm. He is very over-worked.'

'That will be something different for you and useful for him. We will both have new projects. You'll learn about farming and I'll get to grips with my reading. There is something that I want to ask you; something else, that is.' Emily looked up expectantly.

'How would you like to join me and Oliver for a dance at Braunton next Saturday evening? If you come here during the afternoon we can go on the bus and see him there with some of his friends. Then you and I can come back on the bus, or we will get a lift home, and you can stay the night at our house and return to the farm on Sunday. What do you think?'

Emily had caught a bus to Swimbridge on saying goodbye to Doreen, with the promise of thinking about attending the dance the following Saturday. Her aunt was waiting for her in the car as she jumped off at the stop near the church.

'Thank you for meeting me, Auntie. I hope we'll be back in time for the milking.' Emily climbed into the front seat of the little car and Barbara roared away from the bus stop and shot up Station Hill travelling at the usual unforgiving pace with little regard for the actual capacity of the modest engine. 'He's gone in the milking parlour to make a start and knows that you want to join him to learn the ropes. I want you to wear some stout shoes. I've got an old pair, really tough boots with steel-tipped toes. Cows can be very casual where they put their feet.' Aunt Barbara forced the gear into third as they reached the top of the hill, taking the corner wildly and throwing Emily against the inside of the passenger door. Returning to the upright position, Emily gripped the sides of her seat and stared ahead through the last of the afternoon light. To take her mind off the journey, she said conversationally, 'Doreen asked me if I would like to go with her on the bus to a dance in Braunton next Saturday. She's asked me to stay at her house that night and then I'd come back on Sunday. What do you think, Auntie?'

'It's about time you had a bit of life, Emily. That's wonderful!' As if in celebration Barbara forced her foot to the floor with the accelerator and the little car responded with a jolt as it laboured dutifully up the hill to West Buckland, Emily closed her eyes as they took a blind corner at speed, just avoiding tipping over. The road was deserted and Emily was grateful to have survived another lift in her aunt's car. Three minutes after leaving the village and with the light fading, Barbara turned in at the farm gate. The lights were on in the milking parlour. It was time for Emily to learn a new skill.

Chapter 15

'Not many eggs today, Auntie.'

'Never mind, dear. Perhaps it'll pick up again in a while, but there aren't many hens so we can't expect miracles. Where's your uncle?'

'Stan's arrived, and he's outside looking at that cow's leg. It's healing very nicely. We're going to let her out in the field; the one near the milking parlour.' The kitchen door opened and Stan came in carrying their post.

'Mornin' Barbara, Emily. 'Tis cold and dry. Us don't mind that, do us?'

Fred walked in and they all sat around the table.

'No. This is good weather, Stan, for the time of year.'

'Help yourselves to a mug of tea and there are some shortbread biscuits that I made yesterday in that tin on the table.' Barbara turned to her husband.

'Fred, I've just had a phone call from Mr Hooper in Padfields. He said that if I'd like to go in some time on Saturday he'll have a very smart sofa to show me. He's having it picked up on Friday afternoon.'

Fred Baxter sighed and looked at the place where the old sofa had sat for so long. 'I see you've taken the part outside that I think I could repair, and put it in the lean-to by the back door. What about the rest of it? I'm sure I could do something with it.'

'Yes. I can do something with it, Fred, and that is to break up the wooden parts and use it for firewood. After decades of service, Stan, that sofa finally gave up and collapsed under us.'

'I wondered where 'n was. 'Twas a strong piece of furniture. My Granfer an' Granmother 'ad one very similar, as I recall.'

'Exactly, Stan. Have another biscuit.'

'Thank you. They'm very nice.'

'But Barbara, you said that Mr Hooper can only get what he calls "good second-hand" furniture. What's the point of that?'

'The point is that good second-hand furniture is far better than war-time utility furniture. And you can rely on Padfields, so I told Mr Hooper that I'll drive in Saturday afternoon to have a look at it. And if I'm driving in to Barnstaple, Emily, I can take you to meet your friend.'

'I hadn't decided whether or not to go to the dance with Doreen, Auntie.'

'Of course you must go. Will you see her at her house or meet her from work?'

'I think I will meet her from work.'

'Good. That's settled then. You can come with me to Padfields first, and we can try out the sofa.'

'You see, Stan? One word from me and she does as she likes!'

'I can't say nothin', Fred. Lil is off to a weddin' in March and 'er says 'er 'as to 'ave a new 'at, so 'er's goin' to Banburys on Friday to get one. I said 'er 'ad 'ats 'er could sell they, but no, 'er 'as to 'ave a new one 'cos everyone'd know if 'er wore one 'er already 'ad to some other weddin'.'

'Ooh Stan, Emily helped with the milking last night, didn't you love?' Barbara smiled at her niece, happy to change the subject.

'I don't think I was much help, but I'm learning to milk by hand and by machine. Uncle thinks it's better to know both methods. You never saw such a muddle as I made of it, especially by machine.'

'You need a nice docile animal to start you off, Emily.' Fred smiled at her encouragingly.

'I only milks by 'and. I've never done machine milkin' but I've only got three cows. 'Ow many be you milkin', Fred?'

'Twenty-four, Stan; a mixed bunch, Friesians and a few Dairy Shorthorns.'

'Uncle showed me how to wash the udder and the teats but it took me ages to get any milk with the hand milking. Then suddenly it came streaming out and made a lovely sound as it hit the bottom of the bucket. But when I tried to use the milking machine, no sooner had I fitted the cups on three teats and attempted to fit the fourth one, then they fell off the other three. I felt sorry for the cow I was practising on. She turned her head and looked at me, and mooed loudly.'

'You'll do it, Emily. In any case, I don't expect you to help me every milking time.'

'I enjoyed it, though. There's a lot to learn. The Land Girls will come more often now they've recovered from that nasty chill, won't they?'

'Yes, but our neighbours' farm is much bigger, so they need more help. They milk about forty cows there, and do the milk round in our area.'

'The problem is that many of the young farm workers in the country have joined up to fight. That's why we're relying on the Women's Land Army. And they do a good job too.' Barbara gathered the mugs and plates and took them to the sink.

'Back to work then, Stan.' Fred stood up and walked towards the door.

'Yes, and yer's a few letters; one for you, young lady. Thank you for the tea and biscuits, Barbara.' He and Fred left the room.

'Goodbye, Stan. Ooh, Emily, perhaps that's from your friend, Isaac, in London.' Barbara looked disinterestedly at the other two pieces of correspondence and put them on the desk in the corner of the room.

'No, Auntie. I'd know his writing immediately.

I don't recognise this at all.' It was a rather official looking envelope, and Emily tore it open and read the letter aloud.

Dear Miss Ward,

As the Secretary of the Barnstaple Orchestral Society, I am writing to invite you to join our group of happy music-makers. I understand that you are an accomplished violinist, and as you have recently arrived in the area, you may not know about us. Our Society has long been established but our numbers have been diminished over recent years since some of our players have been conscripted and are sadly far from home. We are looking for players in all sections of the orchestra and it has come to our attention that you would be a very welcome member of the string section.

Our conductor is Mr Alcwyn Evans and our Leader is Miss Clara Stone. We meet to rehearse once a week and hope to give concerts three times a year, although our choice of programme has needed to be more modest of late as we have had difficulties in obtaining the sort of membership numbers we had before the war.

I enclose a stamped-addressed envelope for your reply. I assure you that you would receive a very warm welcome from our members, should you consider joining us.

I am,
Yours Very Sincerely,
Michael White. (double bass)

Emily held the letter out and shook her head. 'I don't understand. Who is this man and how does he know about me? Only you and Uncle know that I play the violin.'

'You've only played it once since you've been here.' Barbara was silent and both women looked at one another in bewilderment. 'You played it the day that the cow tore its leg on the barbed wire.'

'Yes, that's right. And someone other than you must have heard me playing.'

'It was Daniel who heard you, Emily. Daniel Smith, the vet.'

Chapter 16

'**Bromleys Tea Shop** for a cup of coffee, Emily, and we deserve it. Look, here's an empty table. My treat, dear. You were a great help to me in Padfields.'

'I should treat you, Auntie. You've given me a lift to town.' The two women sat at a table for two as a waitress came towards them.

'What will it be, ladies?' Her black dress and white frilly, starched apron with matching hat looked smart and her smile brightened up the afternoon.

'Coffee for me and a coconut cake, please. What about you, Emily?'

'The same for me, please.' The waitress bustled off humming.

'Well I'm pleased with the sofa. It doesn't even look second-hand. I think someone must have been moving into a smaller house and that sofa was too big for the sitting room; a stroke of luck on our part.'

'It's very comfortable, and just the right size for where it will go. Do you think that Uncle will approve of it?'

'Eventually, once he's sat in it a few times. He has to accept that it will be lots more comfortable than the old one, but he won't actually admit it, of course.'

'Perhaps we could re-cover some of the cushions that went on the old one; you know, buy a bright-coloured remnant. What do you think, Aunt?'

'Yes, that's a good idea. Fred likes orange. The sofa is brown, and orange cushions would cheer it up. I'll pop up to Banburys before I drive home and see what I can find. Ah, here comes our coffee.'

'Aunt, what do you think about the dress I've brought with me for the dance tonight?'

Barbara poured the coffee and passed Emily a cake. 'It's very pretty, dear, and it suits you.'

'It's not very fashionable though, is it?'

'I wouldn't know about that, Emily. I don't have much occasion for dressing up, and with rationing, the coupons wouldn't stretch to high fashion anyway.' Barbara took a sip of her coffee and looked enquiringly at her niece. 'The question is, can you dance?'

'I can waltz a bit.' Emily bit into her coconut cake and looked solemnly at her aunt.

'You might need to do a little more than that, dear. There'll be Americans there, won't there?'

'Yes. The dance is at one of the halls in Braunton, and the soldiers come in from the camps around the area. Doreen's boyfriend, Oliver, will be there with his friends.' Emily swallowed the rest of her coffee. 'And I can quickstep a little.' Her aunt leaned forward across the table.

'I saw some of the American soldiers dancing on a newsreel when I went to the pictures in Barnstaple with a friend from the village. It's not your ordinary dancing. No. It's more frenzied than that. Let me think what they call it.' Barbara frowned, her coconut cake half way to her mouth as she recalled the newsreel she'd seen a few months ago

'I know, it's called, "Jutterjugging". The soldiers throw the girls up in the air and they do lots of wriggling and jiggling.'

'I think you mean "jitterbugging", Aunt. Yes, I've seen that on a film. I may have to sit those dances out.'

'Oh, I think you'll be fine,' she paused, 'as long as you're wearing a good pair of knickers.' Barbara stood up and went to pay the waitress. Emily sat and wondered what she had let herself in for.

'Emily, I'm going to make my way to Banburys and I expect you will be off to meet Doreen from work soon. Phone me from a phone box and let me know what bus you will be taking to Swimbridge on Sunday and I'll come and meet you.'

'Are you sure, Auntie? I'm hoping to be back to help Uncle with the afternoon milking,'

'Yes, I'm sure. Now you have a wonderful time. I shall look forward to hearing all about it when I see you.'

They hugged one another and Barbara went

scuttling off up the High Street.

Emily reached the bakery and saw her friend through the window tidying the shelves and preparing to close the shop. The door to the shop was locked so Emily knocked on the window. Doreen looked up and went to unlock the door.

'Come in, Emily. I've just got to hand over the day's takings to Bert. He's finishing up in the bakery and won't be a minute.'

'No hurry, Doreen. Am I too early?'

'No. You're fine. I've cleaned up in good time. It all went quiet early this afternoon so I don't have to hang about.'

'All done then, Doreen? I'll take the money and we can get off home. Is this the friend you've been telling us about?' Emily looked up as a jolly-looking man came into the shop from the bakery at the back.

'Yes, Bert. This is Emily. We're going to a dance in Braunton tonight.'

'Hello Emily. Well you two have a good time. I hope you've got plenty of energy.'

'Hello. I don't expect to do much dancing but I shall enjoy watching Doreen and her friends.'

'We'll see about that, Emily. Bert, here are the takings for today. We'll be off now, if that's OK?'

'Yes, get along, and get dressed up. Bye, Emily. See you Monday, Doreen, all in one piece, hopefully.'

Doreen and Emily left the shop followed by Bert, after he had first pulled down the blind showing the closed sign, and locked the door.

'Look at the queue for the bus to Braunton, Doreen. Do you think we'll get on?'

'If we don't, we'll have to wait for the next one. It's cold, isn't it?'

'Freezing. Ah, here comes the bus.' The long queue of well-dressed young women in front of them began to shuffle forward.

'Come along, ladies!' The bus conductor leaned out of the double-decker bus and beckoned the glamorous young women inside. 'My, this is my night. Where's the party and why didn't I get invited? Two more, please. Yes. you'll do nicely but you'll have to go upstairs,' he said winking at Doreen and Emily.

'That was lucky, Emily, but I'm wondering if all these girls have tickets. The dances are very popular.'

Emily looked at her friend and frowned. 'But I don't have a ticket. I thought we would pay at the door.'

'No, don't worry. Oliver and his friends have our tickets and we will meet them outside.'

'Oh! Doreen, let me know who bought my ticket.'

'They won't let you pay. They're glad you're turning up, Emily.'

'I think they may change their minds when they see that I can't dance much.'

The bus pulled in at the bus stop in the middle of Braunton village and the passengers poured off and thronged towards the Village Hall from where, although in total blackout from the outside, there was already emitting the sound of lively music and loud voices.

'Doreen! Hi!' A handsome young American in uniform came towards them and kissed Doreen on the cheek and smiled politely at Emily.

'Oliver, this is my friend, Emily.'

'Nice to meet you, Emily. Shall we go in? My friends are already inside. It's cold out here for you.' Oliver handed in three tickets at the door and they followed him to the cloakroom and left their coats.

'Please let me know what I owe you for my ticket, Oliver,' Emily said.

'Nothing, Emily. This is my treat.' They followed a line of young people into the hall. 'Let's go and sit with those guys.' Oliver pointed at a group of American soldiers sitting around a table near the raised stage where the band was preparing to play the next number.

'Hi guys. You know Doreen and this is her friend, Emily. Carter and Dylan came with me from Woolacombe, along with this young lady who lives outside the village on a farm near Morte, - Mortehoe, is it? Sorry, but I get some of the village names wrong.' Oliver shrugged his shoulders apologetically and smiled.

'Oh, Imogen, I didn't know you were coming. We haven't seen each other for ages.' Doreen looked around the group, wondering what the other young woman's connection was with the American soldiers. 'Immy and I know each other because our fathers are cousins. We met last at a family wedding, didn't we?'

'Lovely to see you Doreen. It was a last-minute decision for me to come. A nursing friend from the hospital passed me her ticket because she is having to work. Yes, our Dads like to find an excuse to meet for a chat sometimes and prop up the bar in The Three Tuns in Barnstaple.'

'Do you like dancing, Emily?' the young man called Carter asked. He was black and very handsome. Emily noticed that most of the negro Americans sat together apart from the white soldiers. She thought that they were also billeted separately too. Emily smiled and shook her head.

'I haven't done much dancing really, so will be happy to watch you all,' Emily replied nervously. The young man grinned at her, showing his beautiful white teeth as the band started to play its rendering of 'In the Mood'. Just about everyone in the room stood up and started dancing. Carter held out his hand and beckoned Emily to join him on the floor. The rest of the party were already active and looking very competent.

'I'm not sure if I can – ' 'You'll be fine, Emily. There's nothing to it. I'll show you.' With that, Emily found herself twirled and twisted, thrown and lifted and in no time, she was back in her seat flushed and breathless, amongst a noisy, laughing group, all friends together.

'Well done, Emily,' Doreen laughed. 'I thought you said you couldn't dance.'

'It was Carter doing all the work,' Emily shouted back against the noise of the crowd. Carter shook his head. 'No, you've got a great sense of rhythm, and you know what people say about us black guys.' Dylan interrupted and nodded laughingly. 'Well you sure **do** have a great sense of rhythm, Carter. He's "King of the Jive", Emily. Hey, what about that guy on the liquorice stick? He's really something!' Imogen leant forward to try to make herself heard.

'He's new to the area but I've seen him driving a van around Woolacombe and Ilfracombe from time to time. Our local dance bands have lost some of their players, so he fills in occasionally.'

'Drafted, I guess,' Oliver said. 'He's a great clarinettist. I wonder if he plays classical, too? OK, it looks as if they're off again. Anyone for a drink before we get back on the floor?'

Chapter 17

Emily didn't know if she could dance any longer. Where were the sedate waltzes and dignified foxtrots she had tried to learn when she was at college? There were a few slow dances but everyone was so exhausted after all the jiving and jitterbugging, that as soon as one was played, the couples just leaned on each other and dragged themselves around the dance floor in order to recover for the next fast number. So many men, mostly American soldiers had asked her to dance, surely it was time to go home. The only men she hadn't danced with were the ones in the band. The clarinet player was amazing and was starting up with 'That's a Plenty'. She'd heard it played by Benny Goodman but this man was a wonderful instrumentalist too. Everyone was gathering around the bandstand to listen to him and she was taken forward with the throng, clapping and cheering. It was very hot and she was feeling thirsty. Some of the soldiers broke away from the group and started dancing as the music became more and more rhythmic. She was dragged into a space behind her by the man who had served them the drinks, and twirled and lifted into the air. The drumming became louder and the clarinettist took his extemporising into the top register of his instrument. The sound was shrill; it was loud; it was wonderful. She was weightless and floated slowly above her dance partner, up to the ceiling, looking down on everyone.

'I can't dance any more,' she shouted above the noise of the music and the cheers of the listeners. 'I can't dance any more. That's a Plenty, I tell you. That's a Plenty.'

'Wake up, Emily! I've brought you a cup of tea. Wake up!'

What was happening? Where was she? Someone was shaking her arm. She wasn't dancing or floating in the air.

'Wake up! You've been dreaming. Sit up and drink this tea.' Doreen put the tea cup on the bedside table and shook her friend's arm and helped to prop her up in the bed.

'I think you're still dancing.' Doreen laughed as Emily opened her eyes and looked around the room.

'Oh, I'm in your sister's bedroom, Doreen. I thought I was still at the dance in Braunton.' She sighed and reached for the tea. 'Thank you. I hope I'm not too late getting up.'

'No, there's no hurry. It's Sunday and as you know, my parents and young sister went on the train to visit Mum's sister and her husband in Taunton for the weekend. Are you feeling all right?'

'Yes, just tired, but last night was the most fun I've ever had. I had no idea it would be like that. My dancing lessons didn't amount to much.'

'No, not with our American friends. Everything you thought you knew about dancing might as well go out the window. Do you want to come again some time?'

'Let me recover from last night first.' Emily drank the last of her tea and handed her cup and saucer back to Doreen.

'You know where our little bathroom is. Get washed and dressed and come downstairs when you're ready. We've got two of the eggs that you kindly brought from the farm, and I'll fry some bread to go with them. See you when you're ready.'

Doreen handed a plate of fried egg and bread to Emily and they sat to enjoy a quiet breakfast together.

'Mum used to make marmalade before the war, when you could get Seville oranges. She loved to make jam and chutney. We picked lots of blackberries last September and she made as much jam as she could, but it was a matter of being able to get enough sugar. She kept hiding our rations away from the family and telling us that we had run out of them. She's quite devious at times. Anyway, yesterday she brought out a jar from the cupboard so we can have some with our toast.'

'Oh, lovely! It's so kind of your family to let me stay, Doreen. You can come to the farm when you have a free weekend but I expect you see Oliver when he's not doing whatever they do at Woolacombe.' Doreen cut some bread from the loaf and handed some slices to Emily.

'I'm not really sure what they do there, but Immy said the firing and explosions start early in the morning and lots of soldiers are practising driving different sorts of landing craft and vehicles. And there are tanks too, Immy said. They're training for something or other but what for we don't know, and they never talk about what they do. They say that the soldiers get very good rations sent from back home and they're always giving things to the locals; you know, chocolate, sweets, bananas. Everyone likes the American soldiers and there are lots of friendships formed with them, especially with the local girls.'

'Yes, Doreen. I think you've proved that.' Emily looked up from her breakfast. 'Oliver is really nice, isn't he? And he loves you. Anyone can see that.'

'Well, he hasn't found out that I'm not nearly as clever as he is yet, Emily. But I'm going to work on that. I got some books from the library and I'm borrowing some from friends, including Margaret.

Do you want another cup of tea?'

'Yes please. I'm so thirsty after last night's efforts. What have you been reading, then?'

'I started with "Pride and Prejudice." I've almost finished it.'

'Really? Well done! What do you think of it?'

'It's not fair, is it? I mean, just because you're a woman you have to clear out of your home if your dad dies and it passes to some bloke, a cousin, and all the sisters are homeless. So, before that, they have to hope they can find a husband and marry him, even if they don't love him, just so they have somewhere to live. I mean, it's not fair, is it?'

'You're right, Doreen. That's exactly what Jane Austen was writing about. I think she made a story out of it and protested at the unfairness of the law at the same time. Well done! You've got it exactly!'

'Have I? Do you think so? I'm going to read another one of her books next. What about "Sense and Sensibility"?'

'Good choice, Doreen. I might read that one again too.'

'Then we can talk about it. Another thing; Oliver said that he will tell us when there is a concert we could go to with him. He's keen on all sorts of music. You could come with us.'

'Surely you would rather go on your own? I don't want to be a gooseberry.'

'You wouldn't be. Oliver suggested it. He'd get up a small party, and Immy might come too.' Doreen poured herself another cup of tea. 'Do you play your violin sometimes?'

'I didn't play it for months but I picked it up again recently. I've had a letter inviting me to join a local orchestra. I'm a bit rusty but I expect they're short of players, what with the younger men away in the forces, fighting.'

'Oh, Emily! You make it sound as if you can't play, but I'm sure you can. That has to be your task, getting back to what you used to do, just like catching up with my education is mine.' Doreen looked at her friend and giggled. 'Well, I know which of us has the harder job, and it's not you!'

Chapter 18

Five days in a row she'd practised. Emily packed her violin away in its case and sat on the bed and leafed through her music. It was good that she'd never minded working on scales and arpeggios because that was what she needed to do in order to regain her technique. She would ask her mother to send on her book of studies. Not that she didn't like playing some of the pieces she knew, but if she were to join the local orchestra, she would have to get her playing up to scratch. Emily had written to the secretary saying that she would like to attend some rehearsals, but that she would understand if it was felt that her standard of playing didn't meet their requirements. She tidied away her music and looked out of the window. Her mornings were starting to settle into a routine. After breakfast, she'd collect the eggs, feed and clean out the chickens, and let them out to forage for themselves. She knew all their names and found the creatures full of character. Then she'd come in for coffee, when they were usually joined by Stan. After that she'd go to her room and practise her violin for half an hour before helping her aunt to prepare dinner. She couldn't help feeling guilty about not working.

She knew she was not ready to go back to teaching but felt that she was not doing enough when many women were working in factories or carrying out voluntary work to help the war effort, even those caring for young children or elderly relatives. She would discuss her concerns with her aunt. It was fascinating helping her uncle with the afternoon milking, not that it was much of a help at first but she was starting to improve. There was so much more work involved than she had realised; sorting out the milk that had been collected, measuring it, cleaning all the pails and equipment, letting out the cows and cleaning out the milking parlour. It was endless, and twice a day too. Her uncle wouldn't allow her to help with the morning milking. One of the Land Girls was sharing that with Uncle Fred but had to rush back to the neighbour's farm as the two girls were responsible for the milk round in the area. They were nice girls and strong, and worked hard. One of them was tall and heavily-built and the other one shorter and skinny. They were like a female version of Laurel and Hardy, but fortunately for Uncle Fred, cleverer and very efficient. The big girl was called Henrietta but everyone called her Hen and the skinny one was Philippa and was known as Pip. It was Hen who usually came to help with the morning milking. The girls were able to carry out all sorts of work on the neighbour's farm;

drive the tractor, plough, help with the lambing. It was a much bigger farm, of course but she'd heard her uncle saying that the Ministry wanted him to plough up more land for tilling vegetables. There'd be lambing soon. Emily remembered her aunt telling her that their daughter did most of the night shifts at lambing time. How many sheep did they have to lamb, Emily wondered? She opened the door to the kitchen and saw her aunt topping up a large saucepan with boiling water in which was sitting a steamed suet pudding.

'I hope I haven't been too long upstairs, Aunt. I'll peel the potatoes if you pass me the peeler from the drawer.'

'No, dear, I love to listen to you practising but am not so keen on those scale things you do. I suppose it's to get your fingers working again.'

'It is, and I'm very out of practice.' Emily paused and said, 'Auntie, there is something I want to ask you.'

'You're looking very serious, Emily.' Barbara replaced the lid on the saucepan and moved it along the hot plate on the Aga. 'Let's sit on the sofa and you tell me what it is.' They sat side by side and Emily took a deep breath.

'Well, I'm feeling very guilty that I'm not doing enough. It's like paradise here in the country for me, but very hard work for you and Uncle. You've given me a chance to start to regain my health and although I know I couldn't return to teaching yet, I can do something more than I'm doing at the moment.'

'But you are helping us with the chickens and the milking.'

'It's not enough though, is it? I don't just mean helping on the farm, although I think I could do more. Perhaps I could do some sort of voluntary work.'

'Oh, you mean volunteering for the WVS for instance; the Women's Voluntary Service? The problem is that we are out in the country and it's easier to serve if you live in a town or city.' Barbara smiled. 'There is one thing you could do. Darn socks.'

'Darn socks? I don't understand, Aunt.'

'The WVS are sent bags of socks to darn and return, and I've started darning some in the evenings. You could help me because I can't get them darned fast enough before Mrs Smale from Swimbridge drops off another lot for me.'

'Oh, do you mean that those socks I've seen you darning some evenings are not Uncle Fred's?'

Barbara laughed. 'Good gracious, no! When the socks have been mended, they are sent back to our troops. It's the little bit of work I do for the WVS. Most of the voluntary workers buy their own uniform but as I don't leave the farm to volunteer, there's no point in me doing that, but I can do my bit without leaving home. What about helping me out on some evenings?'

'Yes, I'd love to help, if you'll show me how to do a good job.'

'You have no idea what you've volunteered for, Emily. Some of the socks appear to have bigger holes than they have feet. We get sent all sorts of coloured yarn from local people to do the job. It is very boring so I'll be glad to have someone to keep me company while I work.'

'If it's boring, we could listen to ITMA on the wireless together.'

'Good idea, Emily. It's on tonight. We'll get started.'

Chapter 19

There was a breath of spring in the air as Barbara left the milking parlour and made her way back to the farmhouse. She had risen early to help her husband with the milking knowing that Henrietta wouldn't be working for him as she had gone home to see her family for the weekend. Barbara opened the door to the kitchen and started to prepare a good breakfast for Sunday morning. She had saved some bacon and found that Emily had already placed a basket of eggs in the larder. They would have a leisurely breakfast. Occasionally they went to church on Sundays, mainly at Christmas or Easter and always at Harvest Festival, but she and Fred were not regular churchgoers and tried to take things a bit easier on Sundays. At some point she would have to take the bundle of darned socks to Mrs Smale at Swimbridge, and would probably be given another bag sent on to the WVS from the fellows in the Army and Air Force. Barbara laid the table and sliced the bread. Poor chaps! She looked out of the kitchen window at the first signs of spring; the catkins almost finished on the trees and the primroses coming out in the hedges. The kitchen door opened and Emily and Fred came in together.

'Hello, Emily. Where have you been?'

'It was such a lovely morning that I had a little walk after I'd let out the hens. Uncle has just finished in the milking parlour and told me that you helped him this morning, Auntie. I could have done that.'

'No, Emily. We don't want you doing the morning milking. Now when you've washed your hands sit down at the table both of you, and we'll enjoy a peaceful Sunday morning breakfast.'

'Just the job, Babs. You know the way to a man's heart, don't you, love?'

'Through his stomach, isn't it, Uncle?' After a few minutes the three were gathered around the table with their cooked breakfasts in front of them. Suddenly the phone rang.

Barbara sighed and went to answer it. 'Oh Doreen. Of course, you may speak to her. She's here.' Barbara handed the receiver to Emily and resumed her breakfast.

'Hello, Doreen. Is everything OK? You saw Oliver last evening? Yes, you told me you were going to the pictures together. He said he has managed to get three tickets for a concert, for him and you and – me? Really? No, I'm not busy. But it's this afternoon? Where? Sorry, I lost you for a minute. I thought you said at the Woolacombe Bay Hotel. Oh, you did. At 2.30? But how can we get there today? There aren't many buses running on a Sunday. Really? Oliver is driving into Barnstaple to pick us up in a Jeep at 1.30? But I'd have to get to your house by that time. Oh, I don't think I can, Doreen. He said that I've got to be there because the brilliant jazz clarinettist from the dance band is playing some classical pieces. I thought the hotel was the Headquarters of the High Command for the Assault Training Course. Hold on, Doreen. Auntie Barbara is saying something to me.'

'Emily, I'll drive you to Barnstaple and call at Mrs Smale's about the socks on my way back. We'll work out how to get you home later. Tell Doreen you'll be thrilled to go. She'll be thrilled to go, won't she, Fred?'

'Thrilled!' Fred remarked, taking a large bite from his fried bread.

'Auntie will drive me to your house for 1.30, Doreen. Do you know what the clarinettist is going to play? Oliver does, and he'll tell us later. Yes, I'll be there in time. Oh, the pips are going! Thank you for phoning. Bye.'

Emily replaced the receiver and sat at the breakfast table. 'What a surprise! Are you sure about taking me to Barnstaple, Auntie?'

'And have you got enough petrol, Babs? Are there any petrol coupons left for this month? You can't just gallivant around the countryside, you know. There's a war on.'

'Fred, I've hardly been anywhere. There's nowhere much to go. Anyway, I can do with calling on Mrs Smale so I can kill two birds with one stone.'

'That's the sock woman, isn't it?'

'Eat your breakfast, Emily. It's not nice when it's cold. Yes, Fred. That's the sock woman, as you like to call her. If I'm going to Barnstaple, I might call at the British Restaurant to see what the WVS, you know, the women volunteers are doing there. I've heard all about it but as I hardly ever get out of this farm I'm in ignorance of their efforts. It's good to keep up with the times. We'll have a light, early meal today at about 12.30. I want to get you there on time, Emily.' Barbara stood up and picked up the tea pot. 'More tea, anyone?'

'The thing is, Auntie, I won't be able to help Uncle with the milking this afternoon, will I? If the concert starts at 2.30 it probably won't finish for about an hour and a half.' Emily slid sideways in her seat as Auntie Barbara took the corner suddenly onto the main road to Landkey.

'I've thought about that, Emily. Uncle will have help from Pip later as she's going to start off the milking on our neighbour's farm and leave the rest to him, then dash over to us. It's only for the one time and we have been very light on the help from the Land girls so far this year. Our neighbours say that themselves. And, – ' Barbara braked suddenly as she started going down the hill into Landkey faster than was manageable. There was a squeal of breaks and a cat dashed across the road, saving one of its lives. 'And, I'm thinking of staying on at the British Restaurant, maybe to help them out. I think they do three-hour shifts. That would work, if Doreen's boyfriend can drive you both back to Barnstaple.'

'It's all very complicated, Auntie and too many people are putting themselves out for me, including you.'

'Nonsense! I'm quite keen to see what goes on at the restaurant. It used to be the Albert Hall but was badly damaged in a fire in 1941. I think part of the building is used for dancing and concerts occasionally. Living in the country, like we do, it's easy to be unaware of what is going on in town.'

'That's the building where Boutport Street meets Butchers' Row, isn't it?'

'Yes, That's right.' Barbara drove past Rock Park. 'It's a lovely day, Emily. Woolacombe will look beautiful in the sunshine. And it will be so exciting to have a ride in an American Jeep.' Barbara drove up through the town and headed for Boutport Street.

'That's funny,' Emily muttered. I thought you could only get two people in a Jeep.'

Barbara drew up outside the British Restaurant, parking the car with a screech of brakes. 'Well dear, that'll be a cosy, ride, won't it?'

Chapter 20

The **Woolacombe Bay** Hotel looked elegant and welcoming and must have been the perfect place to holiday in peacetime. After a breezy and exciting ride from Barnstaple, Oliver had parked the Jeep in a road near the entrance to the building and taken them inside, showing their tickets at the door. The room where the concert was to take place was wood-panelled and smelt of furniture polish. Rows of chairs had been laid out in readiness, their wine-covered seats and high backs adding to the feeling of luxury and comfort. The sun was streaming in through the huge windows and the waves were breaking on the golden sand across the bay. At the far end of the room was a grand piano and a music stand with music laid out on a small table nearby. At the opposite side of the room to the door was a table with cups and saucers and plates covered with white paper napkins. The war and the training that was going on all around North Devon seemed far away. It was Sunday and all seemed well in the world.

'I'm sorry if I've gotten you both here so early,' Oliver apologised as they were shown into the room and told to sit where they liked.

'Better than being too late,' Emily smiled. 'Couldn't you two take a little walk around outside for ten minutes or so?'

'I guess we could.' Oliver looked at Doreen. 'People will start to arrive soon so can you hang on to a couple of seats next to you, Emily?'

'Of course. I can put my bag on the seat by me.'

'And I can leave my bag on the other one,' Doreen added. 'Look, Em, It's Imogen coming in. She could sit the other side of you. We won't be long.' Doreen beckoned to her cousin and the two lovers left the room.

'Imogen.' Emily waved and indicated a seat next to her. 'Good to see you here.'

'Hello, Emily. Oliver got me a ticket. I expect he got one for you and Doreen as well. He is so generous.' Imogen sat next to Emily. The room was starting to fill up as local people and American soldiers, mostly of high rank, started to file in.

'Although I've lived up at Mortehoe all my life I've never been in the hotel. Isn't is lovely? Really classy! I wonder if I'll know anyone here.'

'I'm sure that I won't, Imogen. Oh, is that a programme you have? I'd like to see what the clarinettist will be playing.' Imogen passed the programme to Emily. 'Have a look. You're a musician, Doreen told me, so you'll have more idea than me.'

'I wouldn't say that, but I'll look and see if I recognise anything. Thank you, Imogen.' Emily looked down through the single page and saw that the clarinettist was called William Taylor and his accompanist was Robert Stone. They were playing Weber Concertino, Opus 26, some Brahms, and Five Bagatelles by Gerald Finzi, and there would probably be something really popular as an encore. Emily handed the programme back to Imogen.

'They have dances here sometimes. I don't know why I've never been. I'm going to make sure I go when they have the next one. I think the organisers will even arrange transport if you don't have your own.' Imogen looked very determined.

'Well, you live within a few miles, don't you?'

'Yes, off Station Road up at Mortehoe, but they are long miles; "farmers' miles." ' Emily laughed and pointed to the door. 'Ah, here come Oliver and Doreen.'

'Yes, and someone I recognise.' Imogen nudged Emily. 'You see that beautiful looking woman behind them, standing next to that handsome American officer? She's the new relief doctor around this area. I'll tell you about her when we get a moment.'

The woman was a natural blonde, tall and slim and looked as if she had just stepped out of the pages of Vogue. She walked with the man at her side to two seats in the front row, sat down and crossed her slender, silk-stockinged legs and surveyed the room.

'Crikey!' Emily whispered to Imogen. 'What a head-turner!'

'It was lovely outside, Emily.' Doreen's face was flushed and her eyes shone. Oliver smiled at her and squeezed her hand. Imogen leaned forward. 'Hello, Doreen. We meet again, thanks to your kind friend, Oliver.'

'He spoils us, doesn't he? We have to think of a way to make it up to him,' Doreen looked up at Oliver.

'It looks as if things are gonna get started.' Oliver nodded towards the door where the soloist and his accompanist were standing, waiting to be introduced. A man entered the room behind them, squeezing past apologetically, and moving quickly to the back of the room. Emily recognised him immediately. It was Dan Smith, the vet from South Molton. But a senior ranking American soldier was standing in the front of the room and waiting to introduce the soloists.

'Good afternoon, Ladies and Gentlemen and welcome to our afternoon concert. I think some of you know our soloist, William Taylor in another guise, and we are truly fortunate to welcome him here to entertain us by playing some very different repertoire. We are in for a treat, I assure you. Accompanying him we have a well-known local musician, Robert Stone, piano and cello teacher from Ilfracombe, brother of our own Clara Stone, violin and piano teacher here in Woolacombe. William and Robert are both giving their time this afternoon and the proceeds from the sale of the tickets will go to the American Red Cross. Following the performance, we will be serving afternoon tea. So now, please give our musicians a very warm Woolacombe welcome.'

There was enthusiastic applause as the musicians took up their places and William checked his tuning.

'Did you enjoy that, Doreen?' Emily asked as the friends were offered tea and refreshments after the performance.

'Yes, it was so special hearing music played right in front of us. It made me feel part of it. What did you think, Emily?'

'It was really wonderful. William is a fine player and Robert is such a sensitive accompanist. Thank you, Oliver, for treating us.'

'So, what did you like best, Emily?' Oliver passed a plate of iced cakes to the little group.

'I liked all of it, especially the English music; the Gerald Finzi pieces are a favourite of mine.'

Oliver nodded. 'Yes, they sound English, don't

they, especially the slower numbers. What do you think, Doreen?'

'I liked the first piece, the one by Weber, was it? But my favourite was the slow one of the English pieces. It was called Forlana and it was so forlorn too.'

Imogen swallowed the last of her ham sandwich and was offered an iced cake by Oliver. 'I could hardly believe that the man who played the clarinet was the same one who played at the dance the other night. He was wonderful.'

Oliver nodded. 'Yes, such an able guy. He sure is versatile.'

Emily looked across the room and saw Dan sitting on his own. 'Would you excuse me a minute? There's someone I know over there.' She took a cup of tea and a plate of sandwiches and walked across the room. Dan was sitting looking at the programme that he had just picked up from the empty chair next to him.

'Hello! May I offer you a cup of tea and something to eat?' Emily sat down beside him.

'Oh, hello. That is so kind of you. Are you here with friends?'

'Yes, Oliver, an American soldier. He bought three of us tickets. We'd heard the clarinettist play at a dance in Braunton, jazz and swing. He was wonderful and when our friend heard he was giving a concert here, he managed to get some tickets. He even came to Barnstaple to collect his girlfriend and me and drive us here in a Jeep.'

'I was late. There was an emergency at the last minute and I nearly didn't make it.'

'What did you think?' Emily looked at Dan. He was quite tall and looked tired and serious.

'What a lovely tone he gets out of the instrument.'

'Yes. Don't they say that of all the instruments the clarinet is most like the human voice?'

Dan smiled. 'Yes, I think they do.' Suddenly he looked younger and more relaxed. 'I think I should apologise to you. May I call you Emily?'

'Yes, but apologise for what?'

'I put your name forward to the secretary of our orchestra and asked him to invite you to consider joining us. I should have asked you first. You must have wondered how you received the invitation.'

'I did, but then Aunt Barbara and I worked it out. No, it was fine. I didn't mind, but I have played very little for most of last year and am really rusty.'

'You haven't heard our string section yet!' They both laughed. Emily stood up. 'I must go because Oliver is going to drive us back to Barnstaple and I have to meet my aunt at the British Restaurant. I think she was offering to do some volunteering there this afternoon for the WVS. Then she will drive us home. She isn't happy driving in the dark so I don't want to delay her. To be honest, I'm not happy with her driving at all, but she is so kind. She's always doing something to help me.' There was a short silence and Dan stood up and smiled. 'Perhaps I'll see you at one of our practices some time.'

'Perhaps, if I can pluck up courage.' Emily walked back to join the others who were preparing to leave.

'We'll say goodbye then, Imogen.' Doreen hugged her. 'I think Dad wanted to see your Dad some time soon. He said it's been far too long, so he'll probably be in touch.'

'Fine. Bye, Doreen, Emily, and thank you, Oliver. It's been a lovely afternoon.'

'Goodbye, Imogen. I'm going to give the two ladies a draughty ride home now.' They walked out through the front of the hotel. It was not as sunny and the air was much colder. Time to get back to the Jeep.

Oliver drew up outside the British Restaurant just behind Aunt Barbara's little car.

'Thank you again, Oliver. Doreen, I think my aunt is still inside but we're losing the light so I must drag her out. She doesn't like driving in the dark.'

'Bye, Emily. I'll be in touch with you soon.' She and Oliver waved and the Jeep pulled away, heading for Doreen's house.

Emily opened the door to the restaurant and saw a woman in the uniform of the WVS.

'I'm looking for my aunt. Barbara, she's called.'

'Oh yes. She's come to our rescue today. We've got some of our volunteers off with the flu. She's in the kitchen. Go through that door there.' There were still a few groups of American soldiers sitting around, drinking coffee and playing draughts. Emily pushed open the door leading to the kitchen and immediately saw Aunt Barbara at the sink, washing dishes.

'Auntie, I think you should leave now or you won't get back in the daylight.' There was only one other woman in the kitchen. She thanked Barbara profusely for her help. It had obviously been a difficult day.

Emily thought that Aunt Barbara drove better than at any time she had been subjected to being a passenger. Perhaps it was because she was tired after three hours at the kitchen sink. Was she going to stop at Mrs Smale's house to swap darned socks for undarned ones? No. Her aunt said she would wait for Mrs Smale to come out to the farm and they would swap the bags then.

Barbara turned the car into the yard and they got out and hurried indoors and took off their coats and hats.

'I'm so glad you enjoyed the afternoon, Emily.'

'I'm only sorry that yours was so busy, Auntie.'

'It was all for a good cause, but not the most relaxing Sunday afternoon I've spent, that's for sure.'

Chapter 21

'**Babs! Babs!**' **Fred** Baxter called out from the bottom of the stairs. 'Barbara! Are you up there? The sock woman is outside. Are you up there?'

'Yes, Fred. Emily and I are sorting out the spare room and making up the bed for the new Land Army girl. Show Mrs Smale into the kitchen. We'll be right down.' The two women shook the eiderdown and pulled up the counterpane. 'We'll have to finish this later, Emily.' They closed the bedroom door and hurried downstairs.

'Hello, Mrs Smale. I'm sorry that I didn't call on Sunday to hand over the socks we'd repaired. I was doing a shift at the British Restaurant and was there longer than I had expected. I don't like driving in the dark. Please sit down. Let me make you a cup of tea. This is Emily, my niece.'

'Hello Mrs Smale. Shall I take that bundle from you? We have one to give you of darned socks. Auntie did most of them. She's much quicker at it than I am.'

'Oh, what a state some of them are in, dear; more holes than socks. I don't know how they get them so bad, lots of marching, I suppose. I guessed you'd been held up somewhere when you didn't come on Sunday.'

'With the blackout regulations limiting lights on vehicles, I avoid driving at night if I can.' Barbara cut a slice of madeira cake. 'How did you get here, Mrs Smale?'

'With my husband in the van. He works at the big school as one of the groundsmen so I left him at West Buckland School and walked the rest of the way. It was further than I thought and the bundle got heavier.'

'Here's your tea. It was good of you to come. What are you going to do until your husband finishes work?' Barbara put the tea cup on the table next to the sofa and Emily handed the lady the cake. She and Barbara sat either side of the visitor and drank their tea.

'I want to see a friend in the village. She hasn't been well and could do with some company. She's worried about her son. He's in the army and she hasn't heard from him for weeks.'

'We keep hoping that it will be all over soon, but this war just keeps going on and on. Now Fred's been told he has to plough up more acreage for vegetables. We have had one piece of good news though. We're going to have our own Land Army girl. She'll come to live in and go to relatives some weekends.'

'Where does she live, Auntie?' Emily asked. 'It

can't be far. They get Saturday afternoons and Sundays off usually, don't they?'

'Yes, unless it's harvesting time or lambing. Then they can't always go home when they want to. She stays with her aunt and uncle in Taunton at weekends but she grew up in Eastbourne, and her parents still live there. I think she will travel to us from Eastbourne, by train, of course. She has had time off since her last work on a farm. We're not sure why she left that job.'

'May I get you some more tea, Mrs Smale?'

'Thank you, dear. I must say that this is a very comfy sofa. Ours is in a bad state, what with the dogs and the cat spending so much time on it. I have to sit at the table and have a good light to mend the socks. That reminds me, there are several odd balls of wool in the bag, different colours. I've got feelers out all over the village and beyond for unused balls of wool. People are very kind but sometimes send me them in very striking colours, yellow and red. Still, beggars can't be choosers, can they?'

'Well done to do the job, dear. Will your husband collect you from your friend's house when he finishes work?'

'Oh yes. He shouldn't really be working today but the school has managed to track down some second-hand garden machinery, lawn mowers, that sort of thing, and he wanted to go and look at them. Grass cutting time will be on us soon and the groundsmen like the lawns in front of the school to look good.'

'Would you like me to drive you to your friend's house in the village?'

'No, Mrs Baxter. Now I've had two cups of tea and a lovely piece of cake, I'll make my way slowly. It's downhill all the way too. Where's the bag I've come to collect? I don't want to take back the socks with all the holes by mistake.'

They all laughed and saw the lady off, just as the phone rang. Barbara hurried back to the phone. 'Barbara Baxter speaking. Yes, who's speaking, please? Eleanor who? Elly Reed. Oh, yes, you're the girl who is coming to work on our farm.' There was silence as the caller was giving information to a slightly confused Barbara. 'You're coming today! No, we didn't receive a letter from you. In fact, we haven't had any post recently. Of course, I'll meet you off the train. Will you be coming from Taunton? Oh, from Exeter. I see. You've been home to see your parents. I will meet you at Barnstaple Junction. Yes. I can be there at that time. Goodbye, Elly. We'll see you later.' Barbara looked at Emily. 'She's coming today.'

'We'd better go upstairs and finish cleaning the bedroom, Auntie. Better still, let me go and do that.'

'That would be such a help. I can get the dinner ready. The morning seems to be slipping away.' Emily ran back upstairs as Barbara went to the sink and cleared the dishes. She looked out of the kitchen window as she heard the sound of a vehicle coming into the yard. Now who could that be? Fred came out of the milking parlour and walked towards the vet's van. The two men chatted for a while and Daniel got out of the van and followed Fred to the field behind the big barn. What was the problem? Barbara went out the door at the back of the farmhouse to see what was happening. They were both striding across the field and had stopped to look at one of the cows. It was the one whose leg had been stitched after the animal had caught it on the barbed wire. Strange, Barbara thought. Surely it was better by now. The two men were both walking back towards the farmhouse. Fred showed Daniel into the hall and on into the kitchen. Barbara hurried through the back hall and opened the kitchen door.

'Hello, Daniel. Oh, good. I see that Fred is making you a drink.'

'Yes, Mrs Baxter. I was passing and thought I'd just check to see how that cow's leg was healing, the one who had caught it on some barbed wire.'

'And how is it healing?' Barbara asked, wondering how Fred had managed to get the shy vet into the house after several years of trying.

'Very well. Very well indeed.' Daniel looked around the kitchen as if he were searching for something. Suddenly, the kitchen door opened and Emily entered, flushed and dishevelled, carrying a duster and a mop.

'All done, Auntie. Oh, hello.' Daniel stood up and Emily put her mop and duster in the corner of the room and pushed her hair out of her eyes.

'Sorry to intrude but while I'm here to check the cow, I thought I could give you the details about the next orchestra practice.' He put his hand in his pocket, pulled out a crumpled envelope and handed it to Emily.

'Here's your tea, Daniel. There's no sugar in it, that's right, isn't it?' Fred passed the mug to Daniel who smiled and nodded, and Barbara cut him a slice of madeira cake and handed it to him. She busied herself at the sink, observing Emily out of the corner of her eye.

'Thank you.' Emily looked at Daniel and then opened the envelope and read the details of the time and venue of the next rehearsal. 'There's a name and phone number here, Daniel but I don't know who this person is.'

'Ah, yes. Well, he is one of the staff at West Buckland School. He is in the orchestra and comes to rehearsals. I've been in contact with him to tell him that if you do decide to join us, perhaps he could give you a lift. He's a brass player. But don't hold that against him.' They all laughed.

'That's very thoughtful of you, Daniel. I was wondering about getting there and back each time, and I don't want to bother Auntie, especially if any of the rehearsals are evening ones.'

'I can collect you from the big school, Emily, and take you there for your lift,' Uncle Fed smiled at his niece.

'There's no need. Edward intends to collect Emily and bring her home after the rehearsal. She will be driven door to door.' Daniel swallowed the last of his cake and drained his mug. He stood up and smiled at Barbara. 'Thank you very much, Mrs Baxter. What delicious cake! I must be off now.' He smiled at everyone, averting his eyes quickly from Emily. 'Goodbye. That cow's leg has healed well, Fred. Nothing to worry about.' He left the kitchen and walked out of the front door towards the van. Fred looked at Barbara and frowned. 'I wasn't worried anyway. It healed days ago.'

Chapter 22

Barbara was starting to cook the breakfast as Emily entered the kitchen with a basket of eggs.

'Not many today, Aunt, I'm afraid.'

'Better than none, dear. Put them in the larder, please. Do you know if our Land Army girl is up and about? She is probably tired after her journey yesterday and we told her to take a day or so before she starts work. Hen was coming this morning to help Fred with the milking but from next week she and Pip will work most of the time at our neighbour's farm.'

'Yes. Uncle will have Elly here all the time, except when she goes home to see her family. Actually, I saw her driving the tractor an hour or so ago. She was heading towards the field that uncle is intending to plough.'

'Really? I wonder how good she is at ploughing. Fred's very fussy about ploughing. I suppose he knows what she's doing. I just hope that **she** knows what she's doing.' Barbara beat some eggs with a fork and placed some bread onto the hotplate on the Aga to toast. 'They should be in for breakfast soon, that is if Fred has told her when we have breakfast.'

'I'll lay the table, Auntie. I can see Uncle coming across the yard.'

'He knows when it's breakfast time, or his stomach does,' Barbara grinned.

'Guess what, Babs?' Fred Baxter went to the sink and washed his hands.

'We've started lambing.' Barbara placed the plates on the table and Emily poured the tea into four mugs.

'No. Well, yes, just one ewe so far, but not that. No, while I was doing the milking this morning, I could have sworn I heard the sound of a tractor.' Fred dried his hands and sat at the table. 'That girl, Elly. You know we were talking last night about ploughing up the field the other side of the bridge, the one the Ministry said we have to plant potatoes and green veg in?'

'Yes, Fred. You were moaning about it when Elly was asking about the farm. Poor girl had only just got here and you were telling her about all the jobs there were to be done.'

Fred took a sip of his tea. 'Well there are lots of jobs to be done. That's why she's here.

'I know, Fred, but give her a chance to get her breath and get to know us.'

Emily looked at her uncle and passed him the salt and pepper while her aunt place two pieces of toast on a plate, topped it with some scrambled egg and passed it to her husband with a frown of impatience.

'The thing is, Babs, with this war on there isn't time to take a breather. We farmers have to work the land to feed the nation and we're being asked to produce more and more. What with lambing starting now it'll be all hands on deck.'

'Well there's one pair of hands missing. Where is Elly? You must have seen her drive the tractor off? You saw her, didn't you, Emily?'

'Yes. She looked as if she was going to do some ploughing.'

Fred put down his knife and fork. 'Ploughing? What? Where? You mean she had the plough hitched up? I don't know if she can plough.'

'Well, there's only one way to find out. And did you tell her what time breakfast is in this house?'

'No, because I haven't seen her this morning. I've been doing the milking with Hen. I thought she was still in bed.'

'Oh, no, Uncle. I think she was up very early. She must have gone to find the tractor and the plough.'

Fred Baxter took a large bite of his scrambled egg and toast, swallowed the last of his tea, and stood up and pushed his chair back. 'Well, I'm going to find her. I don't want my farming machinery messed up by an amateur. Keep that warm for me, Barbara, and I'll have it when I've investigated.'

He left the kitchen and slammed the door behind him. Barbara placed her husband's half-finished breakfast in the warming oven and hurried to the window to see him striding determinedly in the direction of the bridge over the stream on the far side of the shippon. 'Emily, run after him and keep him calm. Tell Elly to leave what she's doing and come in for breakfast. I don't know if she's even had a hot drink this morning. Your Uncle Fred never gets rattled but he does panic if any of the machinery looks like breaking down, or if anyone looks like breaking it.'

'Right, Auntie.' Emily ran into the hall, put on her coat and wellies and pulled a woollen hat over her head. Barbara sighed as she heard the outside door bang shut. How long had Elly been trying to plough that field? She can't have done much, even if she had got the tractor going. Didn't Fred say there was a problem with it and he'd have to get George Tucker out to sort it before he could do any ploughing? Barbara poured herself a mug of tea and sat at the table and munched absentmindedly on a piece of toast. She stared into her tea cup and thought how much she and Fred missed their daughter, Helen, not just her cheerful and loving character but all her help in running the farm. She'd phoned two days ago to say that all was going well on her father-in-law's Exmoor farm but that he'd had bronchitis and wasn't over it and wouldn't be able to do any lambing work at night. Getting up in the cold would not help him to recover. She and Don would do shifts. They lambed later on the farm there. It was very exposed to the wind up above Exford and all the sheep had to be brought inside. Barbara opened the fire door of the Aga, threw on two logs and slammed it shut. She looked up as she heard voices. It sounded like loud cheerful voices and she could pick out her husband's laugh as the front door opened and the noise of the group removing coats, hats and boots prompted her to put on the kettle and make some more breakfast.

Fred came into the kitchen first, his eyes shining, followed by a red-faced, wind-blown Elly who went to the sink and washed her oily hands. Emily walked quietly to her seat at the table, giving a sly wink at her aunt and averting her eyes from her uncle.

'You must be starving. Elly. I'm sorry you didn't know what time we have breakfast. I didn't think that you'd be up so early on your first morning with us. Come and sit down at the table. Cooked breakfast coming right up,' Barbara smiled.

'Oh, I like to get on with it. I heard Mr Baxter saying last night what a lot there is to do.' Elly had a fresh complexion and her smile lit up the room.

Fred Baxter sat at the table and looked at the new recruit with admiration. 'And get on with it she did, Babs. And Elly, please call me Fred and you can call Barbara Barbara, can't she, Babs?'

Barbara put her husband's half-eaten breakfast in front of him and set about making scrambled egg on toast for Elly. 'And you know Emily, my niece, don't you, Elly?'

'Yes, of course.' The two young women looked at one another and smiled.

Fred Baxter could contain himself no longer. He gulped down the last of his breakfast and blurted out his news to his wife. 'What do you think, Babs? What do you think young Elly has been doing?' Barbara took a breath to offer a reply but was interrupted. 'Ploughing. That's because she'd repaired the tractor and hitched up the plough.' Fred paused dramatically as he sensed he had every eye and ear in the audience upon him. 'Yes. She's made a wonderful start on that field. She can plough a straight line better than me or any man that I know.' Barbara winked at Emily and turned to Elly with a serious expression on her face.

'That's amazing seeing that she's just a woman. I suppose you'll want to keep her on, Fred?' The three women all turned their straight faces on the only male in the room.

'I'll say I want to keep her on.' Fred looked from one woman to another as their expressions of comic indignation matched one another. His face broke into a grin. 'That is, if she'll agree to stay.'

Chapter 23

'Emily,' Barbara called up the stairs. 'Emily, the fellow from West Buckland School is here in his car. Are you ready? Don't forget your violin.'

'Coming, Aunt. Just getting a warmer cardigan.' The young woman ran down the stairs and grabbed her coat and hat from the hallstand and hurriedly put them on.

'That's right, dear. You don't know where they're going to rehearse but you can be sure it will be in some freezing cold hall with no heating. See you later.' They hugged one another and Emily rushed out of the front door and got into the waiting car.

'It's so kind of you to pick me up, Edward. I hope you don't mind me calling you Edward?' The ginger-haired driver smiled and started the engine. 'That's my name, and Dan told me that you are Emily.' He pulled away and drove smoothly across the farmyard and turned quietly onto the road. Emily loosened her grip on the sides of the seat and relaxed. Edward's driving was certainly an improvement on Aunt Barbara's.

'I have to call back at the school for my colleague. He was finishing duty supervising Prep. He's called Gareth. He's Welsh and mad on rugby and music.

'Is he a brass player too?' Emily asked.

'Yes, he plays the trumpet and I play the trombone. But he also plays the harp when he's back home in Wales. Couldn't be more different from the trumpet, could it?'

'I like the harp but it's not easy to carry it around, is it?' Emily commented. Edward turned into the entrance to the school and spotted his colleague coming out of a door at the side of the main building.

'Good job he doesn't play it in the orchestra. We'd never get it in the car, would we?' He stopped at the door just as it began to drizzle, and Gareth quickly jumped in the back of the car.

'Gareth, Emily, Emily, Gareth. We have gained a string player.' Edward drove out of the grounds of the school and set off at a steady speed for Barnstaple.

'Hello, Emily. A string player? They're in short supply these days. We're trying to recruit more but some of the problem is getting the transport to attend rehearsals, what with the petrol rationing.'

'We get coupons because we often have to run boys to South Molton or Barnstaple for various things but even then, we can't come and go just as we please.'

'Are there any boys who could play in the orchestra?'

'We have some boys who are quite musical but they mainly play in smaller ensembles. You have to be a good sight reader to keep up with the sort of thing that Alcwyn does.' Gareth remarked. Emily hoped that she would be a good enough sight reader to keep up with what Alcwyn does.

'Alcwyn is the name of the conductor, isn't it?' Emily asked. Edward drove steadily up the hill out of Landkey, smoothly double declutching and moving into first gear.

'Yes, that's right. Alcwyn Evans. He's Welsh too. He's trying to rebuild the orchestra. So many of the younger members were conscripted, and it's not easy to find new players to fill their places.'

'Have you both been in the orchestra long? You must be kept busy with your work, teaching at a boarding school.'

Gareth leaned forward to reply. 'No, we are newish members. We haven't been working at the school for long. We both started in the Autumn Term. I teach in the Science department and Edward teaches languages, or should I say Classics.'

'Dan said that you teach languages too, Emily.' Edward stopped the car at the top of Newport Hill to allow a car to cross from the other side of the road and drive into the entrance to a large house.

'Yes, I was teaching French and Music, but I've been – ' She paused. 'I've not been very well, and so I took time off from my work in London to stay with my aunt and uncle at their farm in the country.'

'Working in London?' Edward shook his head. 'I should think you hardly know what's happening from one day to another. Mind you, when I have a bad teaching day, I feel like I don't know what's happening from one day to another.' He turned the car into a small courtyard and parked it between a van and a smart Humber.

'That's teaching for you, though isn't it? Well here we are at the church hall where the rehearsal is to be held. Everybody out!'

The room was well-lit and warmer than Emily had expected. About thirty to forty people were milling about, sitting on chairs that had been laid out in the room, warming up their instruments, and leafing through sheets of music set out on music stands. Emily noticed that the group consisted of some very young members, probably still at school and some much older. The age group that was less represented was obviously the conscription group aged between eighteen and forty-one. She could see Dan sitting with two other cellists. He looked up and smiled encouragingly. Emily stood at the side of the room, waiting to be told where to sit. Almost all the chairs were occupied except two near the front of the violin section and one in the woodwind section. A man of about fifty with a shock of grey hair was talking to another man holding a double bass. Emily wondered if he could be the secretary from whom she had received the letter inviting her to join the orchestra. The group settled down as the two men stopped talking and the grey haired one came to the front and stood on a podium. He took up a baton and tapped it against a music stand. The double bass player went to join the bass string section at the side of the room.

Suddenly the door creaked open and a woman entered the room, carrying a violin, and shaking the rain off her beautiful blonde hair. All eyes turned to her and silence fell upon the group as they took in her film star-like appearance. She was beautifully groomed and striking. She smiled apologetically and looked unblinkingly at the conductor.

'I am so sorry, Maestro, to be late. I had an emergency call just as I was leaving.' The musicians dragged their eyes away from the newcomer and looked at the conductor, who appeared simultaneously flustered and honoured to be addressed as 'Maestro'.

'No, no. Not at all. We haven't started yet. Would you be Dr Miller?'

'Yes, but please call me Anna.' The woman walked towards the side of the room where she had spotted Emily waiting to be welcomed into the gathering. The conductor waved at Emily and smiled apologetically.

'This is wonderful. We have two violinists joining our orchestra and I believe you are Emily. Welcome to you both. Our librarian has set out two chairs and a music stand over there, so would you please share a stand. A round of applause and a warm welcome for our new members, everyone.' Enthusiastic applause rang out as Emily and Anna walked towards their places near the front of the violin section and sat down.

The conductor drew himself up to his full height, which was not as high as he would have liked, but was elevated by his one-foot high podium, which in itself posed a slight problem in getting on and off.

'Let us warm up with an old favourite. You have the music on your stands, "Hail the Conquering Hero Comes" by George Frederic Handel. Oboe, may we have the A for tuning, please?'

The orchestra attacked the chosen piece with some gusto, and as the majestic sound of the final chord died away, the conductor punched his baton into the air.

'You see folks, that's what we want our boys to give old Hitler; a real basin-full of brass, a welling up of woodwind, a striking resonance of strings and a punch-up of percussion. Yes, indeed to goodness! That's what we want to give old Hitler.'

There was gentle applause and some tittering from members of the orchestra. One of the violinists seated behind Emily and Anna leaned forward and whispered to them.

'There's no stopping him when his Welsh blood is up.'

'Now, sit back for a bit as we have to discuss what new repertoire we are going to work on for our next concert. I have some ideas and I'd like to hear suggestions from you. Of course, bear in mind the size of our orchestra, and whether we have enough players in each section. Let me say that I think we should start the programme with that old favourite to wake them all up. There's nothing like a bit of Handel, is there? He knew how to put on a good show.'

The first oboe player raised her hand.

'Yes, Muriel? Any suggestions?' Muriel cleared her throat and wriggled in her chair.

'Well, Alcwyn, I feel uncomfortable playing the Handel. He was German, after all.' Alcwyn Evans put his head on one side and looked at the ceiling for inspiration.

'I never think of him as German. He spent so much time in England. We practically adopted him.' Muriel licked the double reed of her oboe and sat back in her chair.

'What about some Beethoven, for a change?'

one of the viola players suggested.

'German!' Muriel spat the word out as if it were poison. The first clarinettist raised his hand to speak. It was William Taylor, the wonderful player who had given the concert at the Woolacombe Bay Hotel. Emily hadn't noticed him sitting in the woodwind section. She took the opportunity to look around the room while people muttered to each other. She noticed that one of the cellists was Robert Stone, the accompanist at the concert.

'What about some Mendelssohn?' William suggested. Alcwyn nodded enthusiastically.

The second oboe seated next to Muriel waved her hand and shook her head. 'He's German too.'

The leader of the orchestra turned her head to address the woodwind section. 'Yes, but he was a friend of Queen Victoria and Prince Albert.'

'Who were also German,' Muriel murmured.

Alcwyn gripped his music stand with both hands and rolled his eyes heavenwards. He took a deep breath and sighed.

'But that's not their fault, is it? Their nationality, I mean. They have nothing to do with this war. We can't just wipe out every piece of artistic and scientific contribution to society because of someone's nationality. We'll be like Hitler if we do that!'

Silence fell on the room then the tuba player

said, 'My little boy has German Measles.' Seated in front of him, Gareth lowered his trumpet and commented, 'That's dangerous, if you're expecting.'

Ripples of laughter broke out across the room and Alcwyn looked at the leader of the orchestra and shook his head.

'Well, the last time I checked, I wasn't expecting, but as to choosing our repertoire for the next concert, I will discuss it with our leader, Clara, and we two will come to a joint decision. You can expect us to do that by the next practice.'

Chapter 24

Thinking back to the orchestra rehearsal she had attended on Saturday afternoon, Emily had found the people friendly and the music enjoyable. The discussion at the start of the practice about choosing new repertoire had amused her and she found herself giggling as she recalled the exclusion of some composers because of their nationality. Emily had decided to keep out of the arguments and noticed that Anna, with whom she was sharing a music stand, made the occasional 'tut' but otherwise kept silent. The rehearsal continued with some fairly well-known favourites, which Emily managed to play without too much difficulty. It was obvious that Anna was a very good player, producing a beautiful tone and playing sensitively without dominating the violin section.

When Emily arrived back at the farm, there had been a telephone message from Doreen to ask her if she would like to go with them the next day and visit her cousin's family at Mortehoe. Aunt Barbara was going to help at the British Restaurant for about three hours. They were short of staff as so many of the WVS volunteers were ill with the flu. Her aunt would drop her at the restaurant in Boutport Street and they would meet there about three hours later. Doreen had said that she and the family would go by car, leave Barnstaple at about half past one and stay at the Mortehoe farm for two or three hours. Aunt Barbara said that would suit her plans, and as the daylight hours were starting to draw out, she should be able to drive home before it got dark. Elly would be able to help with the milking so there was no need to worry on that account. She had told them that she had no plans to visit her family in Eastbourne or in Taunton for some time as she wanted to settle in to her new job on the farm. It was such an improvement on the last job she'd had, she was glad to say.

Emily finished sorting out the hens and had collected some eggs. It was a lovely bright spring morning and she sat on the old wooden garden seat with the basket of eggs on her lap and looked up at the blossom coming out on the apple tree nearby. It would soon be Easter. Wouldn't it be lovely to have an Easter egg? Chocolate! She tried to remember the last time she'd had some. Her mother used to make hot cross buns and a Simnel cake, and she thought that Auntie Barbara did the same. You need ground almonds and sugar for that, and dried fruit and – Emily sighed. Best not to think about it.

After she had returned from the orchestra practice, she'd had a good chat with her mother until the pips went in the phone box at the other end of the line. Her mother never seemed to have enough change or didn't manage to put the coins into the slot in time to continue the call. Anyway, Emily was able to say that she was feeling better and had joined an orchestra, and her mother told her that everything was fine their end, but that lots of the buildings were unsafe as a result of the bombing, and that children loved playing on the bombsites. Little Jimmy Blades next door said that it was better than any park, and you could find all sorts of good stuff to play with if you dug about a bit. She and Dad were busy at the hospital and her grandparents' shop was going along steadily. Isaac's English had come on very well and he was popular with the customers, and had started singing cockney songs as he worked in the shop. Emily's mum said that people were very entertained by Isaac's increasing musical repertoire. Emily smiled and hurried to the kitchen. Her aunt had planned an early dinner so that she could get to Doreen's house in good time. Aunt Barbara looked up as her niece entered the kitchen.

'I should take your wellingtons, dear, and don't wear anything too smart, even if it is Sunday. It is a farm after all, and you know what this place is like.'

'Good idea, Auntie. Shall I lay the table?'

'Please. I did tell Fred and Elly that we'll be eating at twelve today, so we haven't got long.'

'It's good of you to do some work at the British Restaurant today, Auntie. You're not going to do it regularly are you?'

'No, only while they're short of staff. You wouldn't think they'd be busy on Sundays, would you, but I suppose the American chaps haven't anywhere much to go, so they meet there and chat, and play draughts and chess. It's all very jolly, and noisy.' Barbara bent down to remove a pie from the oven.'

'Ooh, Auntie! What a treat! What have you made?'

Something for afters to hide the fact that the first course isn't very exciting. It's plum pie. I bottled a lot of plums in Kilner jars in the autumn, and with some custard – '

'It'll fill a hole,' Emily added. 'I'll make the custard, shall I?'

After the early dinner, Elly left the kitchen to check on the ewes. Lambing was starting to get going, and Elly said that it was her favourite time of the year, which was a great relief for Fred to hear, who went and flopped down gratefully in the second-hand sofa and picked up the Farmers Weekly.

'Emily and I will be off now, Fred. Glad to see you're finding the sofa comfortable.' Fred Baxter had already closed his eyes and was nodding off.

They hardly saw a vehicle on the road on their way to Barnstaple. It was Sunday, after all. Barbara drove past Rock Park. There were families out enjoying the spring sunshine and soldiers walking with their girlfriends.

'If you park in Boutport Street, I can walk to Doreen's from there, Auntie. I'll come to the restaurant when we get back, as we arranged.' Barbara parked outside the British Restaurant and Emily picked up her bag and her boots and got out. 'Don't work too hard,' Emily shouted as she shut the car door, waved and crossed the road as a large group of soldiers went into the restaurant, laughing and chatting. Barbara slammed the car door shut and waved back at her niece. 'See what I mean, Emily? Never a dull moment!'

Doreen's father was outside the house, organising the seating of his passengers in a rather smart Humber car.

'Ah, hello! You must be Doreen's lovely friend. I'm her Dad, Thomas Edwards, but you can call me Tom. Here's Carol, my wife and here's – where is she? She was here a minute ago. Ah, there you are, Christine. Don't disappear again! We have to be off. Now Carol, you get in the front, of course. Carol smiled at Emily and said hello as Doreen banged the front door shut and hurried to get in the back of the car.

'Hello, Emily. Well done to be here on time. Dad, here is a bag of some of our old shoes in case it's muddy there.'

'Good girl! Of course, it's muddy there! Emily, can you sit in the back by the window, and Christine can fit in the middle.'

'It's so kind of you to take me.' Emily smiled at everyone as Tom sat behind the driving wheel and pulled away expertly.

'Emily, you are here to provide extra ballast in the back, and to keep a certain person under control.'

'What a lovely car, Mr – Tom,' Emily commented.

'It's not ours, Emily. It is used for taxi service and for hire when required, and lives at the garage where I work.' Tom drove confidently along the Braunton road and the passengers looked out of the window at the blue sky and green fields as they left Barnstaple.

'Dad works at Hopgoods as a mechanic, and has been allowed to take the car today as he has to call at Ilfracombe after he has dropped us at his cousin's farm,' Doreen explained to her friend.

'The boss has said that it's all right for us to use it as Mortehoe and Ilfracombe are not far from each other,' Tom said.

'Are you comfortable there, Emily?' Carol turned her head to check on the passengers in the back. 'Christine, you're not fidgeting, are you?'

'No, she's fine, aren't you, Christine?' Emily pointed out of the window. 'Look! There are some baby lambs.'

'Aren't they sweet?' The little girl turned around to look out of the back window as they motored on to Braunton. 'Will there be some lambs at the farm, Mummy?' she asked.

'I don't know when they start lambing, do you, Tom?'

'Later than here. It's higher up and not as sheltered, with the winds and weather coming from the sea.' Tom motored on and the group fell silent as each one enjoyed the pleasure of a ride in a luxury car in wartime and the picture postcard views of the changing countryside as the journey continued. Passing through the crossroads at Braunton, they could hear a train setting off towards Ilfracombe.

'We'll be travelling alongside one another for a while. Can you see the railway track, over there?' Tom pointed at the view from the passenger's window on his left. 'And there will be lots of steam and smoke as it labours up the gradient.'

'Dad,' Doreen moved forward in her seat. 'Don't they have to put another engine on at Braunton?'

'That's right, Doreen. It's a sort of "push me, pull me" affair to get the train up the hills.'

'Can we go on it, Dad?' Christine asked.

'We have been on it, but you were a toddler

and probably don't remember.' Christine's mother turned her head to look at her daughter and smiled. 'We will do that one weekend, dear. Perhaps in the summer when it's warmer.'

'But it's warm today, isn't it?'

'But not warm enough to go in the sea at Ilfracombe, Christine, and in any case, we're going to the farm, so that will be fun, won't it?' Carol looked at her husband and raised her eyebrows in mild frustration.

'They have a horse, don't they?' Christine said. 'It's a big grey one, called Lady.' Tom turned the car left at Mullacott Cross.

'Yes,' Tom answered. 'And they have another horse which they bought to keep Lady company. I don't know what that one's called.'

'Immy told me it's called Monty after Montgomery, because it bosses the big horse about even though it's smaller,' Doreen explained.

'It's a boy, that's why it's bossy,' Christine cut in.

'And you're not?' Doreen laughed. Emily stifled a laugh as Tom pointed ahead to indicate Mortehoe Station but took a turning off to the right just before it which he said led to his cousin's farm. 'We have to turn off soon and go down a lane,' he explained. 'I hope it's not too muddy. In any case, I will have to clean the car when I return it to the garage early tomorrow morning.'

'Who are you calling on in Ilfracombe, Tom?' his wife asked.

'Robert Stone. He isn't too well and he needs some parts for his car. I'll fit them for him while I'm there.'

'What, on a Sunday? Why couldn't it be done at the garage?'

'His car belonged to his late parents. They were great friends of Mr H, and their son hasn't been enjoying good health. Mr H likes to keep an eye out for him.'

'Will it take you long, dear?'

'No, Carol. It's just small jobs. The handle that winds down the window has to be replaced and there are a couple of other things to do. I've met Robert and he's a nice chap. There's something different about him. I think his parents were from Austria originally.'

'I know who you mean, Tom,' Emily interrupted. 'He's a very good pianist and he plays the cello in an orchestra.'

'Oh, yes, Emily.' Doreen leant forward in her seat. 'He played at that concert we went to at the Woolacombe Bay Hotel.'

'Small world,' her father replied as he turned the car into a narrow lane and motored slowly between high hedges which opened out onto a courtyard fronting a large, stone farmhouse. Tom beeped the horn and a man and woman came out of the front door and waved. Imogen appeared from a nearby barn and ran towards the car. There was a lot of hugging and laughing, followed by murmurs of disapproval when Tom explained that he had to make a quick call on someone in Ilfracombe but would be back as soon as he could, so they should keep the kettle boiling, and not allow the girls to eat all the cakes. They waved as he turned the car and drove off. The visitors were bustled indoors, except Doreen, who was held back by Imogen and told to accompany her to the barn.

'There's something I want to show you, Doreen,' her cousin remarked, 'Open the barn door and go through. I'll follow you in a minute.' With a puzzled expression, and a frown, Doreen did as she was bid. It was quite dark in the barn, away from the sunlight, and the smell of hay filled the trapped air. Doreen screwed up her eyes to see through the dim light. There was someone in the barn with her, she was sure of it.

'Hello, is anybody there?' she whispered. A figure stepped forward and put a hand on her shoulder.

'Hi, Doreen. It's me. Oliver.'

Chapter 25

After Tom's cousin Christopher had given the visitors a tour of the farm, they all went indoors for tea. Christine had been seated on Monty and led around the courtyard by Oliver. Imogen had invited him to Sunday dinner, thinking it would be a good opportunity for him to see Doreen when she came with her family in the afternoon.

The young American soldier endeared himself to Christopher's wife, Louise, when he helped to clear the table and wash the dishes after the meal. His praise of the Sunday dinner, especially the Yorkshire puddings. was welcomed by the cook, although she managed to hide her confusion when Oliver asked if he could have some syrup or honey to pour over them. In the morning, Louise had found time to prepare some egg sandwiches and make fairy cakes to give the guests. Tom had not returned and Christopher was showing some disappointment at his absence. However, it was not only cousin Tom's absence that was noted. Louise made the tea and poured a cold drink for Christine.

'I'm sorry, Christine. You and Alex could have played together if he'd come home at a sensible time.' Imogen sighed and looked at her mother.

'Mum, you know that my brother is unreliable when it comes to time-keeping. He knew we were expecting visitors.'

'Where is Alexander, Louise?' Carol asked, taking a sandwich offered to her by Imogen.

'He went on his bike to Sunday School and was joining his friends at the beach afterwards for half an hour. I told him I'd put his dinner in the warming oven, but that he wasn't to be later than one o'clock. He knew we were expecting family.' Emily sipped her tea and looked at Imogen. 'How old is your brother, Imogen?'

'He's ten, and he should know better. He has no sense of time at all.'

'Are the boys allowed on the beach?' Doreen asked Oliver. He nodded. 'Yes, when there's no training going on there. The youngsters have a great time. '

'That's him now,' Louise said, as the kitchen door was flung open and Alex entered, dirty and dishevelled with his pockets bulging.

'Guess what, Mum? Oh, sorry! Hello, I forgot that we were having visitors.' The boy flopped down in a small chair by the door and looked around the room.

'You'd forget your head if it weren't screwed on, Alex,' his father commented. 'Where have you been?'

'On the beach, Dad. It was brilliant. We picked up loads of shells.'

'You don't mean sea shells, do you?' Christopher remarked with a sigh of impatience as Alex took two handfuls from each trouser pocket and dropped them with a clatter on the table.

'No, Dad. We found the most we've ever found and couldn't carry them all home.' Imogen glared at her brother and looked at the visitors apologetically.

'Who have you been with all this time? No, let me guess. Brian, I suppose, to name but one.'

'He's head of our gang, see. And we sure are defending our territory.' Alex looked around the room for approval.

'You're starting to talk like our American friends now, Alex,' his mother said. 'What about your dinner? It's all dried up in the oven.'

'But Mum, we met some Americans off duty, and they had parcels and opened them and gave us all sorts of food. The best was some Hershey chocolate bars. We ate them first.'

'Yes, we can see you've been eating chocolate, Alex,' his sister commented. 'You've still got some of it around your mouth.'

'After that,' Alex continued, 'we ran for cover in case of attack.' He paused and sighed. 'Anyway, I'm full up now so I won't want any dinner.'

'Well, I think you should apologise to our guests

for being late,' Imogen reprimanded her brother. Alex looked at the floor and muttered an apology.

'It's tough when you're on manoeuvres,' Oliver said as he stood up and began to collect the shells. 'Where are you storing your ammunition, Alex? I guess we should hide it somewhere. Can you get a box?' He winked at Doreen and waited for Alex to respond. His parents looked confused and the three young women eyed one another in amusement.

Alex leapt to his feet and saluted 'Yes, sir. I'll fetch one right away.'

The sound of a car drawing up outside served to divert attention from the situation.

'It's Dad,' Doreen said. 'He's just in time for tea.'

'Sorry that I couldn't get back sooner,' Tom apologised as he entered the room and sat in a chair next to his cousin. Louise topped up the teapot and poured a cup for the newcomer 'Don't worry, Tom. Christopher will take you on the grand tour when you've had your tea. Help yourself to the sandwiches.'

'Everyone has had a look around,' Christopher said. 'We haven't started lambing yet, but I'm having problems with my tractor, if you could look at it for me.'

'Christopher! Give your cousin a minute to catch his breath,' Louise chided her husband. 'Did everything go well at Ilfracombe, Tom?'

'Yes, I fixed what had to be done to the car, and Robert said he was feeling better, but he doesn't look very well. Do you know anything about him, Imogen? You're a nurse in the Ilfracombe area, aren't you?'

'Well, even if I did, I wouldn't be able to discuss his health with anyone other than the surgery and hospital staff I work with.'

'No, of course not.' Tom took a sip of his tea. 'He lives in a huge house that belonged to his parents. After they died, he converted the property into flats and he lives in the ground floor flat and some of the American soldiers are billeted in the next two floors. He has a large room with a lovely piano where he teaches.'

'And his sister teaches in Woolacombe, doesn't she?' Emily said. 'Violin and piano. She leads the orchestra I played in recently. The orchestra rehearses in Barnstaple and people come from around North Devon. I suppose they must work out some sort of car sharing to help one another. It's not easy with petrol rationing, is it?'

Tom took a fairy cake and Louise passed the plate around to offer everyone another.

'I think Robert takes several people to the orchestra practice in his car,' Tom informed them, 'and they share the cost of the petrol. He rarely uses the car for anything else.'

'And I know Clara Stone. She gets a lift with another orchestra member who also lives in Woolacombe and has a car. People help each other,' Louise remarked.

Emily looked thoughtful. 'Are neither of them married?'

'As far as I know, Robert has never been married. He's about fifty and Clara's a few years younger. She was married but her husband was a pilot and was killed in 1941. They didn't have any children.'

'There're both so talented,' Imogen commented. 'But didn't Robert have another career first? I don't know who told me that. Perhaps I imagined it.'

'I'm ready to go and see what you've been up to, Chris.' Tom swallowed the last of his tea and stood up. 'And did you say you wanted me to look at your tractor?' The two men left the room and Doreen and Oliver asked if anyone would mind if they went for a walk. Alex had been sent to play outside with Christine although neither of them looked very enthusiastic at the prospect. Louise, Imogen and Emily cleared away the dishes and went out to look at the small flower garden and the larger vegetable garden.

'You have some lovely daffodils, and the primroses are beautiful, aren't they?' Emily pointed at the hedges providing some shelter from the wind coming from the sea. 'But it's like the farm where I'm staying with my aunt and uncle; there's so much work. Unless you live in the country you don't realise that there's no such thing as a day off on a farm.'

'You're right,' Louise replied. 'But there are so many people struggling with what's happening at home and away. I feel so sorry for the young American lads, not knowing what lies ahead of them.'

'What a lovely young man Oliver is,' Imogen cut in. 'No wonder Doreen is crazy about him.' They walked around the vegetable garden. Louise said that she and Imogen did most of the planting. The onions and shallots were doing well and they were planning to put in potatoes. They had dug a trench for the runner beans and were waiting for Christopher to bring some well-rotted horse manure to put in it. They walked on towards the stable.

'That reminds me, Imogen. Where is the grey horse, the one that's called Lady?' Emily saw that Monty had been put back in his stall.

'Oh, yes. we forgot to tell you that Lady was taken out for exercise just before you came and should be back very soon. Dad is having trouble with his back and can't ride her these days, but she is ridden regularly, and expertly too. And she gets groomed and fussed over. We're really lucky that she is cared for so well, aren't we, Mum?'

'Yes, we are. We have a tenant in our cottage. It's about a quarter of a mile away and a bit spartan, although it has a Rayburn to heat it and there is a telephone, but the tenant likes it there and enjoys the isolation and the rugged beauty of the surroundings.'

'The cottage was empty from the end of the summer when our previous tenant moved away to get married,' Imogen explained. 'He'd been working at the hospital in Ilfracombe and met one of my nursing friends who was working there. They both live in Ilfracombe now. Some of the local doctors needed extra help so the new tenant moved here to North Devon last November to take up a medical appointment. It has all worked out very well.'

At the sound of the clip clop of horse's hooves, they all looked towards the back lane.

'Ah, here they come,' Louise pointed to the beautiful grey mare carrying an elegantly dressed rider and trotting tidily towards them in the courtyard. Rider and horse stopped just in front of them.

'Good afternoon, Mrs Huxtable, Imogen,' the woman said, smiling.

'Hello, Anna. What a surprise,' Emily greeted her fellow musician.

'Oh!' The smile disappeared momentarily from

the woman's face. She removed her hat and jumped down from the saddle and went towards Emily with a laugh and a warm greeting, holding the reigns.

'Yes, what a surprise, Emily! What a lovely surprise to see you here!'

Chapter 26

Fred Baxter washed his hands at the kitchen sink and warmed them over the Aga. The weather had suddenly become colder, the wind had got up and it had started to rain heavily. It was the sort of weather that farmers hated at lambing time. He had been up most of the night and Elly had just taken over in the lambing shed. Things were going well and the young Land Army girl knew what she was doing. Perhaps he'd have a few hours' nap and try to catch up on lost sleep. The morning milking was being done by Pip, and Emily was helping her. The kitchen door opened and Barbara walked in.

'What a blessing that Gordon could spare Pip to do the milking, Fred,' Barbara hurried to start preparing the breakfast. 'How was it last night?'

'It all went well, apart from the weather. Plenty of doubles and one ewe had three but I doubt she will manage to feed them all. Elly has taken over from me for a while. I'll just have a cup of tea and some toast and go and lay down for a few hours, Babs.'

'What a bit of luck getting that girl to work here, Fred. She is so able and a lovely girl, too.' Barbara poured a mug of tea and sliced some bread. 'Where's Emily?'

'She was helping Pip with the milking but I think they've finished.' Fred looked out of the window at the driving rain. 'Yes. Pip's motor's gone. She's using Gordon's little Austin today. Emily must be in the lambing shed or sorting the hens.'

'Surely the girls can leave what they're doing for a while to have some breakfast. They need something hot to eat and drink on a morning like this.'

Fred finished his mug of tea, picked up his toast and left the table. 'I'll fetch the girls in, then go upstairs and lay down.'

'Fred, please don't lay on the bed with those messy clothes on. Take them off and put on your dressing gown.'

'Do you think I would do a thing like that, dear?' He left the room, put on his old raincoat and went to the shed. Elly and Emily didn't need much persuasion to hurry across the yard and into the warm kitchen for breakfast. Fred went upstairs and dutifully removed his dirty work clothes, put on his dressing gown and snuggled under the eiderdown. He was asleep as soon as his head hit the pillow.

'I haven't done the hens yet, Auntie.' Emily looked apologetic as she took a bite of her scrambled egg on toast.

'Of course you haven't, dear. It was very good of you to help Pip with the milking this morning. I'll go and see to the hens today and you two take your time with breakfast. There's more toast and another jar of marmalade from last year to open.' Barbara swallowed her tea, took a piece of toast and buttered it thinly, collected the basket for the eggs and left the kitchen.

'That's the first time that I have seen a lamb born, Elly,' Emily opened the jar of marmalade and passed it to the pretty young woman sitting opposite her. 'In fact, it's the first time I've seen anything born. It's very exciting and frightening all at the same time, isn't it? And then, suddenly the little creature is standing up on its wobbly little legs and moving about. It's all quite wonderful.'

Elly smiled. 'Yes, I never get tired of it although some births are more difficult than others.'

'But you're so good at everything you do on the farm, Elly. You're born to it. A natural.'

'But I'm not born to it, Emily. My parents aren't in farming. My brother is an agricultural engineer and he has always involved me in any tinkering with engines he does and often used to take me with him when he'd go to farms to fix machinery. He'd say, "Go on then, Elly. You have a go at this one." Then I'd learn some of the things that he knew, but it wasn't a girl's job at that time so the career I'd really have liked wasn't open to me.'

'You wanted to do the same work as your brother then, Elly?'

'Yes, that or farming. I spent a lot of time on farms, often when I should have been at school. I used to sneak off, and the farmers never asked why I wasn't at school. It was free labour, after all.'

'But didn't your parents know you missed school sometimes?'

'My brother never said anything. He thought I was learning about what I wanted to do, and I didn't make a regular habit of it. Of course, sometimes my mother would wonder why my school uniform was so muddy. I told her that I was always falling over.'

'Your parents live in Eastbourne, don't they? I've never been there. We went to Brighton on the train for a few days last summer. It was lovely to see the sea. You must miss it.'

'Yes, Emily, but Eastbourne is bombed regularly by the Germans. It seems to be a favourite target town for them.'

'You have relatives in Taunton, haven't you?'

'Yes. My aunt and uncle. I was working at a dairy farm about thirty miles away from Taunton and often went to stay with them when I had a weekend off. It was so much closer than going back to Eastbourne.'

'Yes, so much more handy for you.' Emily smiled. Elly raised her eyebrows and pursed her lips.

'Oh yes, the **farm** was very handy. But the

farmer was a bit too handy, if you know what I mean.' They looked at each other for a moment and Emily remarked, 'So, you left and came here.'

'So, I left and came here.'

The phone suddenly rang, interrupting their conversation. Emily lifted the receiver.

'Hello. Emily speaking. Oh, hello Mrs Roberts. Yes, Pip left over half an hour ago. She was driving straight back to you. And she hasn't arrived?'

The kitchen door opened and Barbara came in and placed the egg basket on the table.

'Here's my aunt. I'll hand the receiver over to her.'

'Hello, Dorothy. No, Pip's not here. She should have been with you nearly half an hour ago. No, don't worry. I'll take the car and go and look for her. Perhaps she's had a problem with the car. I'll phone you as soon as I find out what's happened. Bye, Dorothy.'

'I'll come with you Auntie,' Emily jumped up and went into the hall and put on her coat and wellingtons.

'I must get back to check on our mums-to-be,' Elly said. 'I hope everything is all right when you find Pip.' The three women wrapped up against the cold wind and ceaseless rain, and left the farmhouse.

Chapter 27

Barbara drove slowly through the open gate leading from the farmhouse. The two women leaned forward to see out of the car windscreen which was quickly steaming up while the rain poured down from the leaden sky. Barbara operated the windscreen wipers, which achieved only moderate success with visibility. She drove on for about a hundred yards but there was no sign of Pip and the vehicle she had driven that day. Suddenly, rounding the corner ahead of them they saw a bicycle, a postman's bicycle. It was Stan and he was pushing it, his large, black cape covering most of him and most of his bike. Barbara stopped as he trudged towards them. She wound down the window a little as a sudden clap of thunder sounded.

'Stan, are you on your way to us?'

'Yes, I be, Barbara. The water runnin' off the road is makin' it 'ard to cycle so I be pushin' me bike. But I got to tell 'ee. There's bin an accident back yonder. 'Tis the car one of they maids from Gordon Robert's farm drives. 'Er's not in it, but must 'ave swerved for summat and gone into the 'edge. I thought us could phone from your 'ouse an tell Gordon and Dorothy what's 'appened.' Another clap of thunder, louder this time, interrupted Stan's report and within a few seconds a flash of lightning momentarily lit the sky.

'Stan, I'm going to turn the car round at the next gateway and go back home. We'll see you there. It's no good being out in this,' Barbara shouted. Stan nodded and continued pushing his bike in the direction of the Baxter's farm. Barbara wound up the window, her headscarf wet and dripping into her eyes as she drove on to the next gateway wide enough to enable her to turn the car.

'Poor Stan. He's out in all weathers,' Emily shouted. 'Ooh! Be careful, Auntie. There's a big muddy patch there, by that gateway. I don't want you to get stuck in it.'

'I think I can miss it, Emily, but I'm going to take it slowly in case the tyres won't grip.' Emily looked sideways at her aunt. It seemed out of character for her to be cautious behind the wheel. Barbara turned the car successfully and drove carefully back to the farm as the rain began to abate. She parked just outside the door and they dashed from the car into the hall, hanging up their wet coats and removing their footwear. Stan's cape was draped over the wooden coat stand and dripping steadily onto the stone slabs.

'Stan tells me that you went looking for Pip, Babs,' Fred said as he poured tea into five mugs while his wife and Emily joined Elly and Stan around the kitchen table. 'What's happened then, Stan? Is Pip all right?' Stan liked to be the bearer of news. He just hoped that it wasn't bad news. He took a loud sip from his mug of tea and frowned.

'Well, I was on me way to your place and cycled round the corner up from the village just as the 'eavens opened. I skidded an' fell off me bike an' thought to meself, "Stanley, 'tis no good cyclin'. You'm getting' nowhere vast." I picked meself up an' started walkin' and suddenly sees a car what 'ad gone into the 'edge, right by where they trees is near where us sometimes sees deer up above that there thicket.'

'Yes, Stan, but was Pip in the car? And was she hurt?' Barbara knew that Stan's accounts of events could be almost biblical in their length and detail. She just wanted the short version.

'Well, 'er must 'ave swerved an' stopped sudden for somethin', and banged 'er aid against the front windscreen.'

'Oh no,' Emily gasped. 'So, was she still in the car?'

'Er was **in** a car, but not 'ers. Er 'ad been lifted up and laid in the back of another car. Unconscious, 'er was. Then 'er was took to the infirmary in Barnstaple. I seed the car drive off.'

'Yes, but who was it who drove to Barnstaple with her, Stan?'

' 'Twas the vet. 'E spoke to me afore 'e left. 'E told me 'e 'ad just come from a call at East Buckland an' was on 'is way back to Swimbridge to another call when 'e come upon the accident an' saw the girl 'ad banged 'er aid, like I told 'ee. 'Er was bleedin' bad. 'E asked me to tell Gordon and Dorothy about it.' Barbara walked towards the telephone.

'I'll telephone them right away, Stan.'

'Oh, an' the vet said to say not to worry cause even if there be a lot of blood, it bain't always serious.'

'It's good that you were there Stan to tell us what happened,' Fred commented.

'I wonder what caused her to crash into the hedge,' Elly said.

'It was raining hard. Perhaps she skidded,' Emily remarked.

'More likely 'twas a deer jumped out in front of 'er from the left side of the road so 'er turned sudden to the right so as not to 'it un.' Stan stood up and looked out of the window. 'I best be off now. The sky be clearin'. The vet said that 'e'd try to call yer later when 'e knows more about 'ow the poor maid's doin', "in case you was worried," 'e said.'

'Thank you, Stan.' Barbara looked at Fred and

nodded in Emily's direction as she dialled their neighbours' number.

'See 'ee tomorrow. Oh, and there be no post for 'ee today.'

'Good, Stan.' Fred shook his head. 'We can't cope with any more drama.'

Chapter 28

Three days had passed since Pip's accident. Gordon and Dorothy had driven to the infirmary as soon as Barbara phoned to tell them what she knew. Everyone at Little Bridge Farm had spent an anxious day, not knowing how serious the young woman's injury was. Dan called that evening, as he had said he would, and was able to give them some reassurance. Pip had a nasty cut on her forehead where she had been thrown forward and hit the windscreen as the car stopped suddenly in the hedge. When he found her, she was unconscious and bleeding from her injury. He had decided to carry her to his car and drive her to the infirmary in Barnstaple. On arriving there, she was seen immediately by a doctor and attended by nurses, who prepared her for surgery to attend to the cut. Daniel waited until Gordon and Dorothy arrived and then left to resume his working day. The car Pip had been driving was badly dented on its front right mudguard and wouldn't start, even when Elly tried it. She and Fred had taken the tractor and were able to tow it back to Buckland Farm where Elly said she would go and have a closer look at it later when she had checked on the sheep and lambs. In any case it would have to have some body work carried out, not that its age would ever allow it to regain its once youthful looks. Fred thought that Gordon would be glad if Elly could get it going, but Elly was planning to take off the mudguard and knock out the dents. She said that she had helped her brother to do that. Elly was sure that she could get it functionable but didn't think that it would win a beauty contest. Fred told Barbara he couldn't believe that a young woman could know so much about cars and tractors. Barbara had made them laugh when she remarked that her husband's expertise was with creatures with four legs, not vehicles with four wheels.

The weather had improved and the ground was drying out. Barbara and Emily had planned to visit Pip at the infirmary to see how she was doing. Gordon had been trying to get help to temporarily replace the young Land Army girl until she was fully recovered but it was proving difficult. Fred felt he had to share the help he had with his neighbour but lambing was in full swing for both farms. Emily wondered if she could do more. She was learning all the time but didn't have the skills that took years of practice to develop. She had just entered the kitchen for a drink, too late to join her aunt and uncle as she had been helping Elly in the lambing shed. She washed her hands at the sink and saw that there was a letter for her placed on the kitchen table.

'There you are, Emily. Is Elly coming in for a drink? How is it going?'

'That last ewe had a difficult birth but Elly helped it and it's fine, Auntie.' The kitchen door opened and Elly went to the sink to wash her hands. 'It was good that you were there, Emily, just at the right time.'

'Elly, you're making it sound as if I know what I'm doing,' Emily laughed.

'You're a quick learner, Em, and that last one would have been much trickier if I had been on my own.'

'Well, you two, are you ready for a mug of tea and a cake just out of the oven?' Barbara placed the tea and cakes on the table and the girls sat down. Emily picked up her letter and opened it.

'We know who this is from, don't we, Auntie?' The writing was unmistakeably that of Isaac. Emily read it through and smiled.

'He's very excited, Auntie. My grandparents have told him he can have some time off. He has worked so hard at the shop and they know someone who can take his place and do his job for a while.'

'That will be nice for him.' Barbara poured herself a mug of tea and sat at the table with the young women. 'Will he go away somewhere?' Emily shook her head and took a sip of her tea.

'On holiday, you mean? He doesn't know anyone other than the people he has met in London. And he couldn't afford it anyway.'

'How old is he, did you say, Emily?' Barbara was looking thoughtful.

'He's twenty-two, almost the same age as me.' Emily bit into her cake.

'And me,' Elly cut in.

'Did you say that Isaac spent a lot of time with his grandparents on their farm in Bavaria when he was a young boy, Emily?' Barbara continued to stare unseeingly out of the window. She had a habit of frowning and half-closing her eyes when she was planning something.

'Yes, Auntie. He used to talk to me in great detail about the times he visited them and how he loved to help with the animals.' The kitchen door opened and Fred entered, carrying a lamb that looked as if it was ailing.

'This is the one that isn't getting enough milk, Elly. We'll bottle feed it for a few days and make it cosy indoors.'

'Fred, first of all, you are not to put it on the sofa or give it one of those cushions that I covered especially for you. And secondly, there's something I want to discuss with you.' Barbara looked resolutely at her husband.

'No, dear, to the first thing, and maybe to the second thing, whatever it is. Elly, I have left a box in the hall so we'll make this little chap comfy in it, if you would fetch it for me.' Elly carried the box from the hall and she and Fred prepared a bed for the lamb and set it on the floor in front of the Aga. Barbara looked at the ceiling and sighed.

'Now Babs, when I've sorted out a drink for this lamb, I'll be all ears.'

'It's all right, Fred.' Elly moved across the kitchen and opened a cupboard door. 'I know where the bottle is. I'll get it some milk if you want to talk to Barbara.'

'Thank you, Elly, but she has a look in her eye that makes me think I don't want to talk to Barbara.' He sat on the sofa and looked questioningly at his wife.

'Now, Fred, our neighbours are going to be short of help on their farm and we may have to help them out where we can.'

'That's not going to be easy at this time of year, is it? Gordon can't seem to get a replacement for Pip at the moment.'

'She won't be able to start work for some time.' Barbara commented. 'She has had a nasty head wound. We're going to visit her at the infirmary this afternoon, by the way.' Fred took a breath to discuss the problem further but his wife cut in.

'Now, Emily has had a letter from her friend, Isaac. He's about the same age as the girls here and is a good worker. He has been given some time off from his job in London and can take a holiday. What if we let him stay here, or at Gordon's and he helps out on the farms?'

'What does he know about farming, Babs? He's worked in London, you said.'

'Isaac was a boy rescued from Germany with the Kindertransport. He is Jewish, you see, Uncle. He has no family in this country and doesn't know if he has any family left alive in Germany. When he was a young boy he often visited his grandparents' farm in Bavaria and loved to help them with the animals. We used to talk about it a lot. When he first came to England, he couldn't speak a word of English and because I had studied German at school, he and I spoke to one another in German. It improved my German but now he speaks very good English.'

'I see what you are thinking, Babs. I will speak to Gordon and Dorothy about it. It wouldn't be a holiday for him, Emily.'

'He wouldn't want that, Uncle. He would love to come and help where he is needed.' Elly sat by the lamb and offered it the bottle. 'We could certainly do with more workers. There aren't really enough of us, and the other farm also has the milk round to fit in.' Elly smiled as the feeble lamb sucked hard on the bottle.

'Right. Emily, I'll get an early dinner then we'll drive in to visit Pip.'

'Best not to say anything to your friend, Emily, until I've talked it over with Gordon and Dorothy,' her uncle said. 'I'll phone them and discuss it now, I think.' Fred walked across the kitchen to the telephone.

'Auntie, do you know which ward Pip is on? It's not a very big infirmary, is it?' Barbara had stopped the car in Landkey and bought a magazine and a couple of apples for Pip before continuing their journey to Barnstaple.

'No, but we're not allowed to stay long. Visiting hours there are very strictly controlled. In any case, we don't know how she will be feeling. We don't want to tire her.' Barbara crunched the gears as she changed down on approaching the top of Newport Road.

'You're always driving this car, Auntie. Don't you get tired of it?'

'Yes, I do sometimes. It just doesn't go fast enough for me. I'd like more power really.' Emily's eyes widened as she considered her aunt behind the wheel of a more powerful car.

'You should learn to drive, Emily. I could teach

you. There's nothing to it, really.' Barbara swerved suddenly just missing the kerb on the corner of the road as she stopped suddenly and parked the vehicle in Litchdon Street. They walked along the street and into the entrance of the North Devon Infirmary. Asking a serious-faced woman seated at the reception desk in which ward they could find Pip, they were directed to King George V, and waited at the door until the start of visiting hours. On the dot of half past two, the door was opened by a young nurse and they walked in. They spotted Pip immediately. She was sitting up in an immaculately made bed in an immaculately tidy nightdress with a neat bandage around her head. Emily glanced quickly around the ward as they smiled and walked towards the patient. It was all – well – immaculate. There were two chairs either side of the bed and they sat down and greeted the young woman.

'Thank you for coming to see me,' Pip smiled weakly.

'How are you, Pip? We've brought you some apples and a magazine.' Barbara placed the gifts on the bedside cabinet.

'I'm getting better but I still feel sleepy and my head hurts. I shall be in here for another four days or so but I think they will wheel me out into the observation area in a few days. You can look out from there onto the park because there are so many big windows.'

'What caused you to go into the hedge, Pip?' Emily asked.

'It was a deer. It jumped out and I would have gone into it if I hadn't steered hard to the right. I don't remember anything but I hope I didn't hit it.'

'You couldn't have hit it. Fred and Elly took the tractor and went and towed the car back to the farm. They would have said if they had seen an injured animal.' Barbara looked hard at the young woman.

'I'm worried about not being at work, especially at this time of year. Gordon and Dorothy have been in twice to see me, but I know they are short-staffed.'

'You're not to worry.' Barbara took Pip's hand. 'We think we have found a good temporary solution so all you have to do is get better.'

'I have been worried about that. I was told that I mustn't go back to work until the doctor is happy with my progress. She was very nice but very strict. The nurses here said that she stitched the cut on my forehead. They said it was the best stitching they had ever seen.'

'A woman doctor, and a surgeon. That's not very common, is it?' Emily was impressed.

'Does she work here every day?' Barbara asked.

'No. The nurses said she works here two days a week and works in Woolacombe and Ilfracombe surgeries on the other days.'

'Pip, could you describe her?' Emily looked around the ward.

'That's easy. She looks like a film star. She has beautiful fair, curly hair and very blue eyes.'

'And is her name Doctor Anna Miller?'

'Yes, Em. That's right. how do you know that?'

'I seem to keep bumping into her.' Emily leaned forward. 'Are you feeling all right, Pip? You're looking very pale suddenly.'

'I'll call the nurse.' Barbara walked towards the nurses' station and whispered to the Sister in charge. She immediately hurried over to Pip's bedside and looked at her and took her pulse.

'I think she needs to sleep now,' the Sister said. 'She had a very nasty bang on the head. It was lucky that she came to us so quickly after her accident. The man who brought her in had managed to stem the bleeding. It made all the difference.' Pip lay back on the pillow and closed her eyes.

'We'll see you soon, Pip,' Emily said.

'There's nothing for you to worry about. Rest and recover.' Barbara smiled and she and Emily left the ward.

Chapter 29

Emily stood at the kitchen sink and sighed. She was feeling tired. They were all tired. It had been a very busy week so far with the weather drying up, ploughing the extra acres demanded by The Ministry of Agriculture almost completed, and lambing going well. Elly had driven over to Buckland Farm earlier that morning and after almost an hour of work on the damaged car, managed to get the engine started. Promising to return soon to do some work on the bodywork, Elly drove back to Little Bridge Farm, hurried to the lambing shed and took over from Fred. It was a big juggling act for them all as they tried to fit everything in.

Emily was expecting Isaac to arrive by train that afternoon. He was going to stay for the weekend at the Baxters' farm and then be taken to meet Gordon and Dorothy when they would all talk over how to manage the workload and see where Isaac's help would most be needed. Pip was making steady progress and had been moved to the observation ward. Emily looked out of the window to see her uncle coming in for elevenses, just as her aunt entered the kitchen.

'It's only a little box room and I hope Isaac will be comfortable there until we know where he will be based during his stay,' Barbara looked worried.

'He'll love being here, Auntie, or at Gordon and Dorothy's farm.'

'We'll probably have him helping out at both farms, Emily,' Fred said as he and Elly entered the kitchen, followed a moment later by Stan. 'But not at the same time, unfortunately,' Fred added as they all sat around the kitchen table for tea and scones.

'Don't forget he's new to this, Fred, and the only person he knows here is Emily.'

'Isaac will fit in happily, Auntie. He's easy-going and a good worker.'

'How are you today, Stan?' Barbara asked, offering him a scone.

'Better now that us knows that the poor maid be doin' well in the infirmary,' Stan replied through a mouthful of scone.

'Yes, Stan. What a relief it is to know that Pip is making progress,' Elly commented. Suddenly the telephone rang.

'Emily, you're nearest. Will you answer it?' Barbara asked. Emily put down her half-eaten scone and reached for the receiver.

'The Baxters' Farm. Emily speaking. Oh, hello, Doreen.' There was a long silence in the room while Emily listened to her friend suggesting a night out dancing. 'But Doreen, you mean tonight at the Bungalow Café in Woolacombe? It would be fun, but Isaac, the friend I told you about, is arriving by train this afternoon. And in any case, how would I get to you? Just a minute, my aunt is waving her arms about.'

'Emily, when I drive in to meet Isaac from the station, I can drop you in Barnstaple and you can stay the night at Doreen's, after the dance, like you did before. We can look after Isaac until you get back on Sunday.'

'But Auntie, he doesn't know any of you.'

'We're not that frightening, are we? Go on and have some fun with your friends.'

'Doreen, Auntie Barbara says she will drive me to Barnstaple and will look after Isaac, so I can come, if I can stay the night at your home after the dance.' There was a long pause while Emily listened to her friend giving further information about the evening. Emily said goodbye and put down the receiver.

'I feel so guilty when we are all so busy. Elly, you should be going dancing.'

'If there's a dance nearer to here, Em, Swimbridge, or South Molton for instance, perhaps I might go along. You could come and teach me all you've learned from those American friends of yours.'

'South Molton!' Stan said, as if it were a foreign

town. 'Swimbridge or Landkey be far enough, surely!' Fred stood up and made for the door.

'Any place more than three miles from your house is a foreign place to you, Stan. Well, must get on!' The group left the kitchen and each went to attend to the business of the day.

Emily and Doreen huddled together on the bus to Woolacombe. It was a cold night and even with their winter coats over their party dresses, they were not warm enough.

'We'll soon warm up once we start dancing,' Doreen said.

'Doreen, you said that the Americans have arranged transport to take us back to Barnstaple after the dance?'

'Yes. They often do that. The buses wouldn't be running late at night, so they take the locals back to places like Braunton, Barnstaple and Ilfracombe.'

'That's very good, isn't it? I was wondering how we would get back. Is Imogen going to be there tonight?'

'Yes. She's more or less local, isn't she? Her Dad drops her at Woolacombe and meets her afterwards and drives her back to the farm. She says it's a mixed blessing because she feels that he is deliberately keeping an eye on her. Actually, she quite likes one of the American soldiers.'

It was almost dark, so it was difficult to see where they were but they had been on the bus chatting and hadn't noticed the time.

'Oh, good! We're going down the hill into Woolacombe, Emily. It's always difficult to see where you are at night, what with the blackout regulations and the law on the use of vehicle headlights. I forgot to tell you. Dad said he will teach me how to drive.'

'That's good! Auntie Barbara offered to teach me but I'm not sure if that's a good idea. I told you about her driving, didn't I?'

'You did. But Maggie in the bakery says that all us women should learn to drive.'

The bus pulled up not far from the Bungalow Café. Nearly twenty people got out, mostly young women and a few soldiers who had come from other camps.

A queue of American soldiers in their smart uniforms, and a large group of local girls, laughing and chatting had formed outside the building and the sound of dance music coming from inside filtered out into the cold, sea air. Doreen soon spotted Oliver and his friends and the two young women ran over to them, and they all joined the back of the queue. Tickets were shown or bought and the group of friends moved slowly inside and found some seats in a corner of the room, which

Imogen, having arrived earlier, had saved for them. Doreen sat between her and Oliver and Emily took a seat on the other side of Imogen. The women took off their coats and hung them over the backs of their chairs. The three women knew Oliver's friends but Emily immediately noticed that there was one of the soldiers missing. She looked at the dancers on the floor and glanced around the room. She turned to Imogen with an inquiring look.

'I don't see Dylan here, Immy.'

'If you come out to the toilet, Emily,' Imogen whispered into Emily's ear, 'I'll tell you what I know about that.' She stood up and looked at Doreen and Oliver, who were busy looking at each other.

'We're just going out to powder our noses. Won't be long,' Imogen informed the group, who were paying no attention anyway. She took Emily's hand and pulled her gently out of her chair. 'Come on, Em. I'll show you where it is.' They wound their way through the dancers and out of the main room to the toilets.

'I couldn't say anything in front of anyone else, because I don't know if we're supposed to know. It is common knowledge around the village and up at Mortehoe but the Americans never talk about anything that happens connected with their work and the villagers never ask. It's an unwritten law.' There was a small bench in the Ladies' and the two of them sat on it. There was no-one else in the room. Emily looked questioningly at her new friend.

'What's happened, Imogen? Is Dylan all right?'

'We think he is going to be all right but he was accidentally hit by a bullet during training on the beach.'

'Oh, no! But you say he's not badly hurt, Imogen?'

'I don't know any details and the American lads aren't saying much.'

'Thank goodness it wasn't a real live bullet.' Emily looked relieved.

'Oh, but it was, Em. Didn't you know? They do all their manoeuvres using live ammunition.'

'What? So, it's as if they're fighting a real war, here on our beaches!'

'Yes. And there have been some casualties and losses but the training goes on. Towards the end of last year there was a terrible tragedy here during a storm, when landing craft carrying tanks with men in them were overturned in the sea by the strength of the tide and the power of the waves. But the training's relentless. They never let anything stop them. We hear the firing start at about 6.30 in the mornings. Dad says that it coincides with his milking.'

'Thanks for letting me know about Dylan, Immy. I'll be careful what I say to any of the Americans.

They have a lot to cope with. I wonder how long they will stay here?'

'Yes. And I wonder where they'll go next?'

The two young women checked their hair and make-up in the mirror and made their way back to the dance floor.

Chapter 30

Emily opened the front door of Doreen's house after returning from the phone box around the corner where she'd telephoned her aunt.

'Everything all right, Emily?' Doreen was tying back her long, glossy, dark hair. 'You didn't have much breakfast, did you?'

'I was more tired than hungry, Doreen. Yes, Auntie Barbara met Isaac at the station yesterday and he woke up early this morning and has just returned from investigating the farm. He says that he wants to stay for ever!'

'Oh good! I've just been talking to Dad. He is walking to the back of Hopgoods to collect his car. That's where he always leaves it. He doesn't use it very much, you see, what with petrol rationing, but today, he wants to give it a run and says that he can take you as far as Landkey or Swimbridge, and perhaps your aunt can collect you from there? After that, he's going to give me a driving lesson. There's hardly anything on the roads, especially as it's Sunday, so there will be fewer vehicles for me to bump into. That's what Dad says, anyway.'

'That's exciting that you are going to have a driving lesson, Doreen, and kind of your dad to drop me off later. I'll telephone the farm again when I know what time we are leaving here.'

'Dad says we'll leave as soon as he returns with the car. Do you mind not staying for Sunday dinner?'

'No, of course not. I wanted to go back this morning anyway as Isaac is there and I didn't see him yesterday when he arrived. But we had a good evening, didn't we Doreen?'

'We did, and it was rounded off with a jolly ride back to Barnstaple with a good sing-song all the way home.'

'And Oliver coming just for the ride, there and back!'

'I can hear a car outside, Emily can you go and telephone your aunt and say that Dad will drop you at Landkey or Swimbridge, whichever suits, in about half an hour? I'll bring your things down from upstairs.'

'I want to thank your Mum for letting me stay first, and say goodbye to your sister, Christine.'

'Christine is next door with her friend but Mum's in the kitchen.'

Emily hurried to the back of the house as Doreen's father, Tom, came in the front door.

'Doreen, love, have you seen the special shammy leather I use for cleaning the windscreen? I hope your Mum hasn't been using it for her housework.'

'Dad, have you looked in the usual place?' Emily squeezed past father and daughter and hurried to the telephone box around the corner. It's funny, she thought to herself, but men never look for anything. She was discovering that they don't really know the difference between seeing and looking.

Her uncle answered the phone and told her that he had to go to see George Tucker at Landkey to collect yet another part for the tractor that had given them trouble. Elly had said that she could probably fit it. He would be leaving soon and would see her near the bridge at Landkey in about forty-five minutes. Emily ran back to Doreen's home to see her friend putting her case and coat into the front of the car.

'I'll sit in the back with you, Emily. Dad is nearly ready to go, if that's all right?'

'Yes, that's fine, Doreen. I spoke to my uncle and he said that perhaps you could drop me near the bridge at Landkey. He'll meet me there after he has called on a friend who's an agricultural engineer. Uncle has to collect a part from him for the tractor.'

The two friends sat side by side in the back of the car and talked about their night out while they waited for Doreen's dad.

'Doreen, will you let me know how Dylan is getting on if you hear anything? I told you about one of the Land Army girls who had an accident last week, didn't I? She's doing well but won't be allowed to do any heavy work for a while. I don't know if she'll go home for a week or so.'

'Poor thing. It's hard work in all weathers on the land isn't it? Yes, I'll contact you when I know anything more about Dylan. I think he was hit in the leg but I don't know any details. Immy has her nose to the ground and living where she does she knows more than us. I think she quite likes Dylan, you know.'

'Yes. I wondered if she did.'

'Immy asked if we would like to go out to their farm for the day on Easter Monday and take a picnic. She suggested that we could include Oliver and a few of his friends. We could go on the train from Barnstaple to Mortehoe.'

'That sounds fun. We would need to have good weather. It would be a busy weekend as I have a feeling that our orchestra's concert will be on the Saturday afternoon between Good Friday and Easter Day.'

'Ooh! Let me know about that. I'd like to come and listen.'

'Yes, I'll tell you more when I have the details. Here's your dad, Doreen.' Tom sat at the driving wheel and started the engine. They moved away quietly and headed for the countryside.

Fred pulled into the farmyard and parked the car near the back door.

'I'll go indoors and find Isaac, Uncle. Thank you for looking after him.'

'I think he's looking after himself, Emily. He hasn't stopped helping out since he arrived. He's probably somewhere on the farm. I don't think you'll find him indoors.'

'I'll go in and speak to Auntie Barbara first. What do you have to do now?'

'I'm going to find Elly and we'll see if we can fit this part. This is the second part we've had to have for this tractor recently. We haven't quite finished that ploughing and someone from The Ministry of Agriculture will be coming soon to check that we have completed the ploughing and planting that we've been told to do.' Emily could see that her uncle was not in a good mood, and went into the house.

'Hello, Emily. Did you have a good time?' Barbara was preparing the Sunday dinner and was at the sink washing the cabbage.

'It was such fun, Auntie, and the Americans had arranged transport to take people back to Barnstaple after the dance ended. But how is Isaac getting on? I feel guilty that I went off and left you to settle him in.'

'Don't worry about him, dear. I've hardly seen

him. He's been out helping Fred or Elly ever since he's been here.'

'But has he got suitable clothing for coping with work on a farm?'

'He'd thought about that and came well-prepared. He was even wearing wellington boots when he got off the train.'

'How funny, Auntie! 'll take my suitcase upstairs and help you with the dinner.'

'No, dear. I can manage. Go out and find your friend. I think he'll be with Elly checking the lambs.'

Chapter 31

Alcwyn Evans climbed on to the podium and tapped his baton to gain attention.

'Good afternoon, everyone. As you know we have not given a public performance since the start of the war. It has been difficult to find members and I am pleased to say that thanks to recent recruitment work done by our secretary, Michael White, double bass, we now have sufficient players to put together an ensemble capable of giving a concert. We have booked the hall at The British Restaurant for the afternoon of Saturday, 8th of April. The performance will start at 2.30 but kindly be there at 1.30. I think you all know most of this information, having been contacted by Michael. There are several issues that I wish to deal with now. The first is our name. Since we have recruited players from all over North Devon recently, Clara and I feel it would be better to call ourselves The North Devon Orchestral Society. Are there any objections to that?' Alcwyn looked with a steely eye around the room at the players sitting before him.

'Good. That's what will go on the programme then. Now, what is going to make up the programme, you may ask? We have two practices to put it together so the music we have chosen will not be technically difficult and will include a few items some of us have played before. Of course, you may take home your music and practise as much as you can. As far as the programme goes, we want to entertain, so we will perform some popular items, and I would like to include small ensembles to fill up the time. Our new member, Anna, has offered to direct a small group to perform the Boccherini Minuet, a very delightful and popular work. You may know that the minuet can be performed as a quintet or a quartet, but I will leave that to Anna. Clara has said she will be happy to perform something with her brother, Robert accompanying her. She will let me know what their choice is later, although the sooner the better as we need to print programmes. Ah, I see that Victor has raised his hand. You are offering to take charge of that side of things? Marvellous, Victor! All information about what we're playing and who is playing it must go to Victor soon. Many thanks to him, a longstanding and loyal member of our orchestra.' Applause broke out and one of the flute players put up her hand.

'Alcwyn, what are we to wear for the concert?'

Alcwyn looked uncertain and scratched his unruly, grey hair.

'Well, we always wore black and white in the right places, so if you can manage that, that's what I'd prefer. I know it's difficult with wartime clothes rationing, and I don't want to put you to any expense. Please raise your hands if you can't find, beg or borrow something suitable.' He looked around the room and there were no hands in the air. Emily was wondering if she could borrow something off Auntie Barbara or Doreen.

'So, it's black and white then, everyone. Oh, there's a hand in the air. It's William, I think.'

'Alcwyn, if you need any more music to make up the programme, I could play something, if Robert would accompany me; but only if you feel you're short of items. I don't want to push myself forward.'

'No, no, William. I'm sure we would all love you to play something with Robert.' The orchestra members made sounds of enthusiasm and some turned and nodded at the two players.

'Well, I think that covers everything. Ah, Clara has just reminded me that we haven't discussed the cost of the tickets and where the money is going if we make a profit. Perhaps we could talk about that after our rehearsal. The new music is on your stands. Anna, you have your hand up. Have you any suggestions?'

'Well, Maestro, I work some of my time in Woolacombe and Ilfracombe, and have some contact with the American Army. I could get them to publicise the concert for us. They are very helpful in the local community. What do you think?'

'That would be wonderful, Anna. Thank you very much.'

'Would you like me to design an advert and pass it on to my contacts at Woolacombe?'

'That would be excellent. Thank you.' Alcwyn, elated and somewhat flustered by being addressed once again by Anna as 'Maestro,' shuffled his music about while the orchestra started to tune.

Emily found herself thinking how Anna could have made so much contact with people in Ilfracombe and Woolacombe, having been in the area for a relatively short time. Of course, working as a doctor would allow her to meet lots of members of the public, but how had she got to know so many of the Americans? Emily checked her E string, which was slightly sharp, and then remembered seeing Anna with a high-ranking American officer.

Alcwyn had raised his baton and said that the orchestra should be ready to play the first piece of music on the stands. It was Beethoven's Egmont Overture.

Chapter 32

'**That's settled then,** Isaac. Gordon and Dorothy have agreed that you stay at their farm and help there until Pip is able to return to work. Now that she's out of hospital, it has made sense for her to go home for a week or so.'

'She has to see the doctor to make sure she's fully recovered and well enough to get back to work, Fred.' Barbara looked anxious. 'She had a nasty bang on the head, and farm work isn't exactly a gentle sort of job. Isaac, would you like another cup of tea?'

'Yes please, Mrs Baxter.'

'And Isaac,' Barbara paused. 'Stop calling me Mrs Baxter.'

'Yes, Mrs B – Barbara.'

The kitchen door opened and Emily and Elly entered, followed by Stan.

'Come on you three, or we'll have drained the pot and eaten all the biscuits Babs made.' Fred Baxter smiled. He was looking more relaxed, Emily thought.

'I've finished ploughing that field, Fred, and the tractor is running fine.' Elly sat at the table and took a biscuit. Stan looked at the young woman admiringly.

'George 'ave mended your tractor, then, Fred?' Stan asked, taking a second biscuit from the tin.

'He ordered the part for it, Stan but Elly carried out the repairs.'

'Did 'er? 'Er's a clever maid. There's nothin' 'er can't do, so it seems.'

Isaac looked admiringly at the young woman.

'Elly's teaching me too but there's a lot to learn.'

'You're doing very well, Isaac, and Emily has helped with the lambing, haven't you, Em?'

'Here and there, Elly. But Isaac, how long are you allowed to be away from your job at my grandparent's shop in London?'

'They have another full-time worker and a part-time one too, so they said that I could stay as long as I liked. That is, what I mean is, that I can stay as long as I am needed.' Isaac looked apologetically at Fred and Barbara.

'You're part of the team now, Isaac,' Fred laughed. 'But as you're going to be working with Gordon and Hen, we'll drive you over there after dinner.'

The conversation was interrupted by the sound of a vehicle entering the farmyard.

'Now who can that be?' Barbara left the table and looked out of the window.

'Fred, I don't recognise the man getting out of that van.' Everyone got up to look out at the stranger.

'Goodness, it's William Taylor,' Emily exclaimed. 'He's the clarinettist in our orchestra. Whatever is he doing here?' Everyone left the kitchen and went outside to greet the newcomer, who came forward with a friendly smile.

'Good morning, I'm William Taylor from The Ministry of Agriculture. Is one of you Fred Baxter?'

'That's me,' Fred said, somewhat taken aback. 'Would you like to come into the kitchen and have a drink, and you can tell me what you want to inspect?'

'That's kind. Thank you. Oh, hello, Emily. I'm not used to seeing you without your violin.' William smiled and followed Fred and Barbara into the kitchen.

'Oh! I be off,' Stan said swinging his leg over the bar of his bike and preparing to pedal away. 'I keeps away from the Min of Ag as much as I can. They always wants us to do somethin' that us don't want to do.'

'Bye Stan,' Emily and Elly shouted.

'Good job I just finished that work in the far field. That's what that chap has come to inspect, you see.' Elly said. 'You said that you know him, Emily?'

'Yes, but I didn't know that he works for the Ministry of Agriculture, Elly. He's a wonderful clarinettist. He gives concerts, and plays in our orchestra.'

'Let's all go to the lambing shed. I have to check some of the poorly ones.'

'Is lambing finished, Elly?' Isaac asked as they crossed the farmyard and entered the door to the large shed.

'Yes, thank goodness, just a few late ones left to lamb and some weak little souls to try to save,' Elly replied.

'You will be glad of a good night's sleep, Elly,' Emily commented.

'You're right there, Em. Look, Isaac, can you give these bottles to this lamb here and that one over there. I'm going up to the field in case that chap wants to know anything about the tractor and why we hadn't finished that field sooner. I know your uncle was worried about it, Emily.'

Isaac looked delighted as he walked towards the first of the two little, weak lambs.

'If I can't do anything here, I'll go up to my bedroom and put in a bit of practice on the orchestra music,' Emily said. 'We haven't much time to get it ready for the concert.'

Emily entered the kitchen just as William and Fred were leaving it. William paused and turned to Emily. 'Have you heard anything from Anna, Emily? She has been trying to contact you. She wants you to play second violin in that Boccherini Minuet she's directing.'

'Really? Who else will be playing?'

'Robert will be playing the cello, and, let me think.' He frowned. 'Oh, yes. Dan will be playing the viola part. Here's Anna's phone number. She wants you to telephone her and she will arrange for you all to meet to rehearse.' William handed a piece of paper to Emily, who looked surprised at the news she'd been given.

'Thank you, William. It's all a bit of a rush to get the programme together, isn't it?'

'Yes, but the fact that there is going to be a concert in wartime is an achievement in itself, isn't it?' He smiled and turned to Fred.

'Now, let's see this field you've worked so hard on, Mr Baxter.'

Chapter 33

Elly settled into the passenger seat of the front of the Austin Seven and Emily sat behind the wheel looking anxious. It was good of Elly to offer to teach her how to drive, although Auntie Barbara had also offered to do the same. She had the sewing machine out and was busy repairing the tear in Isaac's trousers which he had made stretching to lift a bag of animal feed. Her aunt had said that she wouldn't be free today but if Elly had time to make a start, and if Emily needed further lessons later in the week, she would be available. The two young women had looked at one another cautiously.

'I think that will encourage you to be a quick learner, Em, so let's get started. Are you comfortable with your view of the road, or should I say your view of the shippon?'

'Yes, but I can't drive forward very far without bumping into it, Elly.'

'No, that's right. I'll tell you about the gears and the clutch first and then you can start her up. Remember to be gentle and don't do any sudden jerky movements with your hands or your feet, like someone else we know.'

After about half an hour, Emily was driving well

around the farmyard.

'Well done, Em. Next time, we'll get you to drive out onto the road. You've even managed to reverse the van to its usual parking place. Now turn off the engine and put it into neutral. Time for dinner. I can see your aunt waving to us.'

'Thank you, Elly. You are a very good teacher.' They walked towards the farmhouse as Fred appeared from the vegetable garden.

'How was the lesson, Emily?' he shouted.

'Not as frightening as I expected, Uncle. Elly is so patient.'

They walked into the kitchen and took turns to wash their hands at the sink.

'It's stew today,' Barbara informed them while straining the potatoes. 'Emily, would you lay the table, please? How did the lesson go?' Fred sat at the table and grinned.

'She didn't knock over anything in the yard, Babs.'

'Fred, I didn't even have a teacher. In the end, I got so fed up with waiting for you to teach me to drive that I thought I'd teach myself when you were out that day.'

'I think that was very brave, Auntie,' Emily cut in.

'So do I, Barbara.' Elly added.

Barbara stood behind Fred, holding the stew

pot, ladle in the air, while she waited for a comment from her husband. He suddenly sat up and woke up to his cue.

'Definitely. Not many women would have done what you did on their own.'

There was a slight pause while Barbara worked out if that was a compliment. Fred turned his head and nodded encouragingly at her. She looked pleased and ladled two portions of stew into his plate. They all sat around the table and the atmosphere became more relaxed.

'Elly, would you drive into Barnstaple this afternoon and pick something up for me? It's something from H R Williams in the High Street. Do you know where I mean? The ironmongers. It's for my toolbox. I'll write it down. I want to do some work on the chicken house, add a bit on.'

'If Elly's going to town, can you go with her, Emily? I want some sewing things from Banburys; more darning needles of varying sizes and some cotton thread for the sewing machine. I'm nearly out of black and grey. I'll write it down.'

'Yes, Auntie.' Emily looked at Elly and smiled.

'I'll need to be back for milking.' Elly looked at Fred.

'Don't you worry, I can start that off and if you get back in time, you can come and help. But you haven't had any time off since you've been here.

Go and have a few hours to yourself, for once.' He tore a sheet of paper off an old notepad and wrote down the details of what he wanted Elly to buy for him at H R Williams.

'Fred, we're getting low on petrol. Shall I call at Hopgoods and fill her up?' Elly asked.

'Yes, but let me give you the coupons for this month. We need to use them or lose them, and here's some money. That should be enough for what Barbara wants as well as what I want.'

'Here's my list, Emily. It's not very much. Is there anything you want to look for while you two are in town?'

'I don't need anything, Barbara. Although I may look for a dress some time or other. I don't have a dress.' Elly looked thoughtful.

'Oh, Auntie, you remember I told you that we have to wear black and white for our orchestra concert? You said that you had a black skirt that would fit me. Well, I think I will look for a blouse.'

'Good. Now you both have something to hunt for, and can help each other. Go and get ready and don't hang about here. I can do the dishes.' Barbara cleared the table and the two young women prepared to leave the room.

'I'll write down what I spend, Fred, and let you have the change when we get back,' Elly said.

'No, we don't want any change. Go in Bromleys

and have afternoon tea.' Fred walked over to the sofa and sat down while Emily and Elly hurried from the room and went upstairs to get ready.

'Here's a cup of tea, Fred. I'm glad you're getting used to the sofa. Very comfortable, isn't it, considering it's second hand?'

'Yes, dear. Very comfortable.' He took the mug of tea and placed it on the small table, laid his head back on one of the orange cushions and closed his eyes. 'You were right, as always.'

Chapter 34

'That dress is lovely on you, Elly. Blue with white polka dots looks so fresh. Do you like it?'

'I must admit that it does look nice but I'm not used to seeing myself in dresses. I wouldn't know what is fashionable and what isn't.' The saleswoman stepped forward and smiled.

'It is the very latest, Madam. But your friend is right. It looks lovely on you.'

'Then I'll buy it.' Elly looked at Emily and grinned. 'And that blouse you bought will be perfect for the concert.'

'Yes, the long sleeves are quite formal but the lace on the bodice makes it look very special. I'm really pleased with my purchase.'

'We've done all the shopping we had to do. I'll pay for my dress and we can go to Bromley's for tea.' Elly grinned. 'This is the most fun I've had for ages.'

After they had left Banburys the two young women walked arm in arm down the High Street carrying their packages. Bromley's café looked quite busy but they could see an empty table across the room. Suddenly a familiar voice rang out.

'Emily! What a surprise! Come and join us.'

Imogen and Doreen were sitting together in the far corner of the room.

'Hello. This is Elly. You've heard me talk about our wonderful Land Army girl who works on my uncle's farm, haven't you? Elly, these are my friends, Doreen and Imogen.'

The four young women were soon chatting and enjoying afternoon tea, a modest wartime treat, all the more appreciated for its rarity.

'Oh, Emily, Dad is trying to get more help on our farm,' Imogen said. 'Don, who works for us part-time is getting on a bit and wants to cut down on his work.'

'I hope he finds someone like Elly. She can do everything; can even repair cars and tractors, and she is bravely teaching me how to drive.' Elly shook her head and looked embarrassed.

'I'm lucky to be working somewhere with such lovely people. Not all farmers are as nice as Fred and Barbara,' Elly remarked.

Doreen leaned forward and smiled. 'I should tell you, Elly, that Imogen and I are second cousins. She called at the bakery this morning, and as I had the afternoon off, we decided to come here and treat ourselves.' Doreen poured a second cup of tea for her and Imogen. 'Where have you two been? I can see you have bought something interesting.'

'Yes, Doreen. I managed to find a white blouse

to wear for our concert, and my aunt will lend me a black skirt.'

'And I've bought a dress. That's in case I should ever go anywhere where I am not wearing dungarees and wellie boots,' Elly laughed.

'Ooh, we'll have to see about that, won't we, Doreen?' Imogen's eyes glinted as she looked closely at Elly, imagining her dressed for a social occasion.

'Immy, how did you come to town?'

'With Dad, in the truck. He wanted to go to the bank and then has to buy some animal feed. I have a day off and felt like a change.'

'Have you heard any news about Dylan?' Emily asked.

'No, not yet. There's been a lot going on around home recently. First it was Alexander's birthday. Dad bought him a puppy.'

Doreen smiled. 'He must have been thrilled.'

'It will give him something else to think about. My brother is such an imaginative boy. We are never sure if some of the things he says are fact or fiction. I don't mean that he tells lies, but he plays these war games with his friends, and they live in their own little world. Alex said that he had seen an American officer drive through our farmyard and on towards the cottage that doctor Anna rents from us. She's not home there much but at weekends, Alex says he writes down the time the Jeep goes to the cottage and the time it comes back. He says that he recognises the sound of the Jeep as it approaches, and hides behind the barn as it passes by.'

'Well, they were arm in arm when we saw them at the concert at the Woolacombe Bay Hotel, weren't they?' Doreen remarked, raising her eyebrows and looking around at her friends.

'I know, Doreen, but Alex is only just eleven, yet seems so knowing. And he's joined the Scouts now. One of the American sergeants formed a Scout Group last year and divided the boys into Puffins, Seagulls and Gannets. They are so lucky to have the opportunity to let off steam.'

'It's very good of the sergeant to give his time and energy to those boys, isn't it?' Emily said.

'It is, Emily. The American soldiers are a really friendly lot and have helped the village in all sorts of ways. Oh, and I must tell you something else. You remember the wonderful clarinettist we heard at that concert, don't you? Sorry, Elly, that you don't know the people I'm talking about.'

Elly smiled. 'Don't worry, Imogen. It is all totally enthralling, and makes me realise that I have been living a very sheltered life.'

Imogen continued. 'You know, he's called William Taylor, and guess what? He works for – '

'The Ministry of Agriculture and Fisheries,' Emily cut in.

'How do you know that, Emily?'

'He came to make sure that Uncle Fred and Elly had completed the ploughing that was required of them. Did he come to inspect something at your Dad's farm, Imogen?'

'Yes, but Dad doesn't really know why. He asked for permission to look at the grazing land and the sheep and lambs that were out on it. Then he drove off in his truck to do just that. He must have had to see some of the land on foot because it is so steep as it drops towards the sea. Anyway, he came back and said he thought that everything was a credit to Dad, and that he wished that all farmers were as conscientious as Dad.'

'Crikey!' Doreen said. 'What did your dad say about that, Immy?'

'He walked around for the rest of the day with a bit of a smirk on his face.'

'William seems a nice man,' Elly looked thoughtful.

'But a bit of a mystery,' Imogen added. 'Why does he do that job when he is such an excellent musician? And where does he live?'

'Not everyone wants to earn their money as a full-time musician, Imogen, especially during wartime.' Emily shook her head. 'It's not a reliable job.

While we're on the subject of music, don't forget our concert the Saturday afternoon before Easter Sunday. William will be playing a solo and Anna is organising a string quartet. I will play second fiddle and she will play first. Robert is playing the cello and Dan will make up the quartet playing the viola. Anna is arranging for us to meet for rehearsals soon.'

'Goodness, she's everywhere, that woman. Didn't you say that she was the doctor who stitched up the Land Army girl's head wound?' Doreen asked.

'And I think she's responsible for the posters that are all over Woolacombe about your concert, Emily,' Imogen remarked. 'She's probably persuaded her American friend to sort out the advertising.'

The four women looked at one another and Emily sighed. 'Crumbs! I'd better get back and do some practice, Elly.'

'Did you have a good afternoon, you two?' Barbara asked as Emily and Elly laid their shopping on the table.

'Very good, thank you Auntie, and a lovely afternoon tea at Bromley's to finish it off.'

'Thank you, Barbara and Fred for the treat. I should change and go and help to clear up after the milking.'

'No, Elly. Fred has almost finished, and anyway,

he knew you wouldn't be back in time, so don't worry. He started early. Just enjoy the rest of the day. Make the most of it! It has been a very busy time, hasn't it?' Barbara turned to Emily as the two women sat side by side on the sofa. 'By the way, Emily, there was a telephone call for you from Dan. He asked if you would call him back.' Barbara smiled a little knowing smile.

Chapter 35

Emily put away her violin and music and sat on the bed. She was playing the orchestral music quite well that would make up the concert programme, and was hoping that the violin part that she would have to play for the Boccherini quartet wouldn't be too difficult. On the farm, lambing had finished, but there was still plenty to do, and she had helped out now and then with milking or working in the family vegetable garden. Uncle Fred and Elly were continuing with planting vegetables on a larger scale in the bottom field. The warmer days and the frequent showers were resulting in a sudden spurt in growth, especially the weeds, as Emily's uncle dryly remarked.

Emily lay back on the bed and yawned. She hadn't slept well recently. Not that she had suffered the recurrence of the dreadful dreams which had plagued her so often in the past. She wasn't sure why she sometimes lay awake. She had been told that people from the cities who went to stay in the country couldn't sleep because it was too quiet. She certainly didn't miss the sound of distant explosions and the noise of sirens and traffic, and the shouts of the ARP Wardens as they gave orders when there was an emergency. In the beautiful North Devon countryside, the night time stillness and the darkness were a comfort to her and a part of the natural order of things. When the sky was clear and the stars twinkled and the moon shone down on the farm no-one told them to 'Put that light out!' No, her unease was connected with something else. She had noticed that her aunt looked at her closely whenever Dan's name was mentioned, or when he called or phoned. Emily looked up at the ceiling above her bed and watched a spider making its way slowly towards the corner of the room. She liked Dan. He was comfortable to be with and showed an interest in other people. How terrible it must have been when he heard that his fiancée had died in the Exeter bombing. All his dreams of their lives together shattered in a moment. How many thousands of men and women in other countries as well as their own had suffered the same shock and the forever loss. Emily stretched her arms above her head and sighed. She wasn't sure what it was that she was feeling restless about, but she thought that it would come to the surface eventually. She got up from the bed and looked at her watch. Five o'clock. Emily decided to go downstairs and help her aunt to prepare tea. Dan was going to collect her in the car at a quarter to six and they would go to Robert's house in Ilfracombe for the first of the practices for the quartet. Having to sight read the new music while sitting next to Anna was causing her some unease. As Anna and Dan would be coming straight from work, Robert had kindly offered to prepare tea and sandwiches to keep them going until they returned home.

'I'm sorry, Auntie. I've been practising and then I flopped on the bed. Can I help you?'

'You look tired, dear. Is everything all right?'

'Yes, fine. I just felt a bit sleepy.'

'Well, there has been a lot happening lately, hasn't there?' Barbara finished making some egg sandwiches and placed them on a plate on the table and made the tea. 'Go and fetch your uncle and Elly, Emily. I did tell them that we are having an earlier tea today as Dan will be calling before six.'

'Thank you, Auntie, for fitting in with my timetable. It's kind of you. I'll go and call them, but they may not have finished clearing up after milking.'

'No, of course not. Tell them that I'll put theirs aside for them for later. Then come right back and have your tea.'

'Right, but we will have a cup of tea when we get there, Auntie so don't put yourself out too much for me, please.'

At exactly a quarter to six, Dan's van drew up outside the door. Emily put on her coat and picked up her violin.

'Goodbye, Auntie. I won't be late back.' Dan got out of the van and took Emily's violin and placed it behind the passenger seat.

'Hello, Emily,' he smiled. 'How are you?'

'I am well, thank you, Dan,' she answered settling into the front seat as he started the engine and drove off.

'I am sorry that you have to drive such a long way for the practice.'

'I think it's unavoidable as we all live some way from one another. There's you near West Buckland and me at South Molton, then there's Robert at Ilfracombe and Anna at –' He paused. 'I can't remember where it is she lives.'

'I have friend called Doreen and she has some relations who live on a farm in the Mortehoe area; Higher Morte Farm. They have a cottage near them that they rent out.'

'And they rent it out to Anna?'

'That's right. It's rather isolated but I think she likes that aspect of it. She also rides the lovely grey mare that belongs to Doreen's uncle. He can't ride her these days so he is grateful that Anna gives her some exercise. I was at the farm a while ago. Anna is a very good rider.'

'She is most accomplished at so many things,' Dan remarked with no sense of envy.

'Her assistance with helping local doctors takes

her to Woolacombe and Ilfracombe but she does some surgery work at the North Devon Infirmary. I think you must know that because she stitched up Pip's head wound. It was very fortunate that you happened to be driving along just after her accident, Dan.'

'I was glad to help. How is she?'

'Pip has gone home to her parents for a break and has to be seen by a doctor and given the go ahead before she can return to work at Gordon and Dorothy's farm.'

Dan drove on, deep in his own thoughts, until he suddenly said, 'Good! That's good! I'm amazed at the work the Land Army girls do. It's really back-breaking much of the time. You help on the farm too, don't you, Emily?'

'Well, now that I'm feeling better, – ' she paused. 'I was suffering from shock when I first came to the farm. I had witnessed a terrible tragedy and tried to go on as if nothing had happened. Eventually, my mother insisted that I see the doctor and he signed me off work and I came to stay at the farm here to – '

'Recover.' Dan said as he stopped at some traffic lights and drove on through Braunton. The journey continued in silence until they reached Mullacott Cross and Dan said, 'You may have heard that I lost my fiancée in the Exeter bombing?'

'Yes, my aunt told me about it. I am so sorry, Dan.' Neither spoke as each tried to imagine the experience of the other.

'We are not alone, Emily, in what we have suffered. There are so many like us who have lost loved ones.'

'But children, Dan; taken before they have hardly lived. That is what I have had difficulty understanding. I've gone through phases of being shocked, tearful and angry. And then I feel guilty if I am enjoying myself. I don't know what I am supposed to feel. Is that how your loss has affected you?'

'Yes, it is.' He stopped the van by the side of the road at the top of a hill and turned off the engine. They looked down on the seaside town of Ilfracombe in the dwindling light. There were no lights to show any sign of life in the town, but the sky above it was clear with stars starting to twinkle as the moon gazed down on the lifeless-looking town. The faint sound of explosions could be heard, coming from the other side of the Bristol Channel.

'The Luftwaffe is bombing Cardiff,' Dan groaned 'Just when we thought the worst of it was over.' He shook his head, turned to Emily and said resignedly, 'Well, we'd better move on, or we'll be late.'

Chapter 36

Robert's house was situated between the town and the beach. Most of Ilfracombe sloped down steeply to the sea affording glorious views of the rocky coastline. The sheer cliffs jutted out into the sea and on the landward side their grassy slopes were criss-crossed with paths enjoyed by walkers. You certainly had to be able to walk well whether you were a holiday-maker or a resident. The beach was shingle and sheltered. Ilfracombe was a very popular destination for tourists and day-trippers, and although the government had tried to dissuade people from going on holiday in wartime in order to keep train use for troop movements, the annual week's holiday was a big event, and no alternative such as concerts, circuses and parties in Britain's parks had succeeded in keeping the population at home. A direct train from Waterloo to Ilfracombe carried the war-weary citizen to the seaside to be rejuvenated. Emily smiled as she remembered the three day stay she had enjoyed with her family in Brighton last summer. Although the enemy frequently bombed the south coastal towns, a day at the seaside was something that the British citizen saw as deserved and justifiable, war or no war.

Dan parked on the road outside Robert's small front garden and he and Emily, carrying their instruments, walked through the iron gate and up the steep path to the front door. There were huge hydrangea bushes on either side of the path that were just starting to leaf up and Emily thought that they must look a picture in the summer. The door opened and Robert welcomed them inside to the long passage with its Victorian tiled floor.

'Please let me take your coats and hang them up here. Then follow me into the front room, which is my music room and where I give my lessons.' The room was large and able to take a sizeable grand piano which stood at the window end. There were bookshelves and music stands, chairs, and a cello leaning against the wall in the corner of the room. A fire was burning in the hearth and although the décor of the room was rather old-fashioned, it was cosy, with a large sofa pushed back against a wall to make room for the musicians.

'Thank you for allowing us to rehearse here at your home, Robert,' Dan said.

'Thank you for coming, both of you. It is quite a drive from South Molton and I expect you met Emily on the way, Dan.'

'Dan met me at the farm where I am staying with my Uncle and Aunt. It's near West Buckland. He is very kind to bring me here and take me home.'

Emily smiled at Dan who looked pleased.

'Anna telephoned to say that she will be a little late coming from the surgery at Ilfracombe. But if you'll excuse me, I'll go into the kitchen and fetch the trolley. I have prepared some sandwiches and will make the tea.'

'That is very kind of you, Robert. I hope you haven't had to cancel your pupils this evening to fit in this rehearsal?' Dan looked closely at the older man.

'No. My last pupil had to cancel his lesson as he is ill and I finish early on a Tuesday, anyway.' He walked to the door and turned and said, 'If you need the lavatory it is along the passageway on the right.' Emily and Dan were left alone in the room with the sound of the fire crackling merrily.

'Should we get our instruments out, Dan, or wait until we are all here?'

'I think it is better to wait until after we have all had tea,' Dan replied, looking closely at Emily. 'Have you played the Boccherini before, Emily?'

'No, that's why I'm worried about it. I've practised the orchestra music a lot and I should be able to manage that, but I've never played this quartet. Surely Anna could have chosen one of the more accomplished violinists in the orchestra to play instead of me!'

'Do you think there are more accomplished

players than you who could have done it?' He smiled teasingly, waiting for her reply.

'Well some of them are older and more experienced and polished instrumentalists. I haven't played much this last year, really. I'm quite rusty, you see.'

Dan looked at her with a serious expression on his face as he said, 'I have to say something important now, Emily.' She looked at him frowning and anxious about what he might say.

'Your rustiness is better than other people's polish.'

There was a moment while Emily thought about his comment and suddenly they both burst out laughing.

The music room door opened and Anna entered followed by Robert pushing a wooden tea trolley.

'Sorry I'm late, everyone,' Anna said.

'Perfect timing.' Robert said, 'Please sit down and relax for a while. I'll bring this low table towards you three. Now, is everyone for a cup of tea. I have some egg sandwiches and some fish paste ones. I hope that is all right.'

'That is wonderful, Robert. It has been a difficult day and it is so good to be spoilt like this.' Anna beamed at him and took an egg sandwich as he placed a cup of tea for her on the low table.

'No, I don't take sugar, thank you, but I don't

know if Dan and Emily do.' She turned her head and looked at them out of her beautiful, blue eyes.

'No, thank you, Robert,' Emily said looking at Dan, who shook his head. Anna laughed as she said, 'That's just as well, Robert as we don't want to deplete your sugar ration.'

'I don't eat any sweet things,' Robert said. 'I have a dodgy ticker, you see, and try to keep my weight down. I didn't suffer with it as a child. It came on after I moved to England from Austria in 1937. It was probably as a result of stress.'

Anna paused, the bone china tea cup half way to her lips. She sat silent, looking closely at Robert while Dan said, 'Well done to keep your weight under control, Robert.'

'You must speak fluent German, Robert,' Anna remarked. 'But you have no trace of an accent.'

'No, that is because my sister Clara and I were brought up bilingually. But you don't want to hear about that. Who would like another sandwich?'

'I would love to hear about your early years in Austria.' Emily looked at Dan who nodded as Anna reached for another egg sandwich.

'My wife's parents, Charles and Alice Wilson, lived here in Ilfracombe, in this very house. Charles was a doctor. In nineteen hundred they went on holiday with their daughter, Clare, to Austria and visited Vienna where my father, Franz Stein, met them at a concert one summer evening. He was a professional musician and was playing in the orchestra. During the days Clare and her family were there on holiday, Franz showed them around the city. They all got on well, especially Franz and Clare, and her parents invited him to visit them in Ilfracombe. You can probably guess that the two young people fell in love. They married in 1902 and settled in Vienna where my father continued successfully with his musical career, both performing and teaching the violin. His favourite composer was Schumann and when I was born in 1904 I was named Robert, after the composer.'

'Oh, and your sister is called Clara after Robert Schumann's wife,' Emily said. 'How lovely! Some people think that Clara Schumann was a better musician than Robert,' Emily added as if she were disclosing a secret.

'There was always music in the house, but I started to train as a doctor and then gave it up after a few years, feeling that I couldn't cope with the responsibility of holding the lives of other people in my hands. It was not a problem on paper but when it came to the real thing, dealing with patients and life-changing situations, I felt I would not be able to sustain that sort of pressure.' He looked at Anna sympathetically. 'You know what I mean, Anna, I'm sure.' Anna smiled back at him and took another sandwich.

'Is that when you started to study music?' she asked.

'Yes, that's right. My sister is two years younger than me but knew what she wanted to do from childhood. Clara and I enjoyed our student days in Vienna and were able to continue living at home. We completed our courses and began to play professionally and to teach from home. They were happy years.'

'What changed it then, Robert?' Dan asked. 'Why did you leave Austria?'

'Our father, Franz, was Jewish. It became obvious that political attitudes were changing and many Jewish people were leaving Germany in the 1930s. In the mid 1930s our mother's parents sadly died within a short time of one another and the house here was left to her. Our parents decided to come to England and settle. It was a big decision for them but at least our mother was familiar with the house and the area in which she had grown up. We moved to England and anglicised our name by changing it from Stein to Stone. Our father sold the house in Vienna but didn't get its full value. The political and social situation was volatile and we counted ourselves fortunate to have escaped it. However, it was our home and Clara and I still share our happy memories of it from time to time.'

'You have both been a great asset to the musical fraternity here in North Devon,' Anna remarked, with a serious expression on her face,

'Why did your sister settle in Woolacombe instead of Ilfracombe?' She continued to look quizzically at Robert.

'Father's health deteriorated rather suddenly after that first year here and he had a heart attack and died in 1939, just before the start of the war. Mother went downhill quickly after that and died a year later. Meanwhile, Clara had met a very nice young man who was in the RAF. He was a pilot. They decided to marry and make the most of their time together, in spite of the uncertain future. They bought a house in Woolacombe, a village which they both loved. Sadly, about six months later, his plane was shot down. Clara says she will never regret marrying him. She has stayed on at the house in Woolacombe and runs her teaching practice from it.'

There was a short silence as they all processed Robert's family story in their different ways.

'If no-one wants another cup of tea, I think we should get on with our practice.'

'Good idea, Robert,' Anna looked at him for a while and then asked,' You said that you have copies of the Boccherini Minuet?'

'Yes, I do.' He handed out some sheets of music

which he had placed on the piano. 'Clara and I played it last when we were in Austria.' They all moved away from the sofa to the chairs placed behind the music stands.

'You have saved me ordering it, Robert. That is very helpful.' Anna looked around at the others. 'Now, are you sure that you are happy for me to direct the rehearsal?'

They all murmured their agreement as they arranged the music on the stands.

'Good. Now let us get started. Today is March 28th. We will probably only have one more practice before the concert. Time goes by so quickly, doesn't it? Please tune to my A.'

Chapter 37

'It's going to be a busy day.' Fred Baxter drained his mug of tea and looked around the breakfast table. 'It's the quarterly vet inspection of the dairy herd today. Dan will be here to do that this afternoon. He's going to inspect the cows at Gordon's farm this morning and come over here afterwards. Elly, I think the milk yield is down a bit. What do you think?'

Elly frowned thoughtfully as Barbara looked at her husband.

'Oh, Fred, I forgot to tell you that Dorothy phoned early this morning to say that Pip arrived back yesterday afternoon and was starting work again there first thing this morning.'

'How is she, Barbara?' Elly took another piece of bread and spread it with honey.

'She'd seen the doctor before she left home and was given the all clear to return to work.'

'That's good news, isn't it?' Emily looked at her uncle. 'Perhaps they will send Isaac here to help, now that they will have the two girls working together again.'

'That's exactly what Dorothy said. More tea, anyone?' Barbara looked around the table. 'No takers? Well, I'll finish the pot then.'

'Fred, I don't think the milk yield is down much,' Elly said. 'Perhaps we should look at it over a period of time. What do you think?'

'There's a lot going on at the moment, Elly. More vegetables to get in the ground, but what is it you are doing with Emily? It looks as if you are building a new hen house?'

'There is so much wood left over from some previous projects that we are using some of it to build a bigger hen house and a good size chicken run.' Elly smiled encouragingly at Emily.

'But, Uncle, we need some strong wire netting, or whatever you call it. We want to make it fox proof, don't we, Elly?'

'Well, we can get some if there isn't enough in the barn. But I thought the hens were fine in the henhouse they already have.'

'Yes, but Uncle, there aren't many of the old hens left. We're planning to get more hens and develop that side of the farm business a little.'

'Oh, I see. At least, I think I do.' He looked at his wife and shook his head. 'I'm beginning to feel I'm outnumbered here. When did you say that Isaac was coming, Babs?'

They all laughed and Barbara looked at Emily.

'I didn't tell you, Emily, but I had a long talk with your mother yesterday. She telephoned from our parents' shop. We were able to talk without feeling that the pips would go and our conversation would be cut off at any minute.'

'Is everyone all right?' Emily looked anxious.

'Yes, they're all fine but our parents have admitted that they are not as young as they were and are finding the daily commitment of running the business, stocking the shop, coping with the rationing and so on, all too much. So, they have decided to sell up. They've thought about it for some time but have waited until they were happy, not just with the financial side, but happy with the person who would be taking over.'

'That's typical of them. When will they give it up, Auntie?'

'I think it will be the end of May but I don't know any more details.'

'It will be a big change for them,' Emily sighed.

'But we know what they are like,' Fred laughed. 'They'll fill their time with helping all the poor and needy folk in their part of Lewisham.' He stood up and looked around and smiled. 'Well, let's get to work, then.'

The morning sped by, each to his own task while Barbara looked at the brass and decided that she could gladly delay its cleaning for another week. She used the morning for cooking and was interrupted, as usual by the elevenses which she took outside and placed on a tray on the old table by the door. The kitchen table had her dough and pastry on it and she hated being interrupted when she was in the middle of a baking morning. Dinner would have to be something simple, she thought.

At around half past two, Dan's car drew up and he and Isaac got out. Dan went off to find Fred and Isaac went into the kitchen.

'Ah, Isaac. There you are. How did you enjoy your time helping at Buckland Farm? Put your things down here and let me have any dirty washing.' Barbara beckoned the young man over to sit by her on the sofa. 'I'm darning socks as you see and will be glad of a chat to relieve the boredom of it.'

'It was very interesting and I hope I can remember the things I learnt. It's a large farm and they are busy all the time, especially as they have a milk round to do every weekday. But Pip is working again now, so is there anything I can do here, Mrs Baxter?'

'Oh, do call me "Barbara" or "Auntie." There's always something to do here, Isaac, and Fred will be very glad of your help. How is Pip?'

'She is well, and she and Hen are planning to go to a dance this evening at South Molton. It will be in somewhere called "The Assembly Rooms." They have asked if Emily and Elly and I would like to go with them. Gordon is allowing Hen to drive everyone in the van.'

'That would be fun, Isaac.' Barbara put down her darning and looked at the young man sitting up straight and serious on the sofa next to her. 'Don't you think it would be fun, dear?'

'I think the young ladies will enjoy it, but – '

'But what, Isaac?'

'Wouldn't it be better that they go on their own? And another thing, I can't dance.'

The kitchen door opened and Elly entered. 'I couldn't help overhearing some of that conversation, Isaac. Of course, you must go, and if it's all right with Barbara and Fred, I'd like to go too. I don't know about Emily.'

'Elly, you have just bought a dress and this will be the perfect time to wear it. Where is Emily?'

'She and I are making good progress with the new henhouse, Barbara, but we could do with your help, Isaac. Dan has started checking the herd with Fred and asked if he could come in when he has finished as he has to talk to Emily about arrangements for the next rehearsal.'

'Of course. Tell him and Emily to come in when they are ready. There will be tea and cakes later. I hope you had some dinner, Isaac?'

'Yes. Dan and I ate dinner at Mr Gordon's farm. They are very kind. You are all very kind to me. I am so happy.' Isaac smiled shyly and looked down.

'Isaac, you won't have heard, but I had a telephone

call from my sister recently and she told me that our parents have decided to sell the grocery business and retire. I know they will write to you about it but I thought you would like to know of their plans.'

There was a long silence and Isaac looked up.

'They have done so much for me. They gave me a home. They are angels. I am glad they will retire. They have worked so hard. Yes, I am happy for them.' He sat very still and looked down at the pattern on the rug in front of the Aga. Suddenly, the ticking of the large clock on the wall sounded too loud as the news the young German man had received was processed by the two women in the room.

'Well, it's early days yet, and there will be lots of things to work out,' Barbara said, comfortingly tapping Isaac on the shoulder. Elly blinked away some tears and cleared her throat.

'Isaac, can you come and look at the henhouse we are building? We've run out of ideas and energy, and can do with some help.' The young man smiled and jumped up. The two left the room and Barbara picked up her handkerchief and blew her nose, wiped away her tears and continued with her sock darning.

'Ah, there you are, you two. How did the inspection go, Dan?'

'Very well, thank you Barbara, I'm glad to say.'

'Emily, when you have brushed some of the wood shavings from your hair, I have put a tea tray in the best room for you and Dan. I think he wanted a chat with you about rehearsals, isn't that right, Dan?'

'Yes, if Emily has time from her construction project.' They all smiled at one another while Emily went to the mirror in the kitchen and shook the wood shavings from her hair.

'Thank you, Auntie. I don't think I've ever been in the other room.'

'We only use it for Christmas and Easter, but you two will get a bit of peace and quiet and a chance to sort out your arrangements.'

Emily opened the door to a cool and tidy room. Dan followed her and they sat side by side on a rather old-fashioned upright sofa in front of which was a low table with tea and cakes laid out invitingly.

'Your aunt and uncle are very kind, Emily,' Dan said, as Emily poured tea into a beautiful china tea cup and passed it to him.

'I am very lucky, Dan. Do you have family living near you?'

'Sadly, no. My parents both died in the Blitz, in London, which was what made me move this way, for a fresh start. I have no close relatives.' Emily poured herself a cup of tea and offered a cake to Dan.

'Did you join a practice, Dan?'

'Yes. The vet was an older gentleman who needed an assistant and we worked well together for several years. He taught me a lot. Then, suddenly, he died and I took over the practice, with a bank loan, of course. It has been hard going especially when – '

'I can only imagine what it must have been like for you.' Emily looked at Dan and put down her cup and saucer as he continued.

'It's only recently that I have realised that I have to sort things out. I can't go on as I have done these last few years. I have a housekeeper now who comes in every day, does some cooking and cleaning and generally bosses me about. She lives nearby in South Street. I have advertised for an assistant vet and will be interviewing some applicants in a few weeks' time. I have to have some help in the business, Emily.'

'Of course, you do, Dan. I am so pleased to hear you say that.'

'I thought you might think so,' Dan replied, looking anxiously at her.

'Would you mind if I talk things over with you again at some time, Emily?'

'Of course not, if you think it would be helpful.'

'I do. Yes, it would. Thank you.' He sighed.

'Meanwhile, there are a few other matters to discuss.'

'That sounds serious,' Emily looked quizzically at Dan.

'I hope that it is not, but I received a telephone call last evening from William Taylor. You know that he is playing a few solos at the concert, and Robert is accompanying him. They rehearse at Robert's house in Ilfracombe now and then.'

'Dan, do you know where William lives?'

'No, but I think it is somewhere between Mullacott Cross and Ilfracombe. I don't know his telephone number either, and don't know anyone who does. He always telephones me. Anyway, William said that he called at Robert's house early last evening to rehearse their concert items, as arranged, but couldn't get an answer when he rang the doorbell. He let himself in and found Robert collapsed on the floor. He did what he could for him and called the surgery and was told that a doctor was on the way. After an hour, William telephoned again and eventually a doctor arrived. William seems to be a man of many parts as the doctor said he had done all the right things. Robert has to rest for a few days and is not in any danger. His medication has been adjusted. The doctor said that the original message had gone through to Dr Anna Miller who has said she had not received it.'

'I don't know what to think, Dan.'

'I think that the years Robert and Clara spent in Austria in the thirties before they left the country, were very stressful. Robert needs to lead a stress-free life with no anxiety.'

'Do you think that performing causes him to be anxious?'

'I don't think so. But I'm no expert. William intimated that it may be something else that is worrying him.'

'I suppose his past is always with him, just as ours is with us,' Emily commented, looking at Dan. 'Was there something else you were going to tell me about rehearsals?'

'Oh, yes. Our final orchestral rehearsal will be at the usual church hall on Saturday and Alcwyn has arranged that all the ensembles and soloists may stay on afterwards for about an hour or more to run through their pieces.'

'That will be easier than going over to Ilfracombe, won't it, Dan?'

'Yes, but I quite enjoyed our little drive there last week, Emily.'

Chapter 38

Emily had woken early and was unable to get back to sleep. Her brain was too busy thinking about what Dan had told her, and worrying about her grandparents and what would happen to Isaac as a result of their decision. She knew that she would have to return home in the not too distant future and felt uneasy about it and guilty at the same time. She got out of bed and looked out of the window. It was a perfect spring morning so she decided to dress and let out the hens and collect the eggs. There was no point lying in bed worrying about things over which she had no control. She could hear her aunt and uncle moving around downstairs and guessed that Elly and Isaac were well into the morning milking regime. She stepped outside. The air was washed clean from the shower the night before and the gentle breeze set the fresh green leaves on the trees in the hedge behind the henhouse fluttering and dancing. It was so beautiful, Emily almost burst into tears. If only she could bottle it and take it back to London with her when she returns. There were more eggs than usual and the hens were happy to get out of the coop. She fastened the door securely and walked back to the house by way of the milking parlour. As she drew near she heard something totally unexpected. There was someone singing. It was a man's voice and it was beautiful. Could it be Isaac, she wondered? Yes, of course it was. Emily stood outside the door and listened, enthralled as the young man sang a song that had become popular in the early years of the war.

Why do you whisper green grass?
Why tell the trees what ain't so?
Whispering grass, the trees don't have to know. No,
no.
Why tell them all your secrets?
Who'd kiss'd there long ago?
Whispering grass, the trees don't need to know.

Then, suddenly a female voice joined in. It was Elly.

Don't you tell it to the breeze 'cause she will tell the
birds and bees and ev'ryone will know because you
told the blab-ber-ing trees.
Yes, you told them once before; it's no secret any more.

Elly stopped singing and Isaac ended the song.

Why tell them all the old things?
They're buried under the snow.
Whispering grass, don't tell the trees
'Cause the trees don't need to know.

The couple went on humming as they worked, accompanied by the clang of the milk pails and the moos of the cows in their stalls. Tears poured down Emily's face as she stood silently outside the milking parlour. After a while, she crept quietly away, dried her eyes and walked back to the house.

Aunt Barbara and Uncle Fred were already starting on their breakfast.

'Oh, Emily. I didn't know you were up. I'll fetch you something to eat.'

'You sit there, Auntie. I'll put these eggs in the dairy and sort out my breakfast myself. Please don't get up.'

'No, Emily. I'll do it. I want to cook Elly's and Isaac's at the same time. I can see they're on their way across the yard now.'

'Good morning, Uncle. I think the hens are laying better.'

'It's probably the fear of competition they'll have when the new ones arrive and move into their luxury accommodation.' He laughed.

'Oh, Uncle, you are funny! Ah, hello, Elly. Hello, Isaac.'

'Morning everyone!' Elly went over to the sink, followed by Isaac and they washed their hands.

'Fred, we think the milk yield is up a bit and we're not sure why. Perhaps we ought to compare yields morning and evening for a while. What do you think?'

'Sounds like a good idea, Elly.' Fred looked up and smiled at them.

'Never mind about all that now, you two.' Barbara stood over the frying pan. 'I'm going to cook you some fried eggs and fried bread and a rasher of bacon each, so no talk about farming until you've eaten something. Sit down next to Emily. Pour yourselves some tea. Now, did you enjoy the dance last night, Elly and Isaac? You didn't go, did you, Emily?'

'No, Auntie. I wanted to do some practice for the concert but I've been looking forward to finding out if the others had a good time.'

'It was such fun, wasn't it, Isaac?' Elly smiled at him.

'It was fun.' Isaac looked rather sheepishly at Elly who said, 'Oh, there was some nonsense at the start of the evening. One of the local lads heard Isaac's accent and picked on him. "Are you a Jerry?" he asked. "You sound like a Jerry, and we don't have Jerries here." Isaac answered honestly, didn't you, Isaac?'

'Yes. I said, "I am from Germany and I was rescued with the Kindertransport by kind English people." And suddenly, Pip and Hen appeared.'

Barbara, Fred and Emily stopped what they were

doing and hung onto every word of the story as it was unfolding.

'Without being rude,' Elly looked around the table, 'we know that Pip is a tough, wiry little thing but Hen is, well, of a much heavier build, shall we say? She went up to this chap and gripped him by his collar and lifted him off the ground. "And what have you got to say about that?" Hen shook him until his teeth rattled then dropped him. He went down on the floor with his mates watching, and got up and brushed himself off with Hen watching, and then said, "Nothing, no nothing. Welcome to England!" Hen continued to glare at him until he looked at Isaac and said, "Let me buy you a cider." Hen smiled and said, "Good. In fact, we'll all have one." It all ended well, didn't it, Isaac, and nobody got hurt?'

'Oh, good for Hen,' Barbara shouted as she rescued the eggs and bacon from the frying pan and passed the young people their breakfast.

'Oh, yes,' Fred looked serious. 'I wouldn't like to cross her.'

'But that wasn't all the excitement,' Elly said. 'Go on, Isaac. You tell them!'

'The bandleader asked if anyone would like to sing with the band. Elly shouted out that I would.'

'Oh, Elly!' Barbara looked anxious.

'Barbara, you don't know but Isaac has a beautiful

voice. Anyway, people pushed him forward and lifted him onto the stage and, – well, tell them, Isaac.' Elly smiled proudly at him.

'Well I sang "We'll Meet Again." They were supposed to dance to it but they didn't.'

'No, of course, they didn't. They crowded around the stage and listened while Isaac sang it. When he finished there was a short silence and then everyone cheered and clapped. He was wonderful. He made the evening, that's what he did.'

Everyone sat around the breakfast table and looked at Elly and Isaac. It was plain to see what the young Land Girl thought of the young man from Bavaria.

'Well, our lives seem rather dull, Babs, after listening to the events at the dance in South Molton.'

'Talking of South Molton, Fred, I'm going to see your mother and father today. I want to take them a few things and see how they are.'

'That's good, Babs. Tell them I'll be over soon and look at Dad's vegetable garden. You know how proud he is of it.' They all stood up and prepared to get on with the day's work. Fred chuckled to himself.

'As I said, compared with the evening you two had last night at that dance, our lives are quite humdrum, aren't they, Babs? Isaac's little adventure was like something from a James Cagney film.'

Isaac looked confused. He whispered to Elly as they left the kitchen. 'Who is James Cagney, Elly?'

Chapter 39

Alcwyn Evans clambered onto the podium and raised his hands to quieten the members of the orchestra who were tuning their instruments and chatting with one another.

'Ladies and Gentlemen, as you know, we are meeting today for our last rehearsal before our concert next Saturday. Let me remind you that the concert will take place in the Hall which is part of the British Restaurant in Boutport Street. Although it will start at 2.30 pm, I want to remind you to be there at 1.30 pm in order to run through the trickier parts of the pieces which we have added to our repertoire recently. I believe that some of you will be at the Hall before that to set out the chairs for the audience and arrange the chairs and music stands for the orchestra. The piano has been tuned recently and is in position. Robert and Clara, you will be pleased to know that.' Alcwyn smiled at the leader of the orchestra and her brother. 'I would like to thank Michael, our secretary for arranging for us to enjoy tea and cakes with any members of the audience who would like to join us after the performance. I believe you have enlisted supporters to serve the tea, Michael.' Michael raised his hand

and nodded. Another hand went up. It was that of Dr Anna Miller.

'Maestro, as you know we have been supported in the advertising of the concert by our American friends. They will be bringing men to listen to us and have offered to provide some food afterwards; cookies and chocolate cakes.'

'Goodness, that will be a treat, indeed. Thank you, Anna for using your contacts with our allies to our benefit. Talking of benefit, the money from the ticket sales (and by the way, tickets can be bought at the door) will be divided between The British Red Cross and The American Red Cross. I hope you are all in agreement with that.' There were murmurings of approval and Alcwyn continued. 'There is one more thing. Our programme contains some items that our long-standing members will have performed before. We have had little time to prepare for the performance so it was necessary to include some familiar pieces, and I must say a big "Thank you" to our new members for all the practice they have done to be performance ready in such a short time. I have added one more item and you will see it on your stand. I have been lucky to have been loaned the parts from the American Bandleader here in Barnstaple whose band plays their National Anthem, The Star-Spangled Banner, every morning in our town. I think we should play it as a tribute to the young American boys who are living and training here in North Devon. Are you all in agreement?' The members of the orchestra shouted out a firm 'Yes' and some of them clapped. 'I knew you would be proud to include it, and so we will play it at the end of the concert, directly before our own anthem, God Save the King. Now, without further ado, we will get on with our rehearsal. I meant to say that the soloists and the quartet will stay on after our rehearsal to run through their items. Michael has arranged to hire the hall here for an extra hour. Oboe, may we have the A for tuning, please?'

William Taylor took out his music and put it on the stand while Robert sat at the piano and adjusted the height of the piano stool.

'Are you sure that you are up to this, Robert?' William attached his reed and blew a few notes.

'Yes, I'm fine; just a bit tired but I've been looking forward to playing the movement from the Mozart Clarinet Concerto with you. It's a pity that we aren't playing the whole thing really.'

'I think this one movement is enough and it's better for the concert programme to consist of more items that are varied rather than fewer that last too long.'

'Yes, I think you are right, William. And your

other piece is a jazzy one which will please our American friends.' William smiled his agreement and nodded. 'Ready to run through the programme when you are, Robert.'

In the small kitchen leading off the main room in which the orchestra had rehearsed, Emily poured boiling water from the kettle into a brown teapot while Dan took the top off the milk bottle and poured milk into three cups.

'I am rather worried about Robert.' Dan stirred the pot and filled the tea cups. Emily handed one to Anna and took one for herself.

'Yes, I hope he's not overdoing it.' Emily looked at Anna and waited for her comment.

'Music is his life, isn't it?' Anna sipped her tea and smiled at them. 'And it is his sister's life too. She is in the hall, sitting at the back to check the balance. She said her brother is always asking her the same question. "Am I too loud? I don't want to drown the soloist." '

'He's a very sensitive accompanist,' Dan commented. 'He'll be playing for his sister's solos, won't he? I think she is going to play Csárdás by Vittorio Monti. It is very popular. Do you know what else they're performing, Emily?'

'Yes. Salut d' Amour by Elgar,' Emily smiled and added, 'It's so romantic and so English.'

'And very sentimental,' Anna remarked, rather

harshly. 'Anyway, they will just run through their programme and then we will go in and run through the quartet.'

'Poor Robert won't have a break during the whole concert.' Emily took the tea cups and washed them at the sink. 'I'll make him a drink and one for William and Clara when they've finished their practice. It was nice of you to remember the tea and the milk, Dan.' Emily smiled at him and he smiled back at her. She turned to Anna and said conversationally, 'You must be so busy, Anna, with your work at the surgeries in Ilfracombe and Woolacombe, apart what you do at the Infirmary in Barnstaple. You'll be pleased to know that the Land Army girl whose head wound you stitched up is back at work in the farm at West Buckland.'

'That's good.' Anna was busy applying resin on her bow.

'Yes, and you can hardly see where you stitched the wound. It's marvellous.'

'Of course. You will not be able to see any sign of the injury in a few weeks' time.' Anna stood up and pointed to the door. 'Ah, they have finished playing. We can go in now. Perhaps they can make their own tea when they come in here.' She walked out of the room and Emily and Dan followed her.

Chapter 40

'**Auntie, your black** skirt looks good with my new blouse but it is rather too big around the waist.' Emily stood in front of the dressing table mirror and held the waistband while her aunt took a safety pin out of the sewing box.

'Let me put this pin in where I have to move the button. You are slimmer than me, dear, I'm sorry to say.'

'Auntie, you are very slim and I am so grateful to you for lending me your skirt. I should have tried it on before instead of leaving it to the last minute. I don't know where the week has gone. Suddenly, it's Saturday and the day of the concert.'

'Take the skirt off now, dear. It won't take me a minute to move that button. Did you say that Dan will be taking you in his van? I thought the young men from West Buckland School used to take you and bring you back.'

'They did but Dan says that it is easier for him to do that.'

'I can't see how, Emily but I'm sure he likes to drive you around. Now, I'll just finish sewing this button on. You know that we are all coming to the concert, including Isaac and Elly, of course.'

'What about the milking, Auntie?'

'Fred said he will start it later. It won't hurt for once. There. That's done. Let me cut the thread and you can put it on. Dan will be here soon. You said that you have to be at the Hall an hour before the concert starts, didn't you?' Emily put the skirt over her head and fastened the button. She looked in the mirror.

'Perfect, Emily. It could have been made for you. Now pick up your things and go downstairs. I can hear a vehicle coming into the yard.'

'It's Dan, Auntie. He's early.' The two women hurried downstairs and Emily opened the outside door to see Dan standing there with a big smile on his face.

'Hello, Emily. You look lovely. Have you got all your music and your violin?'

'Yes, Dan, I think I have everything.'

Barbara passed Emily her coat and smiled at the handsome young man. 'Emily, it's only April so you may be glad of your coat. Don't you think so, Dan?'

'Hello Barbara. Yes, I do. We can leave it in the car in case Emily needs it on the way home.' Emily hugged her aunt.

'Thank you, Auntie, for your help. We'll see you later.' Barbara waved as Dan drove away, and then went across the yard to find the workers. It was time they came indoors and ate the sandwiches she had prepared. They would have to get washed and changed and smartened up before she allowed them to leave the farm and attend the concert.

Dan parked at the bottom end of Boutport Street and they walked up past the Gaumont Cinema towards the British Restaurant. There were already several cars parked along the road and they went in the side entrance, carrying their instruments and music. Michael White was already marshalling orchestra members and asking them to leave their coats and music cases in a room near the concert hall.

'Please don't bring any unnecessary items onto the concert platform, my friends. We don't want it to look like a Jumble Sale, do we?' Michael smiled encouragingly as the musicians took their seats and prepared for the musical warm-up session that their conductor had requested before the concert. Everyone had arrived in good time and a few of the musicians were craning their necks to see Alcwyn Evans making his way to the front and stepping up with some difficulty onto the podium. Emily thought that he presented a somewhat startling figure. His wild grey hair was sleeked back with what appeared to be half a jar of Brylcreem. His black suit with long tails had seen better days and had a somewhat greyish-green hue about it, but his bow tie and white shirt looked very smart, and Emily could only wonder at how much effort he had put into his appearance, and into the work he had done to prepare for the concert. Yes, he is eccentric, she thought; but she was full of admiration for his enthusiasm and musicianship.

He proceeded to pick out the more difficult sections of some of the concert items and after just over half an hour they stopped practising, left the concert platform and returned to the room at the back of the stage. Dan put his viola in its case and went and sat next to Emily. 'That went well, didn't it, Emily, but I was surprised to see Anna arriving so late. She looked rather flustered. I suppose she had some sort of emergency which delayed her.'

'Yes, that's what she told me. Of course, she doesn't need the extra practice. She is such a good player, but there was something strange that happened. You know that Alcwyn had decided not to take some of the repeats in one or two of the pieces? Well, I accidentally knocked the music off the stand we share just as he was reminding us about that, and telling us what number bar we have to skip to. As I was picking the music up off the floor, I whispered to Anna, "What bar did he say, Anna?" Of course, I knew really but somehow, I felt uncomfortable by her presence. I don't know what it was but she was so tense. Then, suddenly she whispered something to me to tell me what Alcwyn had said.'

'Well, that was helpful, wasn't it, Emily?'

'Yes, but it was what she whispered that was so odd.' Emily looked across the room and saw that Anna was talking to Alcwyn.

'What did she whisper to you?' Emily paused and leant towards Dan to talk into his ear.

'Takt siebzehn.' Dan looked uncertainly at Emily.

'That's German, isn't it? I don't know what to think about that. What did you do?'

'I picked up the music and put it on the stand and pretended that I hadn't heard her. "Bar seventeen" is what she'd said. Dan, we'll talk about it afterwards. I think that Alcwyn is trying to attract everyone's attention.'

'Dear friends, our concerts in past years, before the war were attended by musical enthusiasts but were never sold out, as you might say. However, today may be an exception. Anna has just told me that half of Woolacombe will be in attendance. A lorry load of American soldiers has just arrived and several Jeeps and military vehicles are parking nearby. The Hall is filling up. Play like you've never played before.'

The hearty applause after the final concert item died away and Alcwyn Evans turned to the audience.

'Ladies and Gentlemen, in choosing the musical works for our concert programme, our orchestra's leader Clara Stone and I were very conscious of including composers of different nationalities, including two from Germany. Music and Art know no boundaries and do not follow political differences. However, where there is evil, efforts have to be made to combat it. I would like to dedicate this afternoon's performance to those armies of whatever nationality who are engaged in the fight to protect our nation and those of the free world, and to dedicate it especially to the men who are far from their homes and living and training on our beaches here in North Devon. Please stand while we play our National Anthems.'

The audience rose to its feet while the orchestra played The Star-Spangled Banner and God Save the King. More applause followed together with cheers and whistling from the American soldiers. Alcwyn bowed and left the stage with tears in his eyes. Michael White came forward and raised his hand.

'You are invited to join us in the British Restaurant for tea and refreshments, some of which have been kindly provided by our American friends. Thank you.'

Doreen and Imogen were waving to attract Emily's attention. They had secured a large table in the British Restaurant and had been joined by Elly and Isaac, and Hen and Pip. Imogen's parents, Christopher and Louise were sitting with Doreen's mother and father, Tom and Carol, and their daughter, Christine at a table nearby. Emily and Dan, together with Barbara and Fred all sat at Doreen's table.

'We've loaded these plates with food for all of us and the tea pot will be coming around in a minute,' Imogen looked at the two musicians.

'Doreen is keeping a place for Oliver but Dylan didn't come today.' She looked disappointed but smiled and said, 'Well done, you two. We really enjoyed the concert, didn't we?' There were murmurings of approval and Doreen said, 'And at the end, when you played the national anthems, I couldn't stop crying. Oh, look! Here comes Oliver.' The handsome American soldier gave Doreen a hug and sat down next to her. He smiled at everyone and said, 'Great concert, wasn't it? You all worked real hard to get that ready.' Suddenly, Anna appeared carrying a small plate of food and a cup of tea.

'Emily, is there room for me, next to you?' Emily looked up and said, 'Of course, Anna. We can squeeze up a bit, can't we, Dan?' Without waiting for a reply, Anna put down her plate and cup and saucer on the table and sat on the bench between Emily and Dan. Emily introduced Anna to everyone and after a slight lull in the conversation Dan asked, 'Were you pleased with how the concert went, Anna?'

'Yes, I think it all went better than I had expected.' She smiled her captivating smile at everyone.

'Emily, you used to teach music, didn't you? Do you plan to go back to teaching?'

'Yes, I taught class music and French.' The others were chatting amongst themselves but Isaac was sitting very still and watching Anna out of the corner of his eye.

'Oh, I thought you taught German.' Emily took a bite from her cookie, swallowed and said, 'No. I can't speak a word of it.' Isaac sat motionless as Anna looked up at him and asked, 'Did you enjoy the concert?' He cleared his throat nervously.

'I did, especially the music by the English composers.' He looked hard at her and waited for her reply.

'Yes. They know how to write a good tune.' Emily thought that somehow, Anna made it sound like an insult. Perhaps she was just being oversensitive but couldn't quite understand why she had lied to Anna about not speaking German.

'Oh, good. Here comes the tea,' Doreen said as a

woman carrying a huge teapot filled their cups and another woman poured milk from a large jug.

'You aren't British, are you?' Anna took a sip from her tea cup and smiled at Isaac.

'No, I'm German.' He offered no further information until Anna asked how he came to be in England.

'I was rescued by the Kindertransport.'

'You were very lucky.' Anna looked closely at the young man who stared back at her unflinchingly.

'Yes, I was but my family were not so lucky. I don't know what happened to them, you see.' He turned away from her and spoke to Elly who was sitting next to him.

'When we have won the war, I would like to go to the seaside, Elly.'

'Yes. there are lovely beaches around here but I like my town on the South Coast. Lots of people come there for holidays.'

Emily swallowed the last of her tea and turned to Anna.

'Where did you work before you came to North Devon, Anna?'

'I worked on the South Coast, in various hospitals.'

Elly looked across the table and said, 'Oh, perhaps you know my area, then. Where were you living when you were there?' There was a pause while Anna swallowed the last of her tea.

'Where do you come from?' Anna looked enquiringly at Elly.

'Eastbourne is my home town.'

'Ah, I was mostly in Brighton and the surrounding area.'

'We're very proud of our pier in Eastbourne, although they have chopped a piece out of it to deter the enemy from attempting to land on it and attack the town.'

'The south coast towns have wonderful piers, haven't they?' Anna looked confidently at Elly. 'The one at Brighton is also very impressive.'

'That's true.' Elly replied, smiling. Anna stood up and picked up her crockery.

'I'll return this to the hatch and be on my way. I have some paperwork to attend to this evening.' She smiled at everyone and walked away.

'That was interesting,' Elly remarked.

'Yes, I have to agree with you, Elly but perhaps for a different reason.' Emily looked at Dan and raised her eyebrows.

'What was interesting, Elly?' Dan asked.

'Well, there is one pier in Eastbourne but there are two in Brighton.'

The friends sat in silence for a while then Dan turned to Emily and asked, 'Emily, why did you tell Anna that you don't speak a word of German?'

'I don't know at the moment, but perhaps I'll find out later.' She looked across at Isaac.

'Are you all right, Isaac? You look pale. Anna can be rather forceful in her manner. I hope she didn't upset you.'

'Her English is perfect isn't it?' Isaac looked unsmilingly at Emily. 'But she doesn't fool me!'

Chapter 41

'It's a pity that your little group of friends didn't get together today at the farm in Mortehoe, Emily.' Barbara laid out the food for tea on the kitchen table. 'We were going to use the best room over Easter but it is quite cold in there and warmer here in the kitchen.'

'That's fine, Auntie. Where's Uncle Fred?'

'He's lying on the bed upstairs having what he likes to call "forty winks". I was just saying, I'm sorry that the picnic you had planned with your friends was cancelled, dear.'

'Yes. Imogen explained why just before we left the British Restaurant on Saturday, after the concert. She thought it would be better to put it off until some time in May. It can be very cold and windy up at Higher Morte Farm. It's not far from the cliffs and the sea. They'd had quite a lot of rain recently and the ground is very muddy. We're going to meet next Friday in Barnstaple and work out another date for our picnic.' Emily looked at her aunt who was standing staring at the kettle while steam was shooting out of it.

'Auntie, the kettle is boiling. Are you all right?'

'Yes, just a bit distracted, Emily. Oh, here come

Elly and Isaac, back from their walk. It's nice to do something that gets them away from farming. Hello, you two. Tea's ready. How was your walk?'

'We enjoyed it, but it's starting to rain quite hard and it's much colder.'

'Rain, you said?' Fred Baxter walked into the kitchen and sat at his usual place at the table. 'I'm not sorry. We need some rain for the spuds and the veg we've put in the ground.' He sighed and looked at his wife.

'I suddenly feel my age, Babs. Have you told them?'

'Oh, don't be so dramatic, Fred. It's as it should be. It's the order of things. It's life!' She put the teapot down on the table and looked at the young people seated around it.

'You know we went to see Fred's parents in South Molton this morning? Well Helen and her husband Donald surprised us by turning up there too. They told us that we're going to be grandparents.' There were gasps and shouts of congratulations while Fred stood up and left the room. He returned immediately with a bottle of sherry.

'Babs, this calls for something stronger than tea. Where are the glasses?' Sherry was poured for everyone and Emily picked up her glass and stood up.

'Isn't it wonderful to hear some good news? I

think we should raise our glasses to toast Helen and Donald and the soon to be grandparents and great grandparents.' Everyone stood up as Emily said proudly, 'The family and the new baby.' Everyone repeated the toast, drank from their glasses, and sat down. Barbara smiled.

'I'll be going in town next Friday, Emily. I want to buy some baby wool and a knitting pattern. Darning socks will have to take a back seat now. Perhaps we could go together.' She paused. 'You can drive, if you like.'

'That's kind of you, Auntie. I'll look forward to that.' Emily looked around the table.

'We have some news but nothing as exciting as what we've just heard. The new henhouse is finished and we are waiting to find out if you want to buy some more hens to occupy it, Uncle.'

'And what sort, Fred? I haven't had any experience with poultry so it's your choice,' Elly added.

'I'll do some research. There are several articles in recent copies of Farmers Weekly, and I think I'll go in the market in Barnstaple next Friday and chat to some farmers I know who keep poultry on a bigger scale than we do.'

'Perhaps you could see them in the pub, Fred.' Barbara winked at Elly.

'Good idea, Babs. It's amazing what you can learn in The Three Tuns.' They all laughed and

Isaac looked at Elly enigmatically.

'Elly and I have been checking the milk yield. We have discovered something very interesting. You tell them, Elly.'

'Well, Isaac has been more involved in this than I have but we have measured and compared the milk yield over the past couple of weeks. I know that two weeks is not a long time but what we have discovered is particularly interesting. Isaac often sings while we are milking and we think that the cows enjoy that. The milk yield is greater on the days he sings than on the days he doesn't sing. We can show you the figures, Fred.'

'Isaac has a lovely voice and you sing well too, Elly,' Emily remarked. 'I stood outside the milking parlour one morning and heard you both. It was beautiful.' They looked at Fred who was sitting still and apparently lost for words.

'You should write an article about that, Elly, and send it to Farmers Weekly. It is very interesting, isn't it, Fred?' Barbara looked at her husband.

'Yes, it is. I am intrigued. Of course, the cows must be very cultured to appreciate your singing, Isaac. Is there a song they like especially?'

'Yes, they seem to enjoy German Lieder. "The Trout" by Schubert is a particular favourite.'

Everyone burst out laughing and Fred said, 'Who's for another sherry?'

Chapter 42

'Emily, drive into Hopgoods Garage and park by the petrol pump. I need to use some of my coupons for this month, then I'm going to leave the car there to get the radiator checked. You drove very well, didn't she, Babs?'

'Yes, you did, Emily. You can talk now, dear.'

'Oh, yes. Sorry but I can't talk and drive at the same time; not yet, anyway.' A good-looking man came towards them and smiled as Emily stopped alongside the petrol pump.

'Petrol sir?' Everyone got out and Fred handed over the coupons he wanted to use.

'Yes, please, and then I'm going to drive the car around the back to your repair shop. I telephoned yesterday to discuss the problem.'

The man nodded, filled the tank and took the coupons and payment. Emily and Barbara checked that they had their bags and shopping basket and Emily looked at the man and said, 'Excuse me, but are you Jack Partridge?'

'Yes, I am but I don't know you, young lady.' Barbara smiled at him.

'But we know your wife. She asked us to visit her some while back and was very kind.'

'Oh, you are the people from the farm at West Buckland, not far from our friends' smallholding at Sunnybank. Marj told me all about you.' He turned to Emily and looked at her closely. 'How are you?'

'I am much better, thank you.'

'Look, let me drive the car around to the workshop for you, and you can get on into town. I'll tell Marj I've seen you. She will be so pleased.'

'That's very helpful. Thank you, Jack.' Fred turned to the two women. 'Have you got all your bags and bits, girls? We'll meet back here around four o'clock.' With a wave of their hands and shouts of 'Goodbye' Fred, Barbara and Emily walked along Taw Vale towards the town. After leaving her aunt to hunt down baby wool and her uncle to find friends who knew more about chickens than he did, Emily called at the library to look for books that Doreen would enjoy. They hadn't discussed Doreen's progress with her reading recently. There were so many other things going on and Emily guessed that Doreen was seeing as much of Oliver as she could. After all, no-one knew how long the American soldiers would be training in the area and when and where they would be going. She spent over an hour in the little library then decided to walk along the High Street to the bakery.

Being Friday, it was busy in the town and Emily went into the Pannier Market on her way to see what was being sold. With the strict rules of rationing, much of the goods on sale were homemade. There were knitted cardigans, pullovers and socks and children's clothes of every sort, much of it remade from a former life in accordance with the Government's advice to 'Make Do and Mend.' One stall she came upon had cooked brawn displayed in every shape and size. Of course, offal wasn't rationed so people could make chitterlings from pigs' intestines and brawn from a pig's head to name but a few things that Emily couldn't bring herself to eat. With a guilty shudder she left the market and continued on her way past Banburys to the bakery at the end of the street. Doreen was busy serving a small queue of customers and waved at her through the window. Emily pointed to her wrist watch and raised her eyebrows questioningly. Doreen beckoned her inside.

'I finish today at twelve o'clock, Emily, and I'm not working this afternoon. I could meet you somewhere.'

'I'm meeting Imogen at The British Restaurant at twelve thirty and will keep a place for you, if you like?'

'That will be perfect. See you then.'

Emily decided to walk back down the High Street and peep in at The Three Tuns to see if her uncle was there. There were several men hanging around outside and lots of chatter and laughter coming from inside. She squeezed through the doorway and immediately spotted her uncle with a beer in his hand taking to a group of farmers, turned out in their best clothes for Market Day. There was a distinct smell of moth balls mixed with the usual smell of tobacco and beer.

'Red Island crossed with Light Sussex, you say?' Uncle Fred had put down his beer on a table and was writing the information on a scrap of paper. 'The few hens we have were hand-me-downs from when my parents were running the farm, or anyway, descendants of them. I've no idea what they are. Goodness knows what crossed with goodness knows who!' Raucous laughter broke out and Emily slipped away and headed for the British Restaurant. It was only twelve fifteen but Imogen was sitting at a table in the corner together with Alex who was eating a large bun.

'Imogen, Alex, hello. I thought I'd be too early.' Emily sat down next to Alex who looked up and said, 'I'm not at school. I'm too ill to go to school today.' He did a little cough and took a large bite out of his bun.

'Hello, Emily. Sorry that I have this appendage with me. Mum wanted me to take him to buy some shoes. He keeps growing out of everything, you see. As you know, I have a few days off from work and wanted to catch up with you. Will Doreen be coming?'

'Yes, she'll be here in ten minutes or so. I've just seen her.' Emily turned to Alex who had finished his bun and was drinking a glass of squash. 'I'm sorry you're not well, Alex.' He coughed again and smiled.

'Emily, he and his gang went down to the beach last evening and were climbing over the rocks. It was near where there's a pool where they can learn to swim. Of course, Alex slipped and fell in, didn't you, Alex? He came home cold and soaked and then coughed all night and kept us awake.'

'Weren't the Americans training on the beach, Alex?' Emily asked.

'No. They'd finished their practice so we could go and do ours.' His sister sighed. 'Oh, look. Here comes Doreen. Let's order something to eat.'

They all ordered egg on toast followed by the restaurant's speciality, syrup pudding and custard. While they were waiting for the pudding to arrive, Alex went off to find the lavatory.

'Alex,' his sister shouted.

'I know,' he replied. 'Don't forget to wash your hands!'

'Now we have a few minutes to catch up, I want to apologise for cancelling the picnic we'd planned. The weather wasn't good enough anyway, was it?'

'No. We want a good day for it. Your birthday's in May isn't it, Immy?'

'Yes, Doreen. It's May 21st. It's a Sunday this year.'

'That would be perfect,' Emily said. 'We could make it a party for you, if your parents agree, Imogen.'

'I'd love that, and it will be much warmer. Hopefully Dad will have cleared a lot of the farm work by then. He's going to have a new worker soon, who specialises in sheep and shearing. He's from Wales and is called Declan.'

Imogen leaned forward and whispered, 'I should tell you something before Alex comes back. You know that my brother lives in another world much of the time? And you know that he had a puppy for his birthday? Well when we got back from the concert, he couldn't find the little dog. It's called Bullet. Yes, I know. It's not a name I would have chosen. I expect you know that my Mum loves animals but won't have them indoors. Bullet has his kennel in the yard next to the kennel that is Sam's, Dad's sheepdog. I don't think that the puppy had been fastened properly to his lead in the kennel. There was no sign of him. We looked everywhere around the farm and Alex went beyond our farm buildings and fields up onto the grazing land where the sheep are. He'd been gone over an hour and not found the dog. When he came back, he was very quiet. He came into the kitchen and sat at the table and shook his head when mum offered him something to eat. We all tried to reassure him that the puppy would find his own way back. Alex looked so serious and said that he thought we were right, but that was not what was bothering him. He said he'd called out the dog's name until he got near the cottage where Anna lives, then for some reason, he approached it quietly until he reached the front door. Her car was parked nearby and he walked to the window at the front and bent down so he couldn't be seen from inside, and listened. He said he had intended to knock at the door to ask Anna if she had seen the puppy but something stopped him and he decided that he didn't want her to know that he was there. He crouched under the window outside and said he could faintly hear her voice every now and then, with pauses in between what she said. He was tempted to look in the window but was afraid of being seen, so after a while he slipped quietly away and came home. It was unlike him but he hardly said a word for a while and didn't eat his supper.'

'He must have been worried about not finding his puppy,' Doreen remarked.

'Well, on that issue, when Dad went outside to feed Sam, he found Bullet asleep with Sam, in his kennel. We were all so relieved and thought that Alex would brighten up but he just said, "Oh good, but I don't think she was speaking English."' Emily frowned and looked at her friends. Suddenly, Alex returned at the same time as four plates of syrup pudding and custard were placed on the table.

'How many boys are in your Gang, Alex?' Emily asked, as he sat down and picked up his spoon.

'All the ones of my age who are in the Scouts,' he answered. 'We need more really now that the Jerries have landed on Lundy Island,' he said, taking a mouthful of his pudding.

'I didn't know they had done that,' Doreen looked questioningly at him.

'Oh, yes,' he replied, 'but it's not common knowledge, you see.'

Doreen and Emily looked at Imogen who closed her eyes and shook her head.

Chapter 43

Barbara picked up her knitting bag and sat on the sofa.

'I keep thinking back to your concert, Emily. We did enjoy it. I can't get some of the tunes out of my head. It was nearly two weeks ago. When will you have the next orchestra practice?'

'Not for some time, I think. There was a lot of work to do and everyone needs a break, especially Alcwyn.'

'You won't be seeing Dan for a while then, Emily?'

'Actually, he's asked me if I would like to see his veterinary practice room and his house in South Molton.'

'That will be interesting, dear. Didn't you say he is hoping to engage another vet in the practice?'

'Yes. He has received several applications and will be interviewing some candidates soon.'

'Emily, stop drying the rest of the dishes and come over here and sit down by me. I wondered if you would like to go and visit Fred's parents in South Molton. You met them years ago but perhaps you would have been too young to remember that. We told them all about you and Elly and Isaac, and they have asked if you three would like to visit them for tea one day soon. Or you could call on them in the morning at about eleven, if it's easier.' Barbara stopped knitting and counted her stitches.

'That would be lovely, Auntie.'

'One of you can drive you all there and I'll give you some things to take to them.'

'They must be very excited about the new baby. I see you are getting on with your knitting.'

'Yes. I shall finish this little matinée jacket soon and will need some more wool. I couldn't decide whether to buy blue or pink yarn so I chose yellow.'

The kitchen door opened and Elly and Isaac entered.

'The shearing is going along well but Fred's back isn't too good. It's all that bending. We've come to make him some tea,' Elly said while Isaac filled the kettle and put it back on the hotplate.

'I think I could learn to shear,' Isaac said. 'I read about it in one of the farming magazines but you have to make sure the clippers are really sharp and not make too many clips with them.'

'Isaac's right. I can manage to do it for a while although I'm not very quick at it, but it is a strain on the back, and unless you are very proficient there needs to be two of you to each sheep, with one holding the animal still while the other person does the clipping. We won't leave Fred shearing for long. Here's a large mug, Isaac, for when that kettle has boiled. Did I tell you that Isaac can drive well now? He wants to learn to drive the tractor next, don't you Isaac?' She smiled encouragingly at him.

'Yes, I would like that. I want to help as much as I can on the farm. I love the work, you see.'

'The trouble is that farm work is every day and in all weathers,' Barbara remarked, looking up at the young man. 'But you have done wonderfully well, Isaac, and along with Elly and Emily you have come to our rescue.' She smiled and put her knitting away. 'Tell Fred that I'll be out in a moment to see how he's getting on. He may have to rest his back for a while.' Elly and Isaac left the kitchen with a large mug of tea and a coconut cake. The telephone rang and Barbara answered it. 'It's Doreen, Emily. Why don't you ask her if she would like to come out here to see you and look around the farm?' Barbara handed the receiver to her niece.

'Hello Doreen. How are you? Good. Auntie Barbara has asked if you would like to come out here to see us all at the farm? A Sunday would be your best day, you say? Just a minute. Oh, Auntie Barbara is nodding. Sunday week? Auntie is nodding again. And you're going to drive here. But you can't come until after dinner because your Dad needs the car in the morning. Yes, two thirty would be fine. Yes, you turn off after the village. I'll draw a map and send it to you. See you Sunday week, Doreen. Bye.'

'I thought Doreen sounded worried, Auntie. I wonder if she is seeing Oliver as often as she'd like.'

'It isn't easy for young couples when one is in the services, especially when they can't plan a future together,' Barbara said.

Suddenly, the kitchen door was flung open and Isaac entered, flushed and breathless, followed by Elly and Fred.

'I've done it! I've shorned one, sheared one; anyway, I've cut her coat off.' Isaac shouted, triumphantly.

'And it was very good for a first effort, wasn't it, Fred?' Elly asked proudly.

'Yes, the animal looked slightly confused but I think Isaac did very well. Are you going back out there to practise on some more unsuspecting creatures, Isaac?' Fred went and sat on the sofa.

'Yes. Do you think we can shear another six or so before dinner, Elly?'

'I think so, Isaac, but I want to sharpen the cutters first.'

As the sheep shearers left the room, Fred smiled at Barbara and Emily, and picked up the latest copy of The North Devon Journal.

'Is there a cup of tea going spare, Babs? This shearing is back-breaking work.'

Chapter 44

Doreen drove carefully into the farmyard, sending chickens scuttling in all directions, and parked alongside the Austin Seven.

'Well done, Doreen! You found us and drove here yourself.' Emily ran forward to greet her friend.

'Yes. I was so nervous but Dad said that I would be able to manage it.'

'Come inside. My aunt and uncle have gone to see their daughter and son-in-law on Exmoor, and Elly and Isaac have gone for a walk so we have the place to ourselves. Come into the kitchen and I'll make us a cup of tea. It seems a long time since we've seen each other.' The two friends sat at the kitchen table and Emily looked at Doreen.

'You sounded rather tired when you spoke on the telephone a while back, Doreen. Is everything all right?'

'Yes and no. Oliver and I haven't seen as much of each other recently. He's had very little time off but writes to me and I write back, but it's not the same as seeing each other. How are you, Emily? I noticed when we were having tea after the concert one of the orchestra players was paying you a lot of attention.' Emily poured tea for her friend and herself.

'He's called Dan. You may have seen him at that concert at the Woolacombe Bay Hotel; the one when William Taylor played the clarinet. We have seen a lot of each other playing in the orchestra and the quartet, and he comes out to the farm quite a lot to check on the animals.'

'Does he?' Doreen looked at her friend and raised her eyebrows.

'He's a vet, you see, Doreen.'

'Of course. That would explain it.' There was a pause and Doreen said, 'He's very nice, isn't he?'

'Yes, he is and we get on well together. He has a sad history. His fiancée died in one of those bombing raids in Exeter. It was just before they were to marry.'

'Oh, that's terrible, Emily. I don't know what to say.' Doreen shook her head. 'I suppose you and he have both had to deal with tragedies.'

'Yes. It makes us more aware of all the suffering and sadness in the world; things over which we have no control.' There was silence for a moment, then Emily asked, 'But Doreen, tell me how you are getting along with your reading.'

'Oh, that! Well, I've been reading some classics and finding out about American past presidents. Not that I can tell you much about British prime ministers, but I wanted to know more about the American system, so sometimes I go into the library and look up things on American history.'

'Oh, my goodness, Doreen. You're way ahead of me. Oliver must be very impressed with you.'

'He says that he'll have to brush up on his knowledge of American politics to keep up with me.' They both laughed.

'Have another cup of tea, Doreen. By the way, how are things at your cousin's farm?'

'Well, Immy came into town recently and we had a chat in my dinner break. Her dad, Christopher is very pleased with the man who came from Wales to help on the farm. He's called Declan and is an expert sheep shearer, one of those who enters competitions; you know, who can shear the most sheep in the shortest time, sort of thing. It's made all the difference to her dad. After all, their farm is mainly sheep, that's why Christopher had his horse, Lady. He used to ride out over the grazing land to check the sheep. Now that he suffers with his back he can't do that. That's why Anna usually exercises the horse at weekends. Immy says that her Dad wants one of those lightweight motor bikes. He could ride that around to check the sheep. Apparently, he's talking it over with Declan.'

'Does Declan live on the farm?'

'No, he has an aunt who lives in Ilfracombe and he lodges there and drives to the farm in his own car if he has enough petrol coupons. On other days he takes the bus.'

'That sounds ideal. And did Imogen say anything about her brother? He was driving her mad the last time we saw her.'

'As a matter of fact, she did. It's most odd. Even Immy can't work it out. It seems that Alex has been unusually quiet recently. He spends a lot of time with one of his friends, not just on the beach but roaming all over their farmland and writing notes in a book. He keeps the book hidden somewhere and never lets anyone see it. Recently he told his sister that he was worried about something and asked her if she could explain it to him.'

'He is an unusual boy, isn't he, Doreen?'

'Immy told me about his latest adventure. She doesn't know what to think about it. One day last week after school, Alex took the duplicate key to the cottage. His father keeps the key on the hook in the kitchen. When the previous tenants rented the cottage, Christopher had an extra key made in case they lost their key, or in case there was an emergency of any sort. It seems that Alex and his friend Brian intended to break into Anna's home, using the key kept at the farm.'

'How did they know that she wouldn't be there?'

'Alex keeps records of the times she comes and goes, and of when he sees anyone else drive through the farm in the direction of the cottage.

Apparently, he's been doing that for weeks. Well, Alex had told his sister that he knew that Anna wouldn't be at home at that particular time and he and Brian set off to let themselves into the cottage and look around.'

'Oh, no. Surely, Anna would know if someone had been in the cottage?'

'Alex had thought of everything and they had planned to take off their shoes once they had entered through the front door.'

'I wonder what they were expecting to find?'

'Whatever it was they didn't find anything because they couldn't get in. The key didn't open the front door because the lock had been changed so the boys came away with no more knowledge than when they had arrived there. Alex was very confused by it and told his sister what they had done. He asked her if their dad had changed the lock. She said that she thought he must have done, but she could see that Alex was not convinced.'

'Did Immy speak to her father about it?'

'No, because she didn't want to get her brother into trouble. She told Alex not to go near the cottage in future.'

'And what did he say, Doreen?'

'He said he didn't understand why he should keep away from it when someone else was sneaking about the place.'

'Whatever did he mean by that?'

'Immy said that Alex had seen narrow tyre tracks in the area and had even drawn a picture of them in his book. He said that he made sure to scuff the tyre tracks out afterwards.'

'A proper little Sherlock Holmes, isn't he?'

'It's a lot of responsibility for Immy. She doesn't know if she should say anything to her father or just keep quiet about it.'

'Poor thing! By the way, did she say anything about her birthday party? Now that we're on the last day of April, there are only three weeks until May 21st.'

'Yes, it will be a picnic and we can help by bringing food. We can't expect her mum Louise to provide everything. I think Immy is intending to invite some of the American boys, including Dylan. There's still no news of his progress, by the way.'

'We must hope he will be well enough to come to the party. It will mean so much to Immy.' Emily stood up and carried the tea cups to the sink. 'Shall I show you around the farm, Doreen? Look, the sun is just coming out.'

Chapter 45

'**Thank you for** driving me back to the farm, Dan.'

'It's a good excuse for me to have a look at the chicken coop and run you built with Elly and Isaac. Has Fred decided on the breed of chicken he wants to fill it with?'

'I'm not telling you, Dan. I want it to be a surprise.' Emily looked teasingly at Dan as he turned the car into East Street.

'Oh, I see. Well, there is something you can tell me. What do you think of my house in South Molton and the consultation room?'

'I like the house. It is spacious and yet cosy, and it is close to the centre of the town. The little cottage next to the house is perfect for your veterinary practice, and the downstairs rooms make good consultation and practice rooms. You must have done a lot of work on it, Dan. Have you found an assistant yet?'

'Yes, and he'll start in about four weeks' time. He's just finishing his course, is full of enthusiasm and new ideas, and comes from North Molton, so knows the area well. He can live with his parents and I can keep a room for him at the house, for when he might need it. Veterinary work often involves emergencies and irregular hours.'

'That's wonderful, Dan, and how is your housekeeper working out?'

'She's a gem but a bit strict with me, and I have a part-time secretary starting soon. Of course, the Bank owns me now and it'll take some years to get my finances under control but – ' He paused and slowed the car.

'But, it'll be worth it, Dan.'

'Emily, do you mind if I drive past Shallowford and up to West Buckland that way?'

'No, it is so pretty, and probably quicker.'

'We must take a picnic there one day; down by the river. Would you like to do that, Emily?'

'Yes, that would be lovely, but we must do it some time in May. I'll have to go home to my family in London soon. And in September, I hope to start back at school.' Dan slowed the car and there was silence for a while.

'Go home? But you love it here, don't you, Em?'

'Yes, of course I do but it's not that. My mother could do with some help. She and Dad work at the hospital and my brother works strange hours with the Fire Brigade. I think she's worn out. Her parents are selling their grocery business and retiring, so there will be lots to do to help them through that. I feel I'm not much use to anyone at the moment.'

'You're a lot of use to me, Emily, but I mustn't

be selfish.' He changed gear as he drove up through the Deer Park. 'Will you come back to see your aunt and uncle here?'

'I'll come back as often as I can.' She turned her head and looked at him as he drove through East Buckland.

'Good! That's good.' He drove towards West Buckland and turned off towards the farm. 'It's a lovely area isn't it, and you know so many people here, Emily. And everybody likes you.'

'I don't know about that, Dan,' Emily looked at him.

'Well I do. I like you a lot.' There was silence as he drove the car through the entrance to the farmyard scattering ginger chickens in all directions.

'Oh!' Dan shouted. 'Gingernut Rangers! So, Fred's bought Gingernut Rangers. Good choice!' He parked the car and they both got out.

'I thought you'd approve. They're so friendly.' Emily smiled as a curious hen came up to inspect them. At the same time, her uncle came out of the milking parlour and was immediately followed by a hen.

'Hello, you two. Babs has made a cup of tea and is bringing it out here. It's dried up nicely so we can sit on the seat near the door, if you want to join us.'

'Thank you, Uncle. We will.' The three of them sat at the old wooden table, and the hen who'd followed Fred jumped up on his lap and snuggled in for a cuddle.

'Isn't she lovely, Uncle? Have you named her yet?'

'Yes, she's called Ruby.'

'Of course, what else? Gingernut Rangers are Rhode Island Reds crossed with Light Sussex,' Dan explained. 'But I expect you both already knew that. Are they using the new hen coop, Fred?'

'Yes, and they're allowed to forage wherever they like but Babs tries to stop them from coming indoors. She says she thinks they're a bit too friendly and they needn't think they own the place.'

'The old hens are hardly laying much now and there are only a few of them left,' Emily explained. 'They still use their old coop but we keep them in their own run rather than mix them in with the others.'

'Oh, hello, you two.' Barbara appeared with the tea tray. 'I thought I heard the car. Have you approved of Dan's consultation room, Emily?' She set down the tray and poured the tea.

'It's so professional looking, Auntie, and Dan will have an assistant starting soon.'

'What a lot is happening. That's very good, Dan. It's all change here too. We are going to be grandparents soon.'

'Congratulations, Barbara and Fred,' Dan smiled.

'That's very exciting news.'

'We think so but Fred keeps on about how it makes him feel old to be a grandfather.' She looked at her husband and shook her head. They all chatted happily with one another, and then Barbara said, 'Now, Fred, we'll go in the kitchen and leave these young people to talk. Elly and Isaac will be back soon and it'll be time for milking.'

'I might just have forty winks, then, Babs.'

'Steady, Fred!' She stood up and gathered the mugs and placed them on the tray. 'You'll be turning into an old man, if you're not careful.' They both walked away, smiling.

'Dan, before I forget, Doreen's cousin Imogen has invited us to her birthday party on May 21st at their farm near Mortehoe. Can you come? Some of our musical friends will be there and some of the Americans too. We're all supplying food as it's going to be a picnic. Imogen is expecting us around three o'clock. We have to hope for good weather.'

'That sounds lovely, Emily. I don't go to many social events apart from things connected with the orchestra. I could come and collect you and bring you home afterwards.'

'That's so kind of you, Dan. Could I ask you to take Elly and Isaac with us? Imogen has invited them, which is nice because they don't go anywhere much.'

'Of course, Emily. The invitations include the members of the quartet, I imagine?'

'Oh yes, and Clara too. But I don't know about Anna. She usually exercises Lady on Sunday afternoons.'

'Lady?'

'That's the horse on the farm that belongs to Imogen's father, Christopher. He doesn't ride her anymore so Anna rides her at weekends. You know that she rents the cottage about half a mile away from the farm?'

'Oh, yes. That's quite convenient for her with the general practice work she does at Ilfracombe and Woolacombe.' Dan paused.

'I don't know if Robert will come to the picnic. He's not very well. William visits him often and they play clarinet and piano repertoire, but William telephoned me and said that Robert is rather depressed and nervy. He asked me if I knew any possible reason why Robert is feeling so down. He had an appointment with a doctor in Ilfracombe but cancelled it when he discovered that the doctor he was to see was Anna. I have telephoned Robert and he said that he can't talk about it, but I have said he could telephone me at any time, if he feels he needs to talk to someone. Apparently, William is a good listener.'

'It's strange, isn't it, Dan? Isaac won't talk about

her. He said that she doesn't fool him, whatever that means.'

'Well, Emily, we can't get on with everyone, can we?'

'No. But Imogen's brother Alex spies on Anna at their farm and keeps a record of her comings and goings. Perhaps we'll find out more when we go there on Imogen's birthday.'

'Do you know how old Imogen will be, Emily?'

'I heard from Doreen that she will be twenty-one but has asked for no presents. She just wants her friends to be there.'

'And when will you be twenty-one, Emily?' Dan smiled.

'Dan, you know very well that I've passed that milestone! Stop teasing me!' He leaned forward and kissed her on the cheek.

Chapter 46

Dan turned the car into the farmyard of Higher Morte Farm and drew up alongside a Jeep. There were several other vehicles parked nearby although it wasn't quite three o'clock. Emily and Dan, Elly and Isaac took out a ground sheet and a couple of cushions, together with the all-important picnic basket, and walked to the back of the farmhouse from where they could hear the laughter coming.

'Happy birthday, Imogen!' Emily and Dan greeted her and the newcomers spread out their ground sheet on the lightly mown grass and sat down next to the birthday girl.

'Thank you. Aren't we lucky to have a beautiful May day for our picnic? May is my favourite month of the year.' Imogen looked around and smiled at everyone.

'I guess that's because it's your birthday month,' Oliver said.

'No, it's because of all the blossom and green leaves on the trees. It's like nature has woken up and is smiling at everyone.'

'Oh, Immy, that is so poetic,' Doreen remarked. She stood up. 'I can hear some more cars arriving.

I'll go and tell them where we are.'

'I'll come too, Doreen.' Oliver followed her as Christopher and Louise came from the farmhouse carrying a wooden table.

'I know you're planning to go for a walk before you have your picnic, Imogen,' her mother said, 'but we'll set up a few small tables and some chairs out here for when you get back. I'll bring the food out later and if anyone brings any food, I'll cover it up and put it in on a table in the shade.' Isaac jumped up and followed Louise back to the house, offering help.

'You couldn't have asked for a better day, Immy, and it's going to stay fine for another day or so, I think.' Her father waved at the group and turned to see another dozen or so people arriving, all laughing and chatting with one another.

'Thank you, Dad, for bringing out some chairs but most of us can sit on the grass. My friends have brought rugs and things,' Imogen shouted, as one of the Americans offered to help and followed Christopher into the house. She looked around at the latest arrivals, hoping to see Dylan amongst them. Elly leaned towards Imogen and whispered in her ear, 'I'm sure he'll come. Just you see.'

'Time for presents,' Doreen shouted, as she returned with more partygoers, carrying rugs and food.

'Doreen, you know that I sent a message asking for no presents?' Imogen looked at her cousin.

'Well, Immy, it looks like people have ignored it,' Doreen answered. Imogen looked around at the increasingly large circle of friends seated on the grass, and addressed them. 'I think most of you know each other but please introduce yourselves to one another. There are some of my nursing friends here. Thank you all for coming.'

There was the sound of another vehicle drawing up. Imogen stopped talking and looked expectantly at the entrance to the lawned area. There was silence as everyone waited to find out the identity of the late arrival. It was Dylan, walking with a stick and accompanied by Carter. Imogen's face lit up and Oliver rushed to fetch two chairs which he placed near Imogen. Everyone shouted their welcomes to the two Americans, and clapping broke out to see the injured man's recovery. Birthday gifts were given to Imogen and gasps and applause were emitted as the American soldiers handed over pairs of black silk stockings, fruit and chocolate to the lucky twenty-one-year-old, who immediately passed the chocolate bars around and set aside three small bars for her mother, father and brother.

'Thank you so much everyone for coming and for these wonderful presents,' Imogen shouted, and waved her hands to gain attention from the chattering crowd. 'Those of you who would like to take a walk before our picnic, leave when you like. I don't think you will get lost but if you go near the cliffs, do be careful as the ground is steep and can be unstable. Please be back here for our picnic by four o'clock or all the food will have been eaten. Mum has laid out drinks and glasses in the barn behind you, should anyone need a drink. Some of it is alcoholic!'

Cheers and clapping rang out as most of the quests started walking in the direction away from the road, while some went into the barn for a drink. Imogen sat down next to Dylan as Carter wandered off with some of his friends. Emily and Dan joined Imogen, and Dan asked Dylan how his recovery was progressing.

'It's been slow and made life boring, and kept me out of action. It's sure good to come to Imogen's party.'

'I'm sorry about your injury, Dylan,' Emily said.

'It's stopped him dancing too, Emily. We've missed him at the dances, haven't we?' Imogen looked directly at the young man.

'Gee, Imogen, you sure look pretty today.' Dylan moved his stick and turned to face her directly.

'Well, Dan, I think we should hurry or we won't be able to catch up with the others,' Emily nudged Dan.

'Yes, of course, Em.' Dan took her hand as they walked away and Emily turned back and shouted, 'By the way, Immy, where is your brother today?'

'You may see him on your walk. He's doing some detective work apparently. If you see him, tell him I'll be checking on him later, and if he wants to join the picnic party he must be back here by four.'

The ground had dried up well and Emily and Dan could see the others walking a good way ahead. Dan had brought a large-scaled map with him and when they came across a choice of paths didn't hesitate on choosing what he thought was the better one. There were sheep grazing everywhere, with a large part of the land unfenced.

'It's beautiful here, isn't it, Emily?'

'It's having the blue of the sea ahead of us and the coast of Wales in the distance.' She looked up and smiled at him as she said, 'But don't forget that the Germans have landed on Lundy Island. That sort of spoils it, doesn't it?'

'What?' Dan stopped and turned to her.

'That's what Imogen's imaginative brother, Alex has told his family. He and his friend Brian spend hours roaming all over the farmland and surrounding area, keeping notes in a book on who comes and goes, including Anna. He's the boy I told you about recently. He even tried to use what he thought was a duplicate key that his father keeps on a hook in the kitchen which would have opened Anna's cottage door.'

'You mean he was going to break in when she was out?'

'Yes, but he told his sister that the lock had been changed so the key wouldn't open the door. Imogen hasn't told Christopher about this because they don't know if their father had changed the lock before Anna moved in, or if she changed it after she'd moved in. Alex keeps his book hidden from everyone. Of course, he is in another world much of the time, playing on the beach with his gang when the Americans aren't practising their military manoeuvres, picking up spent shells, apart from being given all sorts of things to eat by the kind American boys. They obviously feed his imagination as well as his stomach.'

'He sounds like an intelligent young boy,' Dan remarked as they stopped to sit on a stile and look out across the calm waters of the Bristol Channel.

'It's a pity that Robert and Clara didn't come today, Dan.'

'Yes. I'm quite worried about Robert, but I telephoned him again recently and he told me that he was going to stay at his sister's house in Woolacombe for the weekend, so that will give him a change of scene.'

'Ooh, look, Dan. There's a lovely grey horse in

the distance. Could that be Anna riding it?'

'It's difficult to see from here but I think you're right, Emily. She's disappeared behind that clump of trees.' Dan looked at his watch. 'It's time to return to the farm for the picnic.' They walked back in silence and joined the party just as Louise and Christopher were uncovering the food and pouring drinks.

Imogen and Dylan were still sitting where Emily and Dan had left them, laughing and chatting as if they had known one another for years. Christopher and Louise handed out glasses to everyone and poured drinks in readiness for a toast. Christopher held up his hand for silence.

'Ladies and Gentlemen, thank you all for coming to celebrate this special birthday of our lovely daughter, Imogen. I have a simple toast to propose. It is to Imogen, to Youth, to Friendship and to Peace.' Glasses were raised and everyone sang 'Happy Birthday.'

The food was varied and especially good considering the wartime rationing. It was obvious that the English contingent had been making savings on food during the previous weeks in order to splash out for the birthday celebration. The Americans, as generous as ever, arrived with all sorts of treats never seen by the locals but all the more appreciated.

The picnic almost consumed, Doreen's father suggested a game of rounders. The chairs, table and rugs were moved and the lawned area, which was more of a field than a lawn, was cleared of any objects in readiness for the game. Two teams were worked out and play was explained to the American soldiers who thought it similar to baseball and were showing great enthusiasm. Doreen's father had come prepared and brought the equipment needed including bats and balls. It took some time to get the teams under control and just as the first ball was to be bowled a voice was heard shouting above the noise the players were making.

'Stop her! Stop the horse!' It was Imogen's voice as she attempted to catch the reins of Lady, who had appeared panicked and riderless, cantering towards the barn. Christopher ran forward but wasn't fast enough to stop the animal. Isaac, leapt up and grabbed the reins, talking to the horse and attempting to calm it down. Everyone was frozen to the spot as Isaac brought it to a halt while murmuring to it and stroking its neck. Christopher helped Isaac to lead Lady into the stable and everyone started talking at once.

Where was the rider? Who was the rider? Yes, it was Anna. So, where is she? Has she been thrown and is she lying injured somewhere? There'll have to be a search party to look for her.

After a hasty discussion a large group including Christopher, his cousin Tom, Dan, and some of the American soldiers prepared to set off. Oliver suggested he could cover some of the ground quicker with the Jeep and that Christopher should direct him.

'Shall I come with you, Christopher? I know where Emily and I saw Anna just before we returned from our walk,' Dan said.

'That will be very helpful,' Christopher looked worried. 'I can't understand it. She is an excellent rider.'

'Perhaps something has spooked the horse,' Dan suggested as Oliver started up the Jeep. Under direction from Christopher, Oliver stopped the vehicle at Anna's cottage to check that she hadn't returned home. As usual, the curtains were closed at the sitting room window and there was no answer when Christopher knocked on the door and shouted through the letter box. They drove on for several minutes, scattering sheep in all directions until suddenly they saw Alex running towards them and waving frantically. Oliver stopped suddenly and Christopher jumped out of the Jeep and ran towards his son.

'Dad, Dad, come quick. There's been an accident. I think Anna's dead.'

'Alex, are you all right? What's happened? Lady's

come back to the stable without Anna.'

'Dad, I think Anna must have come off the horse and then fallen over the cliff.'

'What? Where?'

'East of Bull Point. You can just about see her if you look over the edge.'

'Alex, you are not to go near the edge of the cliff. We can't take the Jeep much further so we'll have to walk. Lead the way but once we get near the cliff, you're to stay at the back. Do you hear me?'

'Yes Dad.' Alex was white in the face and breathless from running.

'Well done, Alex. Now, lead the way.'

After walking for over five minutes on steep, rough terrain, they stopped near the cliff edge where Alex had led them. Christopher made sure that his son was sitting on the grass, well back from the cliff edge as the three men went forward and looked down to the rocks below with the waves breaking over them.

'Yes. There she is, lying on that flat rock.' Christopher shook his head. 'I don't think – ' He looked at the others.

'I think she's most likely dead,' Dan said while Oliver nodded solemnly.

'We must hurry back and telephone 999. Sadly, there's nothing else we can do at the moment.' Christopher turned and started walking up the slope towards Alex. They all walked on until they reached the vehicle and then at the top, all four climbed into the Jeep.

'What a dreadful way to end a lovely birthday party,' Christopher remarked as Oliver started the engine and drove off in silence.

Chapter 47

Imogen and Doreen were already waiting at a table in the British Restaurant and drinking a cup of tea when Emily, Elly and Isaac arrived and joined them. They all looked at one another in silence for a few moments until Imogen put down her cup and said, 'Thank you for coming. I feel that I have to share some of what we have discovered since my party ended so tragically. I should order yourselves some tea but we could all do with something stronger.' Elly went to the counter and brought back a tray of tea.

'We didn't like to telephone and pester you but we have been worried,' Emily said.

'I have had two days off and been staying with Immy at the farm,' Doreen explained, 'but I'll let her tell you all about it.'

'It's thought by the medical people that Anna died instantly. Her body was brought up from the bottom of the cliffs and later examined. The police broke into her house as there were suspicious circumstances leading to her death. Dad was shocked to find that his spare key did not open the door to the cottage and that Anna had had the lock changed. Dad was there when the police forced their way in and found a long-range wireless unit in the cupboard. At this point they called in the Secret Service who immediately sectioned off an area around the house and started to pull the place apart. At the same time, some of their team began inspecting the ground at the top of the cliff above where her body was found. When we told them that Alex had been keeping notes on her movements, they interviewed him and took his notebook.'

'How is Alex, Imogen?' Elly looked worried.

'He was very quiet and shocked at first but once the Secret Service started interviewing him he bounced back to his usual self and almost ended up interviewing them.'

'Immy, do you remember that high-ranking American that Anna was with? I wonder if he has been interviewed?' Emily looked questioningly at Imogen.

'According to the records that Alex kept of his visits to the cottage, the relationship ended some time ago. Her boyfriend hadn't called there for several months. We think he must have become uneasy about her. Alex thinks she may have asked him too many searching questions.'

'Your brother is very observant, isn't he, Imogen?' Isaac had been sitting quietly and deep in thought. 'He was uneasy about her, and so was I. She was German, of course.'

'But there was no trace of an accent when she spoke English,' Emily interrupted.

'It was something about her manner,' Isaac replied. 'She was very confident and –' He hesitated. 'Cold. I'd seen it in Germany before I was rescued. I didn't expect to see it again.'

'Are you saying she was a spy?' Doreen looked at her friends. 'If she was, what was she spying on?'

'That's easy. Ask yourselves why the Americans were sent to our sandy beaches to set up the Assault Training Course?' Imogen looked around the table.

'Yes. They're practising at Saunton, Croyde, Putsborough and Woolacombe, and along the estuary,' Doreen said.

'And they're stationed all over North Devon and practising for an invasion somewhere. That's obvious, even to us,' Elly added.

'So where is the High Command planning to invade when the Americans leave here? Surely, they will be joined by other armies, including the British? They will invade France, won't they, to free the French people of the German occupation.' Imogen remarked.

'There's a lot happening around Dover at the moment. Perhaps they will invade near Calais,' Elly added.

'Or perhaps that is what we want the Germans to think,' Emily cut in.

'That was what she was here for,' Elly added. 'She was trying to find out where and when the invasion would take place.'

'But I'm sure very few of the military would know that; only the high command,' Doreen commented.

'Exactly!' Imogen looked at them and Isaac shook his head.

'But Hitler is a very stupid and obstinate man. He has invaded too many countries and has – ' He paused.

'Too many irons in the fire?' Elly finished the sentence.

'Taken his eye off the ball?' Imogen added.

'He has shot himself in the knee!' Isaac said.

'In English we say, "He has shot himself in the foot!"' Emily laughed. 'But it means the same thing. Imogen, is the Secret Service still poking around at the farm?'

'No, they've left but as I said, their investigators have taken the cottage apart, even lifted the floorboards, but have promised to put it all back when the case is closed. They took away all sorts of equipment and took photos of the ground near where Anna must have come off the horse. Dad had returned to the clifftop the same evening that Anna was discovered dead. He had inspected the ground closely and found some faint tyre tracks in the dusty part of the path nearby. Later, he described them to us and Alex showed Dad the drawing he had made of some tyre tracks not long ago. They were the same. Dad told the investigators what he had discovered on the evening of my birthday and they went and examined every blade of grass. Dad was asked to go with them but was told he must not talk to anyone about the matter. Of course, he had already discussed some things with us. I don't think there is anything new that has been discovered that we didn't already know about. Oh, they did take fingerprints in the cottage.'

'There is something that I told Dan about. Do you remember after the concert, Anna came over and sat with us when we had tea and cookies?' Emily looked at her friends. 'She asked me what I had been teaching before I was signed off work. I told her that it was Music and French, which was true and she said that she thought I had been teaching German. Then I told her that I couldn't speak a word of German.'

'Which wasn't true,' Isaac interrupted. 'When I came to England with the Kindertransport, I couldn't speak a word of English. It was Emily who befriended me and spoke to me in German.'

'Not very fluent German, just what I had been learning at school but we muddled though, didn't we, Isaac?'

'I would have been so lonely in those early days without your help.' They smiled at one another and Emily continued. 'It was at our last rehearsal that Anna arrived late and in a bit of a panic. As she sat down, the music fell off the stand that we share just as Alcwyn was explaining that he wanted the orchestra to omit some bars and skip to another one. I bent down to retrieve the music and started to put the pages in order and missed what he'd said. As I shuffled the music sheets, I leant towards Anna and whispered, "What bar did he say?" She seemed rather distracted and out of sorts and muttered, "Takt siebzehn." '

'Bar seventeen,' Isaac said.

'Yes, but I was still shuffling the music and replacing it on the stand and I pretended that I hadn't heard her. Alcwyn repeated his instructions and I nodded my understanding and the rehearsal continued.'

'No wonder she wanted to know if you had understood her after she had slipped up like that,' Elly remarked. 'I wonder why she was so flustered when she arrived at the rehearsal?'

'If we think she was a spy, she must have lived every day with the possibility of discovery,' Imogen said, thoughtfully. 'But what a perfect place to live. The cottage is well away from anywhere and yet she could have seen anyone coming. I'm beginning to realise that my brother is cleverer than I thought, but I can't help wondering why the investigation was stopped so suddenly. There's more to this than we know so far, isn't there?'

Chapter 48

‘Are you sure that you can manage without us for four or five days, Fred?’ Elly and Isaac looked across the table as Barbara placed some cakes, fresh from the oven in front of them.

‘We’ll manage as long as we know you are coming back. George has said he can spare Hen or Pip to help cover your absence.’

‘Fred, of course they’ll be coming back, but you want to introduce Isaac to your parents, don’t you, Elly?’

‘And it will be nice to show him around Eastbourne, Barbara. We’ll try to avoid the parts the Germans have bombed but it is lovely along the coast and we can walk by the pier even if we can’t walk on it.’

The kitchen door opened and Stan came in, placed his bag on the floor and sat at the table. He handed some letters to Barbara and a copy of Farmers Weekly to Fred. Elly and Isaac looked questioningly at one another.

‘Mornin’ volks.’

‘They’re all deserting us, Stan,’ Fred muttered, offering a cake to Stan as Barbara poured tea for everyone.

'But we'll be coming back soon. I've told my family so much about Isaac that it's only natural that they want to meet him,' Elly explained to Stan.

'Sounds serious; sounds like you'm warmin' up for buyin' a new 'at, Barbara. Where's the other maid, or is 'er off somewhere too?'

'Actually, she is, Stan.' The door opened and Emily entered carrying a large basket of brown eggs.

'The new chickens have settled well. Look, everyone. Oh, hello, Stan.'

'We were just telling Stan that you're all leaving us, Emily.' Emily sat at the table and looked around.

'Yes, my father telephoned yesterday to say that my brother has had an accident at work. He was with a team clearing a bomb site when the ground gave way and he fell and broke his leg. He's in hospital but when he comes home there will be no-one there to care for him when mum and dad are on duty at the same time. Mum didn't know that dad was intending to phone me and she kept saying that they could manage. I'll be going back as soon as I know that Jonathan is being discharged from hospital. It's not that I don't want to go back but – '

'It's wonderful here, isn't it, Emily?' Isaac looked at Fred and Barbara. 'Although I love Emily's grandparents and will always be grateful to them, working here with Fred and Barbara, and Elly and

Emily is where I'd always want to be.'

'I know just what you means, Isaac,' Stan said. 'That's why I goes no further than Swimbridge, if I can 'elp it.'

'Oh, Auntie, I forgot to tell you that Dan is going to pick me up in his car and we are going to have a picnic at Shallowford. I won't be gone long.'

'Be gone as long as you like, Emily. Does Dan know that you are returning to London very soon?' Barbara asked.

'Yes, but not exactly when, Auntie.' There was a rather long silence, interrupted by Fred with exclamations of disbelief and laughter as he opened the latest copy of Farmers Weekly and read the headline of an article aloud.

'Sing to your Cows and Increase their Milk Yield' by Elly Reed and Isaac Lander.'

'It's a lovely afternoon, Emily, but I think we are soon going to get some rain,' Dan remarked as he spread the ground sheet on the grass.

'I have brought a flask of tea and a few sandwiches, Dan, but nothing very exciting,' Emily said as they both sat down and looked at the water rushing and sparkling over the stones.

'I have the remains of a cake that my housekeeper made. She is a good cook and I'm lucky to have found her.'

'What about your new partner? Has he started work yet?'

'He's not a partner in the business sense but I'm very happy with the choice I made and lucky too. He knows the area and so many of the farmers and people who are our customers, and they know him. It couldn't be better really. And yes, he has started working in the practice.'

'I'm so glad, Dan. Glad that things are going to be easier for you.'

There was a short silence and Dan suddenly said, 'You're going home, aren't you, Emily? You're going back to London?'

'My brother has broken his leg while clearing a bomb site, and with Mum and Dad both at work, he will be home all day for some time, that is when he has been discharged from the hospital. Then there is the fact that my grandparents are retiring from their grocery business and will need some help to manage that; yes, I have to go home and help.'

'Will you come back to visit your aunt and uncle, Emily?'

'Of course, I will. I don't really want to go home, but that sounds selfish. I want to see my family and help them too, but I shall miss all this.'

'I'd like to write to you, Em, and in July, I will be in London on a course for a week. Perhaps we could see one another?'

'Yes. I'd like that, Dan.' They sat in silence looking at the clear water as it rushed under the ancient bridge forming a deep, dark pool before bouncing over stones and entering a shallower part of the river, where green-leafed branches bent low on either side.

'You know, Angela and I swam here once, in that deep part over there. It was easy to get in and difficult to get out.'

'How lovely! I'll bet it was really cold, Dan.'

'Let's say it was bracing!'

They sat in silence looking at the water and thinking their own thoughts when suddenly Dan sighed and said, 'I drove over to see Robert. He was still at his sister's home in Woolacombe. I'd telephoned him several times at his home at Ilfracombe and there was no answer, so I tried ringing Clara in Woolacombe. She was very keen that I should see him. He had decided to cancel his teaching until he felt better.'

'What was the matter with him, Dan?'

'In short, it was all about Anna. He said that she played tricks with his memory.'

'Whatever did he mean by that?'

'Don't forget that you and he would have seen her quite often with your work with the orchestra and the quartet, and the more he saw her, the more he felt that he had seen her, or someone like her, years ago. It played on his mind until he had difficulty sleeping. He had intended to see a doctor to get some help but shied off when he realised that she would have been the doctor. Eventually, he went to stay with his sister and she decided to take some boxes of old photos out of the attic. They spent hours going through them and talking of their years in Austria and the times they had spent playing in concerts and festivals around Austria, and even at times, in Germany. And then they found a photo that threw light on the whole thing. One of the orchestras in which they both played took part in summer music festivals. In 1929 the orchestra organised a tour playing at festivals in Linz, Salzburg, then over the border into Germany to play in Rosenheim and Munich. They stayed in each place for two of three days. It was when Clara and Robert were looking at some of the photos that they found what had been worrying Robert. One of the photos was of their orchestra standing in rows with an orchestra from Munich, and in the second row from the front on the side where the German orchestra was standing, he found what had been at the back of his mind. It was of a young fair-haired woman holding a violin and looking remarkably like a younger version of Anna. They looked at the photo under a magnifying glass, and on my visit, showed it to me. It was unmistakeable.

'What an amazing coincidence, Dan.'

'Yes, and what an amazing memory, even though Robert took time to unravel the problem.'

'Did they know about what happened to Anna on Sunday?'

'No, not until I told them because I think there has been a block on the news by the Secret Service.'

'There are still questions to be answered, Dan.'

'But I don't think we will find out much more. It's not just a matter of security but of the nation's morale. A situation like this, especially so close to the American Training Centre is not good for their morale either.'

'Do you think that Robert will soon feel better now that he knows what was the cause of his unease?'

'I do, but he is worried that he hasn't heard form William recently. They had become good friends, sharing their love of music.'

'Perhaps William doesn't know that Robert has been living at his sister's home recently.' Emily looked at Dan.

'Perhaps.' He paused. 'Emily, shall we have our picnic now?'

Chapter 49

'**Thanks for coming,** Emily. I didn't know if you could spare the time now that you're off home tomorrow. It's just that Immy telephoned Banburys and asked to speak to Mum. She's never done that before. She sent a message through Mum for us to meet in Woolacombe on Sunday morning, this morning, in other words.'

'But why, Doreen? Do you think she has more information about the terrible thing that happened to Anna?'

'Yes, but there's something else and she wouldn't tell Mum what it was. Dad said that we could use his car, which is good because the weather is turning nasty.'

'What about his petrol coupons, Doreen?'

'He's only used it once this month. That was when he drove us to Mortehoe for Imogen's birthday party. He's kindly left it outside the front door, ready for me to drive.' Doreen looked at her friend. 'Do you want another cup of tea before we go?'

'No, thank you, Doreen. Where is your family this morning?'

'They've gone to church. Christine is doing some performance with the Sunday School and wants Mum and Dad to see it.' The two friends looked at one another and stood up and put on their coats. The sky clouded over as they got into the car. Doreen drove off and they sat in silence until they had left Barnstaple.

'Is everything all right between you and Oliver, Doreen?'

'Yes, but I've hardly seen him recently. They haven't been allowed as much time off. We met in Braunton and went for a walk. He was rather subdued and I thought that perhaps he had gone off me. Suddenly, he turned to me and said that when his training ends they will move on somewhere but wherever it is, he will find me. He will write to me and if he survives the war, he will come back to me and ask me to marry him.'

'What did you say to him?'

'I told him that I loved him and that I would be waiting for him.'

The sky became more overcast as Doreen drove on in silence. As they drove through Braunton it started to rain.

'What about Dan, Emily? Does he know that you are going home tomorrow?'

'It's May 26th today. I've been at the farm for almost five months, and I have to go home to help the family and eventually get back to teaching. Yes, he understands, and he has said that he will write to me and see me when he has to attend a course in London in July.'

'What did you say to him about that?'

'I told him that I would write to him and look forward to seeing him.'

The rain became heavier and Doreen struggled with the windscreen wipers. 'It's steaming up in here. Do you mind if we open the windows a tiny bit, Emily?' They each wound down the windows and were immediately sprayed with rain. 'We're getting wet but at least I can see better.' They drove on, turning left at Mullacott Cross as the weather worsened.

'Are we meeting Imogen at her farm, Doreen?'

'No, she wants to meet us in Woolacombe and suggested The Bungalow Café. By the way, how are Elly and Isaac? They seem very fond of one another.'

'They get on so well. In fact, they have gone to stay with Elly's parents in Eastbourne for a few days.'

'That sounds serious, Emily.'

'I think it could be. I don't think that Isaac will ever want to leave the farm. He and Elly work so hard and are always cheerful and full of ideas, Uncle Fred says that Isaac is like the son he never had, which is just about as much praise as he could give him.'

As Doreen drove steadily down into Woolacombe the visibility worsened.

'What a horrible day. Sorry you are driving in this, Doreen. We can't see the line between the sky and the sea.'

'We can hardly see Woolacombe but I'm going to drive around the back of The Bungalow Café and park, then we'll run to the café and join Immy for a hot cup of tea.'

'I wonder why she wants to see us,' Emily said.

'Yes, I wonder.' Doreen turned left at the bottom of the village and parked the car.

Emily and Doreen took off their coats and sat next to Imogen. The café was unusually quiet as the three young women greeted one another.

'Where is everyone?' Doreen looked at her cousin.

'We should order a drink and a snack soon. It's so quiet they're intending to close early.' Imogen said. They all went to the counter and ordered egg on toast and a large pot of tea, and returned to their seats. The rain continued to lash against the windows of the café, steaming up the windows inside.

'Imogen, have there been any further developments since the investigation was called off?' Doreen asked her cousin.

'I wondered if we could put pieces of the puzzle together. The first piece is that Dad saw a friend of his recently who farms not far from us. Arnold, that's Dad's friend, had been asking William Taylor for advice about managing his sheep. Like Dad, Arnold used to ride out around his farm on horseback. He had a lovely Lundy Island pony who was brilliant for the job, stopping and waiting whenever Arnold wanted to get off and check a poorly sheep or pick up a weak lamb. Then Arnold started to have trouble with his back, rather like Dad, and doesn't ride anymore. Well, one day William Taylor called, supposedly to check something on the farm. Arnold had seen him on a motor bike driving around and looking at the sheep. He asked him about the motor bike because he thought that a small, neat vehicle like that would be a good replacement for his Lundy Island pony. As you know, William has a large van, more of a truck really. Apparently, he keeps this motor bike in the back of it for when he visits farms where a lot of walking is required. He told Arnold that it was a great time-saver. It's a Royal Enfield, nicknamed The Flying Flea, and is used by the army and even taken on aircraft and delivered to our forces abroad because the bike is so compact and reliable.'

There was a short silence while the three women thought about the possible uses of The Flying

Flea. Their food and drink order was brought to the table and Emily poured the tea.

'Elly told me something interesting before she and Isaac left for Eastbourne,' Emily remarked. 'She telephoned The Ministry of Agriculture a few days ago and said that she had a message for someone working there. She gave his name as William Taylor and said he had left his coat behind after visiting the farm, which was untrue, of course. She said she didn't know how to contact him and wondered if anyone at The Min of Ag. could help. After a long wait on the telephone, someone came on the line and said that there was no-one of that name working for them and she must have made a mistake.'

' "Curiouser and curiouser, said Alice," ' Imogen remarked as she frowned at Emily.

'But not exactly surprising,' Doreen added.

'Well, here's another piece of the puzzle,' Emily said. 'Dan visited Robert Stone and his sister, Clara at Woolacombe recently. You know that they teach music and play in our orchestra. They were born in Austria and trained and worked as musicians, until leaving the country a few years before the war and inheriting and settling in their grandparent's home in Ilfracombe. Their Austrian father was Jewish and also a musician. He met Clare, their mother when she was on holiday from England with her parents. It's a long story but you can imagine that with the rise of the Nazi party, the contrast of the life that they settled into in North Devon with the life that they left in Austria just before the war was huge. They became well-known and admired locally through their teaching and performing, and life was good for them, in spite of Clara losing her husband who had been a pilot in the RAF. It was when Anna came onto the scene that Robert started to feel uneasy. He thought that she wasn't what she appeared to be and told Dan that he felt he'd seen her somewhere before. It was at his sister's house in Woolacombe that he and Clara took boxes of old photos from the attic and eventually found a picture of a large group of musicians including their orchestra who had taken part in a Music Festival held in Germany. There, in a photo dated 1929, in the second row of the German orchestra was a younger version of Anna. They showed it to Dan when he visited them and Dan thinks that they may have shown the photo to William the last time they saw him.'

'When was the last time Robert saw William?' Imogen asked.

'Dan telephoned me this morning to say he would see me off at the station tomorrow. He said he'd just spoken to Robert who was back home in Ilfracombe and feeling a little better although he was sorry he hadn't heard any more from William.

Dan asked Robert when he had last seen him. Robert said it was May 20th, the day before Imogen's birthday.'

'These jigsaw pieces are starting to form a picture,' Doreen remarked.

'But the picture will never be shown to anyone, will it? The investigation is closed, you said, Imogen?' Emily asked.

'Yes, apart from the fact that a team of carpenters and builders arrived at our farm to put the cottage back together.'

'And have they done a good job, Immy?'

'I'll say they have, Doreen. Mum and Dad are thrilled and said that it looks much better than it did before.'

'And what about Alex? Is he coping well after such a traumatic time?' Emily asked.

'Oh yes. He said he's going to study hard at school, go to university and work for MI5.' Imogen sighed and shook her head. 'Mind you, it wouldn't surprise me if he does just that!'

'Oh, look! It's stopped raining. Shall we go outside and walk down to the beach?' Doreen looked at Emily and Imogen. They all put on their coats and picked up their bags.

'Yes, Doreen. We must do that. There is one more piece of the puzzle to talk about,' Imogen said mysteriously.

They crossed the road and walked towards the beach. The visibility was still poor and the wind had become stronger.

'Where is everyone, Immy?' Doreen looked around. 'It's like a ghost village.' They walked on until they reached the beach.

'Where are all the tanks and landing craft?' Emily shouted against the howl of the wind and the crash of the waves as they broke onto the sand, wiping out signs of any activity having taken place there.

'That's what I wanted to tell you,' Imogen looked at Doreen and Emily as the rain started again more heavily. 'It's the last piece of the puzzle. They've gone. They've nearly all gone.'

The three women stood on the sand, holding hands and looking out on the grey sea as the incoming tide raced towards them.

'But where have they gone?' Doreen cried.

'That's another puzzle,' Imogen shouted. 'They've just moved on.'

Suddenly, Doreen broke away from her friends, rushed into shallow water and grabbed a piece of crumpled paper which was being tossed around. She turned and ran back to the dry sand, her feet and legs wet and the bottom of her coat dripping with the sea water.

'Whatever are you doing, Doreen?' Emily

shouted as she and Imogen pulled her back up the beach to where they found a seat.

'I had to have it. I had to save it!' Doreen cried as she opened her hand, took the wet, crumpled paper and smoothed it out carefully. She lovingly folded it and put it in her pocket. It was the wrapping of a chocolate Hershey Bar.

About the author

After attending Barnstaple Girls' Grammar School the author studied at The Guildhall School of Music and Drama and had a long career in music teaching, primarily in North Devon. She has written plays and pantomimes, songs and a religious cantata. She is married to Leslie and they have two children and seven grandchildren.

Also by the author

Dia Webb's first book, *Just Making Do* is set in 1943. A close friendship develops between two families in wartime North Devon, one renting a small, terraced house in Barnstaple and the other living on a rented smallholding in the country. While they have to cope with illness, rationing and evacuees, American troops arrive to carry out military manoeuvres on the magnificent beaches, and a mysterious tenant comes to live at a secluded cottage on the Fortescue Estate. Why does he shun all contact?

Make Do and Mend was the wartime slogan put out to the nation in World War 2, and this book tells how the two families, with determination, kindness and humour find different ways of *Just Making Do*.

Just Making Do

Dia Webb

Acknowledgements

I hadn't intended to write another novel. It just sprouted from the first one in the form of a *What if?* There are so many people to thank who put up with me and helped me while I was writing it. First my husband, Leslie for his patience and encouragement, my daughter Debbie and my son David for their interest and ideas, my granddaughter Emily who continues to patiently rescue me when I get lost on my computer and my sister Mary who returns each year from her home in Bavaria to rekindle the love we shared as children of the beautiful North Devon beaches and countryside.

Thanks especially to Yvonne Reed, my wonderful proof-reader, whose eagle eye spotted mistakes that I had missed.

Thanks too to my friend, Cheryl Thornburgh who once again did a marvellous job researching and painting the cover illustrations.

Jenny Saviill and Louise Henderson-Clark have kindly cast their professional eyes over my writing and I am grateful for their interest and advice.

Nearer to home, I have been helped by my friend, Mike Matthews of Lineal Software Solutions for scanning Cheryl's paintings and to Doug Matthews and his wonderful staff when I suffer frequent computer tech problems.

On the advice of my friend and fellow-author, Berwick Coates, I put my first book into the capable hands of Mark and Anne Webb and their staff at Paragon Publishing, and I am grateful for their professional advice and help in dealing with this second book.

Milton Keynes UK
Ingram Content Group UK Ltd.
UKHW010936221123
433051UK00001B/48